MAXIM

MAXIM

JENNIFER GAMBACORTA

MAXIM

iUniverse books may be ordered through booksellers or by contacting:

iUniverse
1663 Liberty Drive
Bloomington, IN 47403
www.iuniverse.com
1-800-Authors (1-800-288-4677)

ISBN: 978-1-5320-4113-6 (sc)
ISBN: 978-1-5320-4114-3 (e)

Library of Congress Control Number: 2018900562

Print information available on the last page.

iUniverse rev. date: 07/05/2018

PREFACE

I always wanted to be a writer. It seems like all I do is imagine new worlds, create new characters, and design scenarios where I challenge my own understandings of things and the limits to which general thinking can stretch and go beyond the common norm. I have a love for languages—though I am not proficient in any tongue other than English, I have studied a few—and different ways in which a single thought or feeling can be conveyed. They say writers have multiple facets to their personalities because they need to understand the many possibilities of any given situation and the expansive mind-sets of their characters so that stories never fall flat. The worlds they invent can forever grow and change. If that does not describe me, I don't know what does. It is also said writers are extroverted introverts or introverted extroverts—I definitely fall into the category of the former.

I was born to be a published author. Nothing feels the same as sitting in front of an open Word document and having unlimited possibilities to explore with a keyboard at my fingertips. I always have an ear to listen and a word to say, so it is only natural that I find some medium to allow myself to communicate with others. I've also been described as an excellent public speaker; while I deny that on some levels, I believe I know how to present myself because I know what I want to bring to other people's attention, and how you present both yourself and your ideas is just as important as what you have to say. That is exactly what this book is: a compilation of my favorite things sewn together to become none other than my first publication.

I could do nothing else with my life other than write, and that is what this book is meant to prove. I have known from early on in life that this is what I was meant to do with myself, and even if taking this first step was a challenge and a half, all that matters now is that I took it, and I am willing to go forward. I believe in self-reflection, and after all of this time with this dream in my heart above any other, this book is going to be the key to a door I have been staring at, sitting in front of, scared to pass through, and impatient to open for far too long. No matter what happens, this is a glorious experience for me that cannot be replicated in any other form. This story encompasses so many things, from history to mythology to romance to adventure, because I genuinely hope there are so many treasures in this world, and nothing is more sacred than what a person can do with anything and everything that he or she knows and holds dear.

I have waited a long time to be published, and now that this moment has arrived and I can say I am indeed an author, I cannot wait to see what happens after this. The future is ever changing, but the past is set in stone, and this publication is truly a gem among the many rocks I've climbed over to reach this point.

ACKNOWLEDGMENTS

I'd like to thank both sets of my grandparents—one for giving me the travel bug that instilled in me the desire to learn about everything I see and the other for teaching me what hard work amounts to, whether on the work front or at home—because they have honestly inspired me in more ways than I could ever convey.

Thank you to my dad for the support that was sometimes a surprise but never in question. There are many eager dreamers out there, but none of them are as fortunate as I to have a parent who stood by their dream as much as you have mine.

To my mom, who never got to read my book, I hope the character Léonie in this novel translates the power you embodied and gives others strength in the way that I know you still empower people to this day.

To my sister, thank you for being the person who participates in discussions that broaden my mind, would travel with me anywhere if we could do so, and always ends up laughing with me until we can barely continue a conversation (which is a major facet of our family).

To my brother, Nicholas, thank you for teaching me about a world I knew nothing of until you were born. I don't think my heart would be this open if not for you.

To Mumei (which is a nickname, because best friends don't use real names after a certain point) for being the person I can talk about anything with without fearing a misunderstanding or overstepping a line; our marriage-like relationship is invaluable, and I hope you know how much you helped me survive this novel's process.

To my twi (another nickname, short for *twin*, something we have always called each other without a second thought), who actually reads with me; will pick up any book I give her, including the in-process mess of this one; and shares with me any story she adores. The ability to analyze and dig deep into the writing process is something I carry with me when I write.

I'd also like to thank Kathi Wittkamper, for being the most supportive, encouraging and sweetest person throughout this entire process! Every phone call and email meant so much to me.

And finally,

To you who so dared to dream and wondered
what it was you were supposed to believe.

To you who knew what you wanted but wondered if it could ever be.

To you because it's true: anything and everything is a possibility.

To you, please keep on dreaming until there
is nothing left to do but sleep.

And thank you, SK, so very much for never ceasing to inspire me.

PROLOGUE

It was almost laughable to see a member of the Nazuré tribe send a combatant into the arena during the tribal sparring matches. Perhaps it was because Van had been told early on in his training that the people who valued peace and equality above all else would never dare to raise a hand against another living creature, or maybe it was simply because of the age of their chosen representative. He had to bite the inside of his cheek to avoid exhibiting his disbelief.

The young girl looked as if she could not be older than ten years of age, and due to the design of the coliseum, it looked as if an ignorant child were standing clueless in the clutches of a demon. She was the fated opposition to his receiving the recognition he righteously deserved. He expected to garner the support from not only his own people but also all of the other tribes in attendance, who cheered for their preferred victor.

"For the Austiant tribe!"

"Nazuré! Nazuré!"

"To the death!"

Van had no right to sneer, given that he had just turned the meager age of twelve, but the Austiant people were known for their brutality and their sheer willpower in both myths and legends. The miniscule warrior before him bore the traditional traits of her people—blonde hair lightly tinted by orange at its ends, as well as a braid that wrapped around her tied-back tresses—which made the situation before him all the more amusing, as she possibly had been no more than a babe being coddled by her mother in the mountains beyond the coliseum the last time the tournament had been held. For hundreds of years, the tribes of Varon K'aii had come together once every decade to live peaceably among each other in the ancient city of Spierté and pit their greatest challengers against one another for the sake of sport and goodwill, and never before had the Nazuré people entered a single battle. The outcasts had finally let go of their Essentia-worshipping characteristics and allowed themselves to take part in tradition while letting their involvement ride on the shoulders of a young girl who, with her bravery and multicolored appearance, resembled Essentia in her own right.

Nevertheless, whether he dueled with a follower or a goddess herself, Van had no intention or expectation of losing the match he had waited his entire life to compete in.

While she posed for battle, her back to the rows of seats filled with impatient tribe members from across the continent of Varon K'aii, Van felt the chilling midnight air flay him from behind; the massive opening at his back reminded him that he could only rise to success in the stadium high upon the mountaintop or sink to the depths of the city below. The arena had the appearance of a gargantuan monster reaching through the unstable terrain of the mountain, and he felt himself relating to the visage: he would reach for his goal—he would defeat the girl—and, in turn, showcase his monstrous strength.

He flexed his hold on the grips of his dual swords as a horn meant to mimic the mighty Grootslang blew, signaling the start of the match. The surrounding crowd cheered for and taunted the two adolescents relentlessly, speaking freely under the darkness of night when addressing the Austiant warrior. The torches that illuminated the arena likely did little to highlight Van's own naturally darkened appearance, but the light gave him a vivid detailing of the brightly colored figure before him. After a moment of examination, he dashed forward and swiped his sharpened blade at the poor inexperienced babe who had dared to enter the coliseum as his adversary. Her whip was much too long for her body, he thought, and Van tried to rush toward her for close combat, rendering her weapon useless.

A shaken yet coy smirk warned him that his goal was too ambitious. The babe of the Nazuré moved her arm from her wrist to her elbow in a wide circle, and the whip followed her instruction like an eagerly obedient pup. Van thought she looked as though she were winding herself up for a powerful yet predictable frontal attack, so he sidestepped around her until he was standing back-to-back with his opponent. Her blonde hair brushed against his left arm just as he raised his other arm to strike her from the side. To his dismay, she somehow knew of his ploy and managed to raise her arm to block his restless blade. The arm guard she wore had many visible sunken dents in the metal, as if something had bitten into it multiple times, disrupting its smooth plating to the point that he could easily assume she felt the impact of his sword through her worn armor. Still, her emerald eyes, as rigid as the stones they resembled, bore into his when they met face-to-face. Van could see the determination of her spirit through the windows of her soul. However, her strength was merely a result of field work and mundane tasks instead of rigorous training—her gaze would surely lose its shine in due time.

"Destroy her!"

"Flog him!"

"Do it!"

Screams from all directions demanded that one of the two combatants make a move. Van knew they were at a standstill once the realization that he had been momentarily bewitched registered with his typically unshakable resolve. Grunting, he tore himself away from their face-off and leaped back a few feet. The babe imitated him, as if she were in need of instruction. Unintentionally, they had switched their starting positions, which supplied him with the feeling of a new beginning, a fresh start after a nearly sentimental blunder.

He took up his swords and crossed them in front of his body as he charged toward the pacifist warrior at full speed.

Van hoped his adversary would be faster at manipulating her whip—she had to be if she was going to be worth any amount of effort he put forth into their duel—and indeed she was. In spite of his wish being granted, his mood disintegrated when he felt the sharp smack of the thong of her weapon against his foot. He halted his forward assault when he swiftly comprehended that the pain delivered to his ribs was also a result of her fast work with her lashes. It wasn't until she struck his face—earning the babe a chorus of enraged cries from the spectators—that Van felt his patience threatening to wear thin. The contact that the bound leather made with his cheekbone created a bruise deeper than flesh, going so far as to temporarily disrupt his vision in his right eye. An undignified rage bloomed in his chest while the pain intensified; in a moment of weakness to his pride, the trained warrior chose to act without restraint and thrust his sword toward the girl—not to strike her but to send her into complete disarray.

With an erratic twist of his arm—as if he were dealing with a flexible arsenal, as his opponent was—Van entangled his blade inside her whip's lengthy body in order to render it useless.

The success of his strategy should not have bolstered his ego as fiercely as it did, yet he couldn't keep himself from feeling as if he had already won. His decisive act had cut down the range of her whip so effectively that it looked as if the Nazuré people's lone entry into Spierté's tournament was all for naught.

Van refused to allow the babe to beg for mercy, regardless of the hopelessness she likely felt.

He raised the sword that was free of interference high above his head before bringing it down toward the young girl. His expectant expression of a bloody demise transformed into one of surprise when once more his attack encountered an arm guard instead of skin. Though her arms quivered beneath his might as she struggled to keep both of his swords at bay, the fortitude she displayed was not at all rattled. Given the proximity of his two weapons, her armor withstood his attack while her hand planted itself on back of his other blade. A slight tremoring motion along the ridge alerted him to her intention: she was hoping to steal away the sword wrapped within her whip.

"Don't let her defeat you!"

"Take him down!"

"End it already!"

Van refused to allow the awareness of her plan to reach the crowd, let alone his people. He lifted his sword that had her arm guard pinned and planned to return the favor from her earlier hit, aiming his slash at her torso. The babe was forced to release the sword she held on to for security and once more used her armored forearm to defend herself against his strike. Now her entire upper body was constrained by his ploys. His spirit was vindictive as he began to apply force toward her, manipulating her stance so that he could push her toward the open edge of the arena. The sound of her sandaled feet gliding through the dirt was almost buried beneath the cheers of the spectating tribes prematurely celebrating Van's masterful end to the match, which would result in the Nazuré girl tumbling down the mountainside on which the coliseum stood. The talon-like pillars, which resembled the bony fingers of a demon, must have looked as if they were towering over him as he shoved her toward her doom.

He watched her expression as she struggled with the reality of her impending loss, and he was thoroughly disappointed when she imitated his sidestep from earlier in their match in order to flee; her whip had become slack and therefore gave her the ungraceful chance to focus her efforts on escaping his aggressive and decisive conclusion to their battle. The people supporting him in the coliseum seats groaned and unknowingly voiced his internal suffering. Van restrained a growl rumbling in the back of his throat as he recalled his stagnant blade from its perch on her arm. Thinking it wise to outwit her positioning, he stepped back a foot beyond her and watched as the babe revealed her shock to him. As her brows rose high above her eyes and her signature hair flew off to the right, she scrambled to strengthen her footing. Her hair represented the heritage of the Nazuré, the passive, credulous, languorous people who had never dared to step into the arena for the past three centuries. What better way to hurt her pride than to cut away her golden locks rather than one of her limbs?

Her green stare darted frantically across his face as Van made his move. His wide movements warned her of his aim, and the young girl did her best to shake her head in a sudden attempt to protect her long tresses. In her moment of evident distress, he decided to end their farce of a duel; the hilt of one sword rammed into her gut, and she fell over like the babe she was, her breath shooting out of her mouth unwillingly before her back slammed into the ground. In the blink of an eye, he planted his feet on either side of her fallen form and dropped to his knees while raising his other sword high. Even with her clenched jaw, the column of her neck was on full display and ready to meet the sharpened, eager edge of his sword—until Van fully comprehended that he was about to murder a child and was gleeful about the prospect of her blood dressing his prized weaponry.

As if freeing him from the most possessive of trances, his awareness of the scene before him struck down the prideful bloodlust that had formed inside him. Voices of outrage and inebriated excitement attempted to compel him to carry out his original intent of beheading his fallen opponent, yet despite everything he had been trained to do, regardless of his revered prowess when he was fighting his fellow Austiant warriors within their own territory, Van had received a horrifying dose of reality that the world outside his borders was frightfully bigger than he could comprehend.

His first opportunity as a warrior would not be at the expense of a young girl's life.

The person he had become was revolting and, in his eyes, did not deserve to—or wish to—represent his clan. Van was overcome with a sense of failure and horror, which bewildered him. Protecting the Austiant name felt unimportant for the first time in his young life as he stabbed his sword into her shoulder instead of aiming for the unexposed target of her throat. She had been fighting his weight while he contemplated his morals, but his sword had finally stilled her. She was shocked; her emerald eyes were wide, and her mouth hung open.

"Stay down," Van ordered with malice strangling his words before rising to his feet to reveal his victory.

Then he left the coliseum, ignoring the officiant from the Waysail tribe who crowned him the victor. He slipped through the congratulating heap of tribal folk, who all held some form of critique of his match, and raced down the steps etched into the mountainside in order to escape the scolding of his chief and find refuge in the city beneath the coliseum.

It mattered not that the locals of Spierté gave him odd looks when he broke through the carved doorway at the end of the staircase, even if their surprise was somewhat warranted. In his eyes, the people housed in the cities of the continent knew nothing of what it meant to be in a tribe and to be expected to do what he had nearly done. They lived their lives in a community, but they knew nothing of his life, and he knew nothing of theirs. To them, the tribes merely carried out their tradition in their city once every decade, and it awarded them a great profit, so Van chose to disregard them as nothing more than features of the city his tribe was housed in during the tournament, especially since the tradition of the coliseum had come long before these people had.

Ignoring them proved simple enough as he wandered the streets of the rugged town. His mind was elsewhere after being faced with the reality of his culture, and only his feet appeared to function while he strolled the limits of Spierté. When he approached the core of the city, he came to a bridge that rose over a river—something natural and calming in a place constructed with unfamiliarity. Van held on to the railing of the bridge and allowed himself to stare mindlessly into the restless waters below; for the first time in his life, he did not know what he was supposed to do with himself, what he was supposed to think, or how he was supposed to celebrate something as loathsome as his victory. After all, no matter how he'd achieved it, he would forever live with the memory of the means by which he'd obtained it. Murdering a child felt more like the twisted circumstance of a war crime than a match in a coliseum. He had won, yet he worried that he might have damaged the young girl mentally more so than he'd ever intended to physically.

"You!" screeched a disgruntled voice, stealing away his reflection.

Van whipped his head to the left and saw the babe from the arena, her blonde hair and bloody shoulder storming toward him. She had a look of great injustice etched into her face. The perplexity he felt kept him still while she stomped over to him and stopped within arm's reach. Unafraid of him despite how strongly he had feared himself after their duel, she blurted out venturesomely, "I may have lost to you today, but sparing me only means that I have the chance to train. And when we fight again, I will defeat you. That's all you have accomplished!"

"Good," Van said before he knew he had said it. He feared he had just misspoken and disgraced his people, and the urge to clarify forced him to elaborate. "Even more of a reason for me to have spared you then."

The cocky grin he had glimpsed early on in their battle reemerged on her face. Crossing her arms, the Nazuré girl said, "You say that now. A victory can make you feel more powerful than you deserve to think." Despite her wound, she stood before him with ferocity and grace. It sounded as if she could not accept defeat.

He knew that her loss that day had only inspired her to become better.

Unable to remain unaware any longer, Van decided to behave just as boldly and risk striking a nerve with his adversary. "Tell me—why did you fight? Your people never participate in the arena, but when they finally pick up a weapon, they let a little girl crack the whip."

The Nazuré girl did not react to his instigating remark. It was evident in the way she repositioned her stance to appear less confrontational and altered her tone of voice that she had been asked that question many times before. "Because I am training myself to be a beast master—I want to protect animals, learn to talk with them, and know how to fight them if they become violent or territorial. I know that is usually the role of someone from the Relic tribe, but I've decided that is what I want to be." Indeed, her words sounded as if she had rehearsed them; they flowed easily off her tongue. Her disposition appeared much sunnier as well, which complemented her tribal appearance, despite her reference to her dream of a role that belonged to a different tribe all together.

The Relics were a deity-focused tribe like the Nazuré in their worship of Essentia; they honored the deity Relic, who governed the land of Varon K'aii and all its creatures. It was rumored that Relic had bestowed on them the ability to communicate with the beasts that roamed the continent in a way that no one else could ever hope to achieve.

Yet the babe believed she had hope to include herself among their ranks.

Van nearly scoffed but restrained himself. Instead, he faced the river once more and grumbled, "That's foolish. You could live a peaceful life with the Nazuré, and you choose to train and enter combat while pretending to be a beast master. You've set yourself up for disappointment with these delusions of yours."

This time, when the young girl addressed him, she did so with an undignified growl. Resembling a beast in her own right, she scolded him. "Don't speak to me as if you understand me or my tribe. You're hardly older than me, so don't talk down to me like you're all-knowing. I have decided what I am going to do with my life, and some Austiant boy isn't going to make me change my mind."

Van figured she'd laced the intentional dig at his tribe into her reprimand in order to offend him, but he was much too taken by her resolve to care much for it. For someone to lose in the coliseum, seek out the warrior who'd injured her, and command him with both her supposed future victory and her dream that exceeded any he had ever had was downright remarkable, whether he voiced his opinion aloud or not. In a moment of selfishness, he pondered his own vision for himself. His goal of being the strongest warrior his tribe had ever known involved a hopeful four or five times competing in the coliseum, so long as the chief or his successor saw him fit to do so. Imagining himself walking down the incredibly narrow path of his future set by Austiant tradition, the once hopeful young man could not fathom the familiar surge of excitement at the thought of fulfilling the role.

Feeling small in stature, Van clenched his fists at his sides. "I apologize. I shouldn't have spoken to you like that."

When he received no recognition of his apology, Van lifted his eyes from the river to the starry night sky and then turned his amber hues to clash with the emerald ones that glowered at him from a few paces away. She was challenging him in every way, this girl from the Nazuré whom he had never met before; it was as if she were destined to skewer him with her words more effectively than he ever could have harmed her with a sword.

"In my tribe," he said, "you are born into your rank. You don't have any opportunities to grow beyond your birthright, regardless of skill; even if you possess all the talent to be a chief, you cannot become one if you are not born into their lineage. I was born to be a warrior, so I strive to be the greatest warrior the Austiant tribe has ever known. To hear you speak of being something that is beyond your entire tribe is ridiculous to me." He softened the tone of his voice despite the words he said, hoping she would understand the intention behind them.

Before she could respond, however, another voice spoke first. "Van."

Behind him stood his sister; he did not need to turn around in order to confirm her arrival. More than likely, the chief had sent Shia to obtain him, and as obedient as ever, she had done just that. His own sense of dutifulness to the Austiant compelled him to bow to his former and future adversary with his arms crossed over his body as he bid her farewell. Unable to say anything else after exposing much more of his inner turmoil to her than he felt was justified, he decided a silent departure was best.

However, his sandals had barely touched the earth beyond the bridge before he heard the babe cry out to him. "Your belief in yourself will always be your greatest weapon! And anyone who doesn't let you sharpen that blade doesn't know what you are capable of! That is my maxim—my creed! See if those words work for you too, and we will learn who is stronger in body and in mind the next time we fight!"

Shia glanced at him after hearing what his opponent had to say, but Van gave away nothing on his face as he followed closely behind her. Her scrutiny never left him as she returned him to the chief and observed the scolding he received, nor did he lose track of her gaze as he sat obediently in his seat in the coliseum for the rest of the tournament. She did not trust his emotionless reaction when he was pulled from the tournament, and Van knew his sister was much too wise to release her suspicion that something dangerous had overcome him that night.

How she must have perceived the creed offered to him when he deserted the Austiant people and his name shortly after the end of the annual tournament, never to return.

Those words became his own maxim as the individual known as Van disappeared and was secretly reformed into a man named Xerus, who was prepared to claim Varon K'aii's capital, the Goodlit Summit, for his own and challenge the structure of the entire country over the course of the two decades to follow until he made it into an idealized country that he could rule with justice and equality.

The young girl who spoke those words to him must have realized how much they mattered to him when he arrived at the Nazuré tribe at the age of thirty-two, asking the chief if he could have the only woman who had ever bested him to be the country's queen.

CHAPTER 1

"I'm sorry to interrupt you all during your meeting," Skylar said, gently introducing the sound of her voice into the meeting place of Yukaih Castle. She strolled along the traditionally elongated carpet that formed a path down the middle of the room as if she possessed sole ownership of it.

Surely it was her sunny appearance shining a beacon of relief on their talks of darker matters that had stunned the room into silence. The antler chandelier hanging above their discussion couldn't hold a candle to her natural demeanor, it seemed. Seated at the eight-pointed star shaped council table of Varon K'aii were the dignified leaders of the major cities across the land, including the always charming, ever gentlemanly Captain General Raibeart Dhrio. Out of all the aristocrats and leaders present, it was the eldest man who offered her a contentious bow while hiding his amicable grin. Seated beside the amused gentleman who sheltered all the manners in the room for himself was none other than her husband, the ruler of the land, King Xerus—or, as she once had known him, Van Austiant.

Skylar's name had changed when she took on the title of queen after wedding Xerus by way of an alliance with her tribal clan. Her mate had forsaken his upbringing in order to do what no other being had dared to dream of, much less achieve—something she was enigmatic in her admiration of. Her relationship with her childhood sparring partner in the long-forgotten land of Spierté had metamorphosed into an almost unrecognizable state.

Then it had changed once again not long ago, as evident in the way his amber eyes stared her down as if she had burst into his chamber of commerce like a wild owlursus hell-bent on destruction.

It was in her nature to offer the awe-stricken leaders a gracious curve of her lips in return.

"There would never be a need for you to apologize for entering your own meeting place, Your Majesty." Raibeart said this in a way that sounded as though he were reminding the other figures of authority of her rights as their queen.

"Of course not," added her husband in his typical expressionless tone. That was how he spoke to her as of late. Arms crossed over his armored chest, lips subtly digging deeper into his cheeks as his frown intensified, Xerus could not have looked any more antagonistic of his own claim if he had rehearsed it first in front of a mirror. The backdrop of sheared furs and burnished leathers that encased the room further demonstrated the tone he tried to maintain; the man was a pronounced workaholic—a fact she had readily accepted—and he made it abundantly obvious he'd rather continue with business than handle some unsuspecting, uncharacteristic interruption on her part, which was contradictory to what he had revealed to her a dozen weeks past.

Nevertheless, she took his reaction as another type of experience to consider when dealing with him in the future and quickly recalled her cause. "I came to report that an important colleague of yours is waiting to see you at your earliest convenience, Your Majesty."

She found formal speak exhausting. Thank Essentia she had a regal captain general patiently instructing her in the ways of royalty; her snowed husband couldn't even contemplate taking the responsibility on himself, perhaps due to his anticipation of her impatience. Though Skylar had never been—and continued to unrepentantly think of herself as presently not—of the vindictive sort, she couldn't resist the pleasure of flaunting his courteous title before him at any given opportunity.

How those amber eyes of his turned molten when he was made to endure her remote civility. "An important colleague?" He nearly growled as he repeated her. Thankfully, he was much more composed than any other foe she had ever faced.

Out of habit, Skylar brought her bountiful blonde hair over her shoulder and stroked the orange-tinted braid wrapped around it to guarantee its hold in her typical style. "He says he is an old friend to both you and Captain General Raibeart. He feared interrupting you, so I offered to do so in his stead, as I imagined you'd want to schedule a moment with someone as dear as a friend."

It was then that she questioned whether or not she had overstepped their unspoken bounds. Perhaps the Goodlit Summit had changed her in ways she'd never dreamed of for herself; though she could be aloof, Skylar was never one to taunt without formidable cause. That said, was not a road show of a marriage without love behind closed doors something to feel passionate about? Even if she never expected Xerus to love her and had merely prayed for an imitation of their relations from their adolescent years in the coliseum, the life they currently shared had deteriorated from the optimistic view he had first presented when he spoke to her chief almost half a year ago. Now they barely acknowledged one another outside of her retrieval of him in the early hours of the morning or late hours of the night.

No amount of foul foolishness between them could ever lead her to forsake her duties as his wife.

That was why Queen Skylar believed herself to be correct in thinking she had done what was right by walking into the meeting place on that day.

Apparently, her mate thought the same, as he nodded toward her. "Thank you. We had just finished conducting our business; I can speak with him now." He offered his gratitude and expertly appointed a date and time for their next convergence before seeing the city leaders off.

The queen stepped off to the side of her carpet with its jagged designs and hourglass details and bid farewell to the six men and women as they went. Some still seemed to be in shock, while others offered her belated congratulations on her marriage and the work she had just completed regarding the Goodlit Summit's knights and armies. She took not an ounce of offense that many seemed surprised a woman from a tribe in the sandy mountains knew how to inform and assist the captains of the snowy kingdom's forces. In fact, her efforts had begun only due to an unexpected suggestion from the very king who had resigned himself to his throne one odd evening many moons ago; she felt only a great deal of pride over her contributions when faced with such an onslaught of open-mouthed compliments.

As the departing authority figures huddled and waddled their way through the expansive doorway, Skylar had every intention of following them, but a booming voice beckoned. "Skylar, you can stay."

She wondered if she had heard him correctly. Or perhaps Raibeart had spontaneously contracted a cold and had spoken the words that had wisped past her and risen into the high peak of the conical roof before crashing down upon her. No, her husband had given her permission to remain in the meeting place while discussing what could potentially be personal matters.

Had he had an aneurism during his previous meeting?

"Very well." She nodded in recognition without meeting his eyes before calling out to the one awaiting her summon, "Sir, King Xerus will see you now."

How foolish she had been in not asking for his name. There was still much for her to be conscious of and to learn; royal pedigree was much more intricate than she had predicted it to be, which filled her with dread and fear. A beast master such as herself was much better suited for instinctive interactions, she'd realized after drowning deeper and deeper into the customs and cultures of such a foreign place.

Foreign was also the word she might have used to describe the man who was to meet with His Majesty.

Messy brown bedhead with equally unkempt facial hair framed the face of what appeared to be a cavalier man. His eyes rested on a flat line and hinted at kindness, but the salute he offered as a greeting was beyond reproach, from what she had gathered in all her fine teachings.

Skylar desperately hoped this man was indeed who he said he was—a former pact member to her mate. If so, perhaps some of his casual ways had unknowingly snuck beneath the Goodlit Summit armor that the king typically donned.

"Hey, guys," drawled the mysterious creature as he sashayed down the carpet she herself had walked upon with much more enforced grace. "Long time no see!"

"Good to see you, Cyril. And what a surprise it is too." Raibeart chortled. His hands left their thinking pose as a fist that had been pressed to his lips moved to rest much more leisurely behind his back. It was a sign that the man was now at greater ease than he had been during the previous meeting.

"Indeed. Welcome," Xerus said curtly.

The man named Cyril merely offered a lopsided grin as he stood next to Skylar. They remained behind the almighty table. Both eyed the deserted seats, yet neither of them seemed to feel fit enough to occupy one for him- or herself. With a poor attempt at a laugh, the remiss man said, "Sorry if I disturbed ya. I just wanted a chance to chat, and lo and behold, I happened upon the queen herself out in the hallway."

"How lucky you must be, since Queen Skylar is a very busy lady," Raibeart teased, arching a brow at Skylar. Their relationship was much more familial than she had imagined it could ever be, so she never minded his quips; rather, she relished any slight challenge they gave.

"Oh, looks like I did more than bother a few ole pals o' mine. And we weren't even properly introduced! What a clod." He must have been referring to himself, as he trailed off, bowing with a sweeping motion of epic proportions. His tone became the biggest farce in its rendition of courtly conduct. His entire businesslike ensemble seemed to fall forward as he lowered himself. "Milady, it is a pleasure to make your acquaintance. I am Cyril, and yes, the stories you hear about me are indeed true."

Skylar performed a sweeping glance of her own up into the eyes of her captain general and teacher before feigning the most delicate curtsy, tugging on the wraps along her sides that cloaked her wing-printed skirt beneath it. "I'm sure they would be."

His tight brown eyes shot open wide and blinked at her as if he stood in disbelief that someone of royalty had made such a bland attempt at humor at his expense. Thankfully, he seemed to be a resourceful sort, and he nearly threw his back out as he straightened. "What? Nothing?

You guys never talk about the good ole days? The queen of Varon K'aii doesn't know about any o' us?"

"I'm sure she is aware of Emery's work," Xerus grumbled thoughtfully.

Raibeart turned to observe the king as he added, "And Kivah and Weswin have visited once or twice since her crowning with Lady Mahina."

A hand found its way into Cyril's tousled hair. "So Dalya and I are the odd ones out, huh? Go figure."

"Oh, come on, Cyril. Don't act so disheartened. I'm sure you'd better enjoy painting your own picture for Queen Skylar of just the kind of man you are."

"Speaking of which." Xerus's voice boomed once again as he leaped onto the end of Raibeart's playful remark, successfully killing the topic in order to gather everyone's focus. "I was told you had something you wished to discuss with me."

"Ah, that I did." Something passed between the two men as business became the reinstated and belated theme of conversation. Straightening again, Cyril cleared his throat before holding out his hands, ready to use them to further illustrate any point he needed to make. "Well, to put it simply, I need the king to help me shoo away some pests."

A scowl encompassed the king's features. "Pardon?"

"It's the same old story: Varon K'aii citizens not being too keen on those of us from Hierony. Only now it's more annoying because it's causing trouble for Rainier and me."

Raibeart scowled now as well. "How so?"

"We're trying to bring our business into Terrinal. You know, the big, open marketplace right near the cathedral? It's a pretty decent spot to open shop; you can take advantage of all the tourism now that the people can travel wherever they want.

"But when we were moving out from Sailbrooke, the charming guards on the west side of Otornot Keep didn't care who I was or that I was with the group who took down the bunch of thieves that almost killed 'em all off—no offense, Raibeart."

"None taken," he said with a dismissive shake of his head.

Cyril immediately went on. "They told us to turn back if we knew what was good for us."

"That is not the kind of military I have built to protect this land," declared King Xerus. His grip on his knees looked as if it would have been painful if not for the shin guards that protected him from possibly self-inflicted pain. However, his armor did not prevent the animosity from seeping out into his words or into his pose.

As someone who had spent time molding and stationing the armies her mate had built, Skylar felt what she imagined to be only a fraction of the frustration and disappointment he must have been feeling.

"You didn't use your charm on them, did you?" Raibeart said. When he received a curious glance, he clarified. "I can only imagine how well your typical demeanor must have gone over with men like that."

"Hey, it wasn't me you should be worried about; Rainier looked like he was about to run over and deck one of 'em. I almost had to hold him back!" Though he laughed in recollection, it was evident that Cyril was grateful the encounter hadn't come to blows. Perhaps this Rainier had had no means to defend himself with. Having to face an impenetrable wall of ignorance—ironically, at such a national stronghold as Otornot—while being the sole combatant for his side of a possible fight must have been distressing for the poor businessman, no matter how blasé he seemed.

None of them cared for any sort of complacent demeanor when dealing with such disobedient soldiers and irrefutable prejudice.

Finally, after a moment of silence, Xerus spoke up. "What is it you have come here for, Cyril? What are you asking of me?" He stared down his supposed friend with a perplexing gaze, surely anticipating a trifling request, and it made him appear all the more troubled, even while demonstrating such a mighty aura on his covenant throne.

Cyril was aware of the king's unspoken apprehension, and it instilled bashfulness in him. "I was hoping that since they're your guys, you could get 'em to knock it off and let us through. I mean, if worse comes to worse, we could backtrack around and sail to Terrinal through Nàmheil, but—"

"But that is not wise for a struggling business such as yours." Raibeart seamlessly—though disappointedly—finished the man's thought.

"Hey, we do all right." His weak try at lightening the mood was thwarted by the heavy tone of the requisition that had been set the moment he began to tell his tale. Cyril grimaced as if he had done something wrong by coming to the king for aid, though helping others was Xerus's foremost drive for living. Even with his passion as it were, it was impossible to ignore the awkward position this put Xerus in as the man who employed the soldiers who were more harmful than cooperative with his ideals.

It struck a chord in Skylar to see her mate wrestle with himself internally so quietly, as if he managed to do so secretively in the expansive space of the meeting place.

"Very well. I will send word to Commander Vergil at Otornot Keep that I wish to meet with him and these men. They will then be further instructed to come here to the summit so that I may deal with them personally."

Raibeart mused aloud after hearing of the king's master plan. "It's an extreme response in pulling the commander away, but this is a cause for concern with Otornot's state of predilection."

"Yes," Xerus said. "Though Vergil has proven himself in the past, I will need to reevaluate the keep's independence if this is the sort of behavior I can expect from his men."

"It is not so easy to determine who has truly accepted the peace between Varon K'aii and the two islands we acquired, Viskretta and Hierony. Queen Skylar, perhaps you could offer us your opinion on the matter?"

At the captain general's sudden request for her counsel, all three pairs of eyes fell upon Skylar immediately. She wasn't so much startled as she was unprepared; many of the men tasked with guarding the people were picturesque in their roles as soldiers and lived much like their king, planning to serve and protect their country—and, in conjunction with the prevailing peace treaty, any human being who stood upon their land—until their dying day.

However, there was a much more effective way of dealing with this entire scenario, in Skylar's opinion, most likely due to her inexperienced ways in the world of politics as a whole. Life beyond her clan had always fascinated her, even if she had only ever revealed such a thing to her husband, whose eyes upon her now still retained their heat, their smolder that implied something lurking deep within should she ever dare to tame the beast behind them. Her manner of doing things might have seemed wild or careless to some, but she truly believed—more now than ever before—that what she thought of as the best course of action was the genuine article.

"I think that rather than calling anyone away from his post, you should simply send me."

Only two pairs of eyes gawked at the queen.

"Skylar." Her title magically disappeared due to Raibeart's shock over her reckless suggestion.

Cyril was surprisingly a tad more articulate in a moment such as this, though his bewilderment was evident. "Your Majesty, you don't have to do something like that for someone like me! I'm sure you have more important things to do than traipse around the world to help me knock a few bullies down a peg."

"Whether I do it at Otornot Keep or here in Yukaih Castle, I will still be a part of the remedial process."

"Remedial?" repeated the king.

Skylar faced Xerus and his captain general, prepared to defend her case. "This is a matter of hatred with these individuals, and we can't make them change. But they are men in the army I have been working with for the past few months—it's only fair that I have a say in what happens to them."

Cyril piped up from behind her. "With all due respect, couldn't you just punish them when they get here?"

"I won't be punishing them." She could have turned to eye the man who had addressed her, but instead, she burned her green gaze into Xerus's amber one. "I will evaluate for myself what these men are so against and what motivated them, and I will give them the chance to be reformed. I may not hold a position in the military, but I do have every right to be concerned when it comes to the morale of a group of soldiers who are tasked with protecting not only the strongest standing fortress but also the people and the security it stands for."

Unintentionally, she had rendered them silent again. Nothing flickered in the eyes of the king, and she was momentarily concerned that she was not being taken seriously. Whether they saw her capable of such a daunting task or thought of her as a wistful dreamer, it mattered not to her in the slightest.

Some good had to come from becoming queen. Wasn't she allowed to have her way from time to time?

The silence felt damning, so Skylar scanned the room's occupants and ventured forth. "If I fired them, I would be allowing them to continue hating; they need to be dealt with by someone who will see them as people with concerns rather than an authority figure who may not take such a delicate approach. I am not committing to changing their views, but I will give them the chance to try to broaden their minds and open their hearts."

Seconds into another pause in the conversation, clapping erupted in the meeting place. It startled her, but she would not appear shaken to anyone when in such an ardent state. After all, it was simply Cyril showing his reverence of her impromptu speech. "Wow, Xerus, where'd you find this one? Did Ordell bless you for all your good deeds or something? It's like she was made for you."

"I was made for a great deal of things." Quick on the draw, Skylar smiled at her future traveling companion. Cyril appreciated her wisecrack and grinned.

"At the moment, it's those unsuspecting soldiers who are the luckiest of all," said Raibeart, praising her in a roundabout fashion, something both common and unnatural of him in terms of expressing his opinion of her. "We just need to assemble your guards, and you two should be able to depart—with the king's permission, of course."

"There's no need for a guard party," Skylar said. Picking up the habits of her mate was a positive sign in some unfounded direction in their relationship; Skylar shot the older man the deepest frown she had ever worn in her entire life. Considering she never moved her lips into any other display than a smile, she imagined it must have been quite a sight. This was a position on which she would not budge, however, and she dared Xerus within her mind to challenge her in regard to her freedom.

No one—husband, king, or otherwise—told a renowned beast master of the tribal world that she needed guards to survive a jaunt to Otornot Keep. If anything, she should plan to hire guards for Xerus, as someone would need to guarantee that he slept and watch over his well-being while she was away.

"I'll wear my warrior clothes while I travel; should I be found out, I will tell the people of the world that I am on a mission to get to know Varon K'aii. I will tell them that Cyril is friends with the king and the captain general, so he offered to accompany me. At the very least, I will go with him to Terrinal and decide from there if I plan to visit any other cities."

"You will write to us about all of your plans, of course." Raibeart sounded as though he had resigned from his previous opinion almost instantaneously after she had concluded her perceived royal tour.

Xerus said suddenly, "There are many ways you can keep us aware of your travel plans—I hope you both will remember that." Just like that, it became clear that she no longer had a case to defend. The king had given her his blessing to do as she wished and, in doing so, had perhaps shown her the most affection she had received from him during the span of their marriage.

Some lovers of a frailer sort might have been worried by his lack of protest in her possibly dangerous, politically challenging mission ahead, but Skylar felt as if she were able to glimpse her foremost wish of having their sentimental companionship of old be ever present in their marriage for years to come.

Maybe it was her dedication or her methodic planning, but somehow, she had gotten him to see her way of things without needing to fret over the hypothetical damage it could have caused. Grateful, she thanked her superiors for their acceptance and did her best to tamp down the excitement she felt inside. She was going to see the world as she'd always wanted—on her own terms—and temporarily escape the pressures of palace life. Her life, with one simple meeting, seemed to suddenly bear upon it a light akin to the spirit Essentia, whom her people worshipped, and it felt perfect.

Less grand was the way her husband's eyes bore into her profile as she faced the businessman turned companion. His stare seemed much more contemplative than one might have expected. Hidden beneath his amber eyes was the mind of a man who felt nostalgia wash over him, sweeping him away as if his cordial demeanor had been capsized and stolen away by the powerful current of a memory he had long since tried to forget.

Recalling the lone act of kindness he had shown her was a dangerous thing to do.

<hr />

"Skylar, please come in." Xerus invited his wife into the meeting place, as he had been far too aware of her presence beyond its doorway for most of the meeting and could no longer resist having her near.

After all, he had a grand surprise for her that he felt nearly desperate to share.

She passed by Raibeart as they traveled in opposite directions along the traditional carpet that emphasized the room, and the king prayed his captain general had enough sense to keep himself composed so as not to potentially obliterate his kind gesture. He had orchestrated as grand of a gift as his time could manage, and it needed to go off without a hitch.

Hopefully, his most trusted adviser wasn't revealing to the queen of the nation how much of a giddy aficionado he could be.

"Raibeart looked to be quite pleased," Skylar said, confirming that Xerus's captain general had failed him for the first time in his career. However, Skylar was obviously unaware as to what had inspired the elder man's visible enthusiasm. Her brilliant eyes hinted at the curiousness she now housed; her fingers skirted her bottom lip as she thought; and her strides slowed, as she was much too distracted by the going-ons she had seemingly interrupted—he was pleased to know he had seemingly intrigued her.

Now he needed to rein himself in if he were to present himself as nonchalantly as he hoped to.

"He appreciates when others have good reason to luxuriate in happiness," Xerus said as an indirect way of explaining his dear friend's glee, though from his position standing before his throne, Xerus could only imagine the expression his wife had seen moments ago.

He would enjoy seeing her wear such a joyous look on her face, especially if it followed what he had to say next.

Clearing his throat, the king hoped to gather his queen's attention. "Skylar, I have something I'd like to tell you."

"Oh?" Personifying intrigue, Skylar snapped her green gaze to focus on his amber one, and he nearly forgot what he meant to say.

After meeting with civilians and entertaining this idea of his for hours, the king of Varon K'aii felt as if he had been possessed in some way, and he blamed his unsuspecting wife for such an ordeal.

Yet he wasn't foolish enough to deny the simple pleasure he always found in her uncommunicated challenges.

"Do you have any other appointments to attend to today?"

His simple question stole away some of her inquisitiveness and replaced it with weak surprise. "I was hoping to meet that friend of yours I heard was here; I was told the famous Emery Mor paid you a visit today."

"She did." Impressed—and, for some unknown reason, slightly worried—by her keeping abreast of the happenings of the castle, Xerus confirmed the rumor she'd heard simply enough. "But I'm afraid she has already departed for her return trip to the Viskretta Center."

Instantly, his adventurous wife was glowing with her insatiable desire to travel. "Viskretta. That's one of the islands, isn't it?" It would seem she had taken to her geography lessons well, what with two new territories merging with the large continent, given that such information was being imparted to someone who previously had known only of the main road between her tribe and Spierté.

Again, he nodded. "I didn't realize you were interested in the islands as well."

The pair faced one another while positioned next to opposite arms of his throne. Skylar gave him a look that showed she could not be fooled. "You know I never left my tribe much; anything beyond the mountains and dunes interests me."

Her remark was the most open, welcoming piece of information Skylar had provided about herself in recent conversation with him. Back when they were both young warriors, surely they had spoken of traveling the globe and exploring its reaches, but not once had she disclosed anything so personal to him since they had been reacquainted and wed.

It wasn't the most telling piece of information, but it was something that hinted at a shared trait between them even after more than a decade's passing.

Xerus was irrefutably determined to bestow his gift upon her then. "What about hot springs?"

"Hot springs?" she echoed curiously. Then she responded after taking a moment to ponder, "I believe I've heard of them."

"Have you ever thought of visiting one?"

"I can't say that I have," she said, and his pride was almost sky high, but she took her time again and responded with genuine heart. "But of course, I would travel most anywhere."

That was all he needed. Exploding at the seams in his stern, orderly way, Xerus told her everything without hesitation. "Tonight I have arranged for us to spend the evening at a hot springs resort. I do have to return tomorrow for a previously arranged meeting with Lady Mahina of Sailbrooke, but we won't need to leave the resort until just before noon."

Skylar was stunned, to say the least; it was as if some invisible force had stolen away her control over the motion of her body. That worried him. Had he gone too far in assuming their walking through the halls and insightful chitchat the night before had meant he could begin pursuing the woman he'd married properly, even if belatedly? He could cancel the outing if she felt reluctant in spending such time alone with him, though in his eyes, the trip would be no different from the nights they normally shared. Nevertheless, he could not necessarily undo any damage he may have inflicted in scarring her and scaring her off too early.

"When do we leave?" she said, and he swore he stopped breathing.

"I can have us on the road in less than an hour."

"Very well." She spoke demurely, but her speedy spin and retreat through the meeting place showed an eagerness in her that he had always suspected was locked inside of his bride and had hoped he would have the chance to see.

In the privacy of his massive meeting place, Xerus smiled to himself for the second time in less than a day. This new wife of his had indeed managed to provide for him something he had never imagined wanting, something Raibeart had made all too appealing. Now it seemed as though the family life he had been desiring and slowly needing was growing ever nearer as a response to one kind action he had dared to take. Her language had been the Skylar of new, yet her behavior had flickered for him a snapshot of the past, of the young lady he had once known and cared for in the back of his heart for all those passing years.

It was unquestionable now that he had made the right choice in having Skylar become his queen.

Hopefully he could someday soon hear her speak of him with the same possessiveness in her willingness to revel in such joys together

CHAPTER 2

I t took a long while for them to set out on their voyage around the world, through no fault of their own.

While Cyril promised to wait for the queen in the company of his friends, Skylar scurried off to her chambers so that she could change into the only other set of clothes she had ever worn, the outfit that represented her as a councilwoman of the Nazuré tribe as well as the warrior she had not been since donning her newest robes and the accompanying crown. She knew exactly where the outfit rested in her closet—like a treasure to which she had memorized the map—and she nearly threw off her tailored royal garbs in order to reacquaint herself with the metal girdle she wore as armor.

Before she could shimmy into the lengthy piece, though, she had to put on her undershirt and accompanying robe to cover her upper body first. The draping sleeves ended just beyond her elbows; however, the feature that made her tribe's robe most impractical to wear while living at the Goodlit Summit was the design of prisms cut into each of the sleeves as a symbol to represent their worshipped deity, Essentia. The etchings on the plate on the front of her armor were also outfitted to show tribute to the deity of peace and equality, yet the cutout designs were representations of the effeminate celestial, who was commonly depicted in art and stories as a rainbow-colored being.

Skylar tied the green beads on either side of her robe's lining just above her chest and then promptly tied her hair into the warrior's-loop style she always wore when heading into battle. The only part of her appearance that did not worship her tribe's deity was the hairstyle designed by the woman Skylar had idolized in her quest to become a beast master: Léonie, the last of the Relics. Though the woman herself had never once tied her hair back and instead let it flow like a silver stream behind her in battle, it had been said, given that no opponent had ever been able to cut off even a single strand, the great warrior had jokingly designed what had become a popular style while on one of the many battlefields she had dominated. Accidentally, she had patented the look of gathering one's luscious, long hair and twisting it to its ends in order to tie it to its roots and create the warrior's loop. Some civilians wore their hair in such a way because they appreciated the look, but Skylar wore it not only to protect her precious hair but also to honor her late hero.

Seeing herself dressed for battle was exhilarating in its own right, but wearing Léonie's signature hairstyle made the queen feel younger, as if her youth could be relocated in a simple attempt to change the way she naturally styled her mane. Bearing witness to herself in the mirror, Skylar nearly lost her breath. She could feel the cold bite of the armor resting from her ribs down to her hips, but observing her reflection in that moment sent an even greater chill barreling down her skin. Impatient in her quest to feel whole, she reached for the final piece of her essence, of what made her a beast master: her dearly missed weapon, the blacksnake whip. The hook on the backside of her armor felt as though it were crying out to be reunited with the bounded leather, and once they had been reunited, she felt as if the world had shifted within her.

Aside from the practical boots gifted to her by Xerus long ago, the traditional appearance of who she once was made her feel as though she had reunited with a second layer of skin; she fit right into it as if she had never left. She had never felt more complete.

Yet her enjoyment of her appearance was not the reason the fashionable queen and her companion set out so belatedly.

After adoring herself a tad bit more than one should, Skylar raced from her royal chamber as if she were trying to escape it. The door slammed behind her in her haste, yet the only sound the queen could seem to register was the clicking of her boots as she made her way down the corridor. She bid good day to the household staff, as she always did, before spying Cyril, who was waving her down at the end of the hall. Instantly, the queen noticed an obvious absence of her husband and her dear teacher. The cause was most likely the dozen or so citizens of the summit and a few of the braver souls who ventured up onto the mountain lining up for a chance to speak with their king in the hopes of alleviating their greatest grievances and woes. The foyer of Yukaih Castle was filled by the worried lot, yet only a few expressions seemed to gaze at her with blank recognition.

Her suspicion was then confirmed: aside from knowing about the king's marriage, many people outside of the Goodlit Summit could not recognize her. Though she had found refuge in studying books and not simply learning through word-of-mouth teachings when Raibeart educated her on the ways of the world, written records had been a mystery to her when she first arrived. Nevertheless, she had assumed receiving information through some sort of public publication was commonplace there. Yet it would seem that a proper print of her appearance had yet to be procured and dispensed across the land. There were such things as newspapers and all sorts of educational materials, as she had come to know over the last few months of her life, yet no one had even drawn a depiction of her to share with the people of the land she supposedly ruled.

Not intending to dwell on the matter, Skylar saw this information for the blessing that it was. Her anonymity would allow her to move about Varon K'aii without the dread of being discovered and forced to hole herself away like a typical royal.

With that in mind, the pair stepped out of Yukaih Castle and into the city of the Goodlit Summit in no time at all. In their moment of reprieve from the crowded foyer, they found themselves facing their cause for delay in their epic departure.

The nipping of the snowy cold reached Skylar's cheeks as she stepped onto the main road of the Goodlit Summit. She flinched and then refocused her gaze in order to stare down at the city she had come to adore despite its opposing temperature to the mountains she had been raised on. She could spy some of the original teepees still standing tall amid the constantly raging storm, but many families had requested plank houses when Xerus had appeared and claimed the summit for himself. The only igloos were those made by children, and it spoke wonders for the people and their city that parents could safely assume their young ones were hiding in a snow fort of their own creation if they weren't at home with them. The queen knew she was blessed to rule and live with such gentle people.

Gentle were they on occasion.

Though Skylar and Cyril had been fortunate in slipping away from the crowd inside, the pair were not lucky enough to avoid many fur-clad citizens of the city who suddenly and effectively bombarded the voyaging queen with offerings of free amenities; gifts, such as food, cloaks, and basic necessities, were supplied to them both, whether they had already packed such things or not. Skylar politely accepted the offerings of her somewhat acquainted people; however, she would only take their gifts in exchange for meetings and tutorials that she committed to participating in upon her return.

"Wow, you're just as popular as Xerus. You've been here, what, six months?" Cyril presented himself as a companion who was easy enough to get along with—he was strong and talkative. Yet when he made comments such as these, he tempted Skylar into her snarky ways, which a queen must forsake.

"And three days." She could not validate her statement's truth; she was merely playing sly while showing a group of children her gratitude for their attempt at sharing their tiny mittens.

There was a sense of impatience as they marched through the summit's main passageway and onto the Tundra Walk, but Cyril was kind and allowed the queen her time to politely address her founded hometown's citizens; many bystanders bid her well on her undisclosed quest with enough adoration to make it appear as if they had known her for years longer than they truly had. It felt as if the entire city of the summit had spontaneously turned up to bear witness to her leaving. Somehow, in a way she could not explain, these people had made her feel incredibly welcome in their land by merely trusting in her husband's judgment in selecting her as his bride, and they'd extended their due courtesies with effortless ease.

Even if their faith wasn't first founded by her own value as a person, she felt obliged nonetheless.

Among the stragglers along the granite curbs was one particular person who caught the queen's eye: Shia, her dear sister-in-law. Skylar had scarcely seen her after moving into Yukaih Castle and had never fully understood why. They had interacted even less. No one had ever revealed what had caused the siblings to become estranged, and she was clandestinely bothered by the detrimental distance between them, even if she had her own suspicions as to the cause. Shia had never fought in the coliseum in Spierté, let alone, if Skylar could correctly recall, picked up a weapon, but she had always been present during the battles to witness her brother's prodigal might.

It was a shame that Skylar did not have an opinion of the only other person who'd known Van Austiant the way she had.

She did know that Shia was just as respectful as her brother, as evident in the way she bowed to her queen. Smiling with a touch of regret, Skylar waved in the young lady's direction. Perhaps they could one day meet, talk, and bond the way sisters did. Presumptuous though it might have been to think the two could become so close after remaining strangers for so long, it was genuinely a dream and assuredly a goal.

For the time being, however, a much more pressing agenda would have to be her focus. While shuffling through the adoring citizens, Skylar led Cyril to the lone entrance and exit of the Goodlit Summit and smiled at the guards who manned the towering gates; she wandered right through the doorway without any sort of fuss, as if she had always been allowed to do so—as if her royal training never had been the reason she hadn't dreamed of such a thing before. The moment she stepped beyond the threshold of the city, the queen couldn't help herself from basking in the moment. Feeling the brush of the wind that flew freely toward her without any obstruction from buildings was exhilarating for something so commonplace, even if the bite of the wintery breeze was unlike the gusts she'd savored in her tribe's desert dunes.

The sounds of her adoring people lost volume rather quickly as they continued on the first leg of her journey: the frigid Tundra

Walk, a lengthy and tumultuous pathway for anyone hoping to exit or enter Varon K'aii's capital. Skylar had only been escorted over the icy stepping-stones once, when she'd had the expertise of Xerus and Raibeart to guide her. Her favored boots stomped through the snow that rewarded one once he or she successfully passed over the frozen lakes and cushioned the trek to the other side.

"So." Cyril started with much uncertainty in one lone word. "How'd you end up with Mr. Strictly Business?"

The nickname drew her attention to his impish face as they walked over the uneven ridges beneath the snow. They were moments away from the largest stretch of its wintery obstacles when he spoke his intrusive question. Though perhaps it was childish, it surprised her that he had not a clue who she'd been before becoming queen or of the heralding journey Xerus had gone on to retrieve her.

Smirking to herself, she turned her eyes back onto their amorphous path. "Are you saying neither Raibeart nor the king ever told you any stories about me?"

"Heh, maybe if I hadn't been so busy working my butt off making an honest living, I'd have been at your queening ceremony and heard the stories myself," Cyril said, referring casually to her luxurious inauguration. In reality, it had been such an overwhelming day that she could not recall if Xerus had spoken of any of their memories as he eloquently gave his gracious speeches. He had praised her and done his best to convince the people that she was a worthy queen they would come to adore, but had he given away some of the precious gems of their childhood? She could not say one way or the other.

Skylar quickly disregarded the thought with a shrug. "I don't know if he ever shared our story with anyone."

"Then maybe you'd like to share it," suggested Cyril.

"How about"—she felt a chill rattle her as she thought of the words she'd say next—"we discuss this further in the next city? Where sunlight is more common than snow? For now, we should focus on what's right before us."

With a wave of her hand, Skylar welcomed Cyril to the frozen lake that separated the Goodlit Summit from the rest of the world. Her companion had crossed it earlier that day in order to seek the aid of the king, but the time difference between the treks could mean great variables in the quality of the ice that littered the surface of the frigid waters. From the constant wintry weather to the seawater that filled the lake with its salty compounds, that portion of the Tundra Walk was second only to the coliseum in Spierté as a test for heroes in the world. She had learned from Raibeart how to test for the safest way to cross, though she wasn't naive enough to believe that a simple chant of "Thick and blue, tried and true" was an apt amount of education in traversing the risky lake.

"Tch, I'll say." Cyril frowned as he watched her work. "Can't you guys make this a li'l' easier on all us regular non-mountain-dwelling folks?"

The queen inhaled deeply as she prepared to offer a formal response. "Currently, we do have volunteers who come to check the density of the ice on either end of the lake when there are scheduled trips coming through. With the meeting of the leaders that took place before your arrival, our volunteers would have crossed with them. However, with the sudden increased interest of citizens across the country visiting the summit, we plan to employ two teams of five on both sides to assist travelers in crossing the lake at all times."

That explanation did not appease the businessman, as evident by the pout he showed her through the fur lining on the hood of his gifted black parka. "Why not just build a bridge then?"

"We are not able to do so, unfortunately." Skylar gave her gentle rejection of the idea as she decided to test a nearby slab of ice by putting half of her weight onto it.

"Oh yeah? Why's that?"

She turned to stare him dead in the eye. The answer on her lips sounded like a question, as if she couldn't believe he would not know the reason himself. "The Agloolik."

The confused expression that filled his hood indicated that he genuinely did not understand the words she had just spoken. "The what?"

"In actuality," she said while moving out, "it's because of the wildlife in this area overall. There are many creatures that would not take too kindly to their territory being covered by a bridge, given that they occasionally breach the water. But Agloolik is suspected to be the zenith who guards the Tundra Walk."

When met with silence filled only by the brisk winter winds, Skylar looked over her shoulder at the rarely expressionless man and knew instantly the reason for his silence. "You don't believe in the spirits?" Given how he had boldly inquired about her relationship with Xerus, the queen assumed he was the sort who could handle a blunt question without taking offence.

And bluntly did he reply. "Given that I'm from Hierony and haven't seen a deity or whatever you just said, I don't have a reason to believe in anything. Never have."

A snappy quip entered her mind as he stepped onto the ice behind her: Cyril should find a deity to pray to—preferably Syvant, as it was her zenith he was denying in its own territory—if he hoped to preserve himself during their venture across the fickle lake. However, it dawned on her then as she caught herself in the midst of the thought that there were sure to be others who thought similarly to him. Whether they were like-minded Hierony citizens, students and teachers at the Viskretta Center, or even people whom she ruled over naturally as natives to Varon K'aii, it was impossible for there not to be more than one nonbeliever in Ordell and the Four Deities. It seemed incomprehensible to someone like her, who'd grown up in a tribe worshipping the deity of peace, that one could be faithless. Ruling over and aiding those whose values in some way conflicted with her own would likely be one of her greatest challenges as queen.

Then she realized that the soldiers she was going to meet at Otornot Keep probably felt an amplified version of her unease. The notion that someone could appear so similar yet behave and act on beliefs that felt divergent from what was thought of as the normalized basis of religion in Varon K'aii's culture had enough power to unsteady even one as gentle-natured as she; if she was not careful, Skylar could glimpse an understanding of how such feelings of instability could lead one astray when seeking balance with the outside islands.

In his own way, Cyril had given the queen insight on how to further assist him with his trouble at the keep.

"A zenith is considered the land-based spirit that acts as a representative for one of the Four Deities," Skylar said, turning to face the icy waters in order to continue toward their goal.

"Really? That's what this Agoogly is?"

"A-gloo-lik." She emphasized the correct pronunciation while doing her best not to show any sign of amusement. "It's the deity of wisdom and philosophy's zenith and is said to live in this lake."

Skylar expected some witty retort from the ever-charming Cyril and was shocked to hear not even a peep from the mouthy man. His response would be on its way, though, and simply slow in its delivery; she realized when turning to examine him that his primary focus was to steady himself on the ice. He spouted some whispered gibberish while fumbling under his large coat, making a poor attempt to balance his stance on the slippery chunk he currently resided on. At one point, she wasn't sure he was ever going to stand upright again, what with the way his back started to curve backward. However, he managed to wiggle his arms enough in order to counteract the falling motion and found his feet firmly planted once again.

When the jittery man finally reclaimed his semblance of control over his flailing limbs, the pair looked at one another in a moment of stillness. Then they each released a laugh that perfectly echoed their thoughts on Cyril's ineptitude to stay upright. Their laughter echoed off the mountain-like walls that encased the Tundra Walk, yet they couldn't find reason enough to lower their voices. When they eventually did simmer down, the klutz of a man chose to conclude their glee with a simple remark: "What's so wise about living on an icy lake?"

The immediate response he received was a rumble from beneath the ice, accompanied by an aquatic cry.

Just as she asked the calculating businessman to put their chat on hold, a rude winter wind rushed past them and pierced them both to the bone. Skylar's knee-high boots and winged stockings peeking out from beneath were not enough to save her legs from enduring the chilly blast as it tossed her floor-length coat behind her back, snapping the hooks with its ferocity. A rumble from beneath their feet nearly toppled them both, as did the set of three similar thundering bursts that followed. It was likely that what they had just heard and felt was a warning of something much more arctic and frightening.

"R-right. L-let's get a move on and avoid finding out!" Cyril shouted over the winds as he attempted to totter off.

"It's too late!" screamed Skylar in an attempt to be heard over the sound of deep ice cracking from the bottom of a nearby hardy slab. "Get your weapon out. We have to fight." Before she could finish her warning, Skylar already had the handle of her whip in hand, squeezing it in her grip in a pulsating motion as she prepared to defend them both. It seemed she had been granted the chance to be a beast master again much sooner than she had expected.

Jagged cracks shot along the ice, weakening its defense for the creature beneath it. Skylar caught a glimpse of an inky black figure beneath her feet before the creature shot forth and disappeared momentarily. Then it emerged by shattering the ice with a strong pierce from its dorsal fin. Skylar and Cyril were forced to abandon their positions in order to locate a place to stand that had avoided the damage caused by the monster of the lake. Another bellowing screech resounded, bouncing around the Tundra Walk as their meager laughter had just moments ago. Shards and chunks of ice flew in every direction as a result of the eruption the beast had caused, and what a formidable one it turned out to be.

"The akhlut," the beast master whispered to herself, stunned momentarily by both reverence and nerves.

Cyril, on the other hand, sounded much more horrified than she. "Iglookik?"

"No, this is"—she decided to avoid using its legendary name, in the hopes that he could pronounce it correctly and remember the species of beast that began to morph before them—"the alpha aquarius."

"And it's supposed to do that?" demanded her partner and supposed world traveler as he stared at the creature with wide olive eyes. He had been forced to kneel before it when finding another place to stand, which surely only made it seem grander in size.

The enormous killer whale that had escaped the lake's waters began to claw at the broken layer of ice it had decimated, using the wolflike claws it grew while morphing between its forms. Slowly, the neck of a wolf emerged and covered most of its neck with fur matching the blackness of the rest of its body. The teeth it dared to bear to Skylar and Cyril had a considerable amount of wear to them, indicating the creature's age and its obvious need to be territorial over the lake. It dragged its body from the water on four giant legs; the muscles in its shoulders and hips bulged beneath the skin, emphasizing the size of the Akhlut in comparison to mere humans.

They could only brace for impact as its ginormous mouth opened and screeched directly at them. Skylar quickly raised her forearm to shield her eyes from the shards of ice that were sent flying under the pressure of the sound, but being unable to see the beast made her instincts run wild when she heard the distinctive noise of the Akhlut bounding toward them. She quickly glanced at Cyril and saw that he was brandishing a set of throwing knives—a practical weapon for a man of business and travel but a death sentence when facing a beast of this size. She realized she might have to fight the beast all on her own.

Throwing down her arm, Skylar demonstrated herself with two harsh snaps of her whip. The crackle was barely noticeable over the stampeding paws headed toward her. It took a great deal of her resolve to remain calm and collected, given that she was losing her ground. A warrior could think; a beast master was strong. What other options were there if she couldn't tame it? It came closer and closer until she was nearly looking up into its massive whalelike face, and an oversize wolf paw prepared to swipe at her without remorse.

Suddenly, in such a position, she realized the akhlut's greatest weakness.

"Skylar, move already!" Cyril begged from off to her right as he attempted to throw one of his knives. However, with the heralding winds being as strong as they were, he must have known how pointless the assault would be.

In response to his plea, the queen said, "Run, Cyril. Now!"

Instead of challenging the beast in a show of physical superiority,

Skylar decided to use its own size and force against it by standing in the way of its attack. She waited until the very last second, watching the black padding of its claw from the corner of her eye, before throwing herself in the way of the underside of the enormous creature's attack. Her slightly curled form collided with the heavy swat, and she nearly lost the wind in her lungs as a result. However, her plan was to utilize the massive swing to land on the forearm of the beast. It required great strength to leap onto its arm and plant herself against the muscles it had built there, but Skylar decided it was best to continue moving rather than try to steady herself and give the Akhlut time to react.

Throwing herself with the extemporaneous power of her adrenaline, the queen let out an unseemly grunt while latching onto the fur that encircled the Akhlut's neck. Its length was short, thereby limiting the creature's ability to snap down at her or turn its head even while in that form. Skylar had wagered her life in the hopes that it would use its paws instead of its teeth to challenge her—now there she swayed, dangling in its fur. The confused beast cried out and immediately began to thrash. Before it could think to rip its nails into her body, she gripped its fur between her hands and climbed.

The Akhlut was wild, but it was not feebleminded; screaming in protest while she scaled its massive form, the beast showed its expertise as a formidable opponent by slamming the side of its body down into the ice. Impacting with a booming thud, the beast master on its back had already made her way over its shoulder and missed the attack by a mere instance. Her experience in scaling the craggy mountains in the desert had prepared her for moments like these—battles in which she needed her body's entire vitality in order to survive.

She needed to move before it tried to thwart her again. Its tail flailed behind its body as Skylar managed to crawl through its ebony pelt and secure herself directly behind its blowhole. It was her goal to lie flat against the Akhlut's forehead until it calmed, but as she positioned herself, the sound of a manly cry caught her attention. Skylar tossed her head high and watched as her companion was sent flying through the air, disappearing into the snow-hauling winds, until she could no longer make out his presence on the lake. The sight was unbelievable;

if the Akhlut was still lying down beneath her, what could have forced Cyril into the air like that?

"Cyril!" she cried, momentarily forgetting her place on the back of the wild beast. Then her breath was stolen from her as she too was forced to endure the same mysterious treatment.

Skylar felt as though a large translucent fin had slapped her sharply. She should have heard the noise over the bellow of the storm. Having no control over her body, she flew across the icy expanse of the lake that had not endured the Akhlut's wrath, soaring at a speed she could not comprehend. When she spotted the smudge that was Cyril trying to collect himself in a pile of snow, the queen braced for impact as she found herself landing face first in a second snowbank next to him. Her companion quickly pulled her free and sat with her while they both did their best to catch their breath. Their wide eyes said everything without their uttering a word: neither of them had any clue what had just occurred.

The Akhlut's waning shriek compelled them to look at the lake they had just magically crossed as the storm raging over it began to subside. Most likely due to the impact of the creature's body, the now familiar sound of ice cracking was shortly followed by a large splash as it assumedly returned to its natural depth before swimming out to sea. Though it wouldn't take long for the lake to repair itself in the Tundra Walk's constant state of winter, their battle had guaranteed a closure of the passageway between the summit and Spierté for a short while, which was something Agloolik appeared to disapprove of.

Before their eyes, the zenith known as Agloolik hovered over the shattered ice with a striking look of disgust on its face. Its scaled body was a cross between a fish and a man, the colors ranging from light greens to cerulean blues, golden yellows to violet purples. At the end of its illustrious tail was a massive crystalline fin that perfectly matched in size and texture those found along its arms and back. Its hair was like a cascading waterfall, but in its spiritual state, the waters seemingly disappeared into nothingness at its end. It had eyes like that of a fish and two trailing whiskers above its mouth. Its facial features only further emphasized how greatly they had angered the lake and its guardian.

The Agloolik faded before their eyes as it turned its back on them, and with its departure, the weather settled into a peaceful state once again. The pair were left sitting in awe at all they had just witnessed, with the most prominent wonder being the assistance of a zenith who surely had just saved their lives. Skylar had yet to cease panting, but she could not refrain from looking over at Cyril the nonbeliever and weakly attempting to smirk at his stunned reaction. "N-now," she huffed as her teeth chattered in protest to her coatless frozen state, "w-what was th-that spirit called-d again?"

As if he were too mindless to protest in response to her chide, Cyril craned his neck to look at the queen with a blank expression. They remained still while she awaited his response. However, instead of granting her the victory, the businessman surprised her by leaping to his feet. He did not bother to dust off his parka or the legs of his suit, which had been soaked by the snow. After standing upright, he kindly helped Skylar to her feet as she observed his suspicious behavior. He blinked a few times while staring down at his once-dry formal shoes and then performed the most awkward and forced bow before turning to face the final, less threatening stretch of the Tundra Walk

"A-all right then, let's m-move out! G-got places to be, and it sure as hell ain't here!" Pointing forward, Cyril mechanically led them on their way again, likely too stunned to notice the giggles failing to be smothered behind him.

CHAPTER 3

When they finally reached Spierté, Skylar stretched out her limbs under the beaming sunshine. She had known this town was just beyond the Tundra Walk, and oh, how she required seeing it, smelling it, and feeling it again. The bridge filled with citizens and combatants stretched out before her, the bustling businesses hosted traveling combatants and tourists, and the coliseum was a perilous hike away to her left. The entire city gave her a distinct flash of nostalgia as she did her best to take it in while still rattling at its entrance, no longer due to the chill that had chased them.

She smiled at Cyril, who was crossing his arms over his chest one at a time and cracking the bones to rid himself of the shivers in a way similar to her. "Feeling better?" she jested.

"Mm, I'll say. Man, I don't know how you live out there. I'd become a Cyril ice pop in a few days. A week tops. Or monster fodder." As he played along with her banter, he escorted her across the bridge she had not finished admiring. The waters rushing underneath were lively and ample, and Skylar believed they reflected her in more ways than one.

She could see the fighting arena from where she stood, and she was amazed at how intimidating it still appeared after all these years. Skylar had stopped competing in the annual tournament between the tribes when she made her choice to seriously pursue the path of a beast master, meaning it had been at least a decade and a half since she had last witnessed its mighty presence. Its design still reminded her of a stony monster clawing itself free through the crust of the earth, even though she had seen the interior of the arena many times and knew that the digit-like towers were meant to resemble spears.

It felt unreal in that moment to think that many moons ago, she had met the sullen, prideful, unmatched king of the land as a young man inside that open dome; there was no way to have known then that he would one day become her husband by the same description.

"I'm sure Raibeart would honor you by putting you on display at the castle."

"You think so? As long as he didn't let Xerus use me as some frozen target practice for the military, I guess I wouldn't mind." They shared a subdued laugh at the picture they had verbally designed.

When the pair had landed on the opposite side of the bridge, Skylar turned around to get a better look at the city. The walls of the hotels and taverns bore many more tribal banners than they had in her childhood, denoting many more victors—and, as a result, local supporters of the champions for those years—who'd braved the Marina Path and the slew of beasts that lived along the way to the yearly tournament, including fiercer beasts than those she had just witnessed. The spirit of life was alive and ever present in that ancient place, and it always managed to bring out the warrior in those who knew it well, with merely the smell of the earth calling anyone worth his or her salt in battle to come to Spierté.

The citizens also honored past champions by erecting statues to their most prominent victors once they had passed on. A rumor had spread among the tribes that Léonie's statue was the only one the builders in the city had begun production on preemptively, due to the indisputable fact that she deserved to be revered and remembered among the league of other heroes. Her statue was stationed next to Skylar when she stepped off the bridge, and the sight of it struck her with awe. She had never met the woman but had heard word of her accomplishments and magnetism as frequently as people spoke of the Four Deities.

Léonie was a fierce giant of a woman, the only medium between beasts and men. She wore the pelt of the first and only beast she had ever slain around her waist, on top of her tribe's traditional robes, in memory of both its life and the immature lifestyle that had led her to kill an ennedi tiger. The instant her ability to communicate with beasts awoke, Léonie worked alone in her goal to bridge the gap between people and the other creatures who lived on Varon K'aii. This led to many battles she fought with her trusty ax, which was ten times the size of the miniscule armor she donned; her chest plate covered only the side of her missing breast. Oddly enough, the story of how she came to lose her breast was never told—it was known only that the injury failed to keep her from fighting until her last breath.

The rock image left Skylar in a state of awe, which nearly led to her failing to recognize the sound of a civilian jogging their way. "Hey, Cyril! You're back so soon." The man sounded somewhat surprised as he greeted his friend.

Cyril stopped and posed in his lazy way the moment he realized who was headed in their direction. "Rainier, perfect timing. How'd you know we were here?"

"I didn't; I was actually thinking of heading to the Goodlit Summit myself to talk to King Xerus with you." Rainier sounded somewhat ashamed that it had taken him some time to consider joining his friend. Cyril's business partner appeared sturdy in his stance, but his heart of gold was an apparent weakness of his. The feeling the pair emitted when standing so close almost made it seem as if they were related—like brothers who had had their fair share of dispensed hardships together— if only their appearances weren't drastically different. Rainier clearly had a second profession as one of the many builders in the city; his tattered clothes and muddied hands contrasted the well-tailored suit his friend wore.

Hissing, Cyril soothed in his unique way. "Aw, you didn't need to worry about me. I can handle talking to the king on my own. Besides, I brought back someone who's willing to help us out more than I ever expected. Rainier, meet Skylar." He motioned to them with his limp arms in a lame introduction.

Her companion had been wise in refraining from using her title or further developing her station in the streets. Rainier was confused for a few instants before confounded realization shone in his weary eyes and tone. "You mean you brought *the* Skylar? The quee—"

"It is very nice to meet you." Skylar stepped in and silenced him politely. Acting naturally meant she could not scan the intersected roads for possible onlookers or suspicious parties, both of which she did not appreciate. Gossiping young ladies or past challengers roaming the streets could have overheard the exclamation, and it risked complicating their journey. If they moved on quickly, she'd have nothing to fear most likely; it had been a simple mistake, one she would not hold against the Spierté native.

The understanding of her silencing act registered with Rainier, and he blushed due to his carelessness. "You as well. Come. We can talk inside my home."

"Good idea. Now that I'm starting to warm up again, I wouldn't mind a nice cold beer. You're stocked up, right?" Cyril chuckled, walking off intuitively after his friend.

They went up the stairs to their right, took another flight carved into the cavern-like walls that housed the city, and entered the first door on the second level of apartments with relative ease. It was a small space that spanned out into one and a half rooms at the most, and its size reminded Skylar of the tent she had grown up in. It had only what one needed to survive and live amicably rather than halls, pillars, separate dressing rooms for royalty, and river-long bathtubs. It was cozy, and she found it charming.

"Vérène not home?" Cyril's sudden question was different from his others as he stood next to the single bed in the designated bedroom of the flat, stealing her silent fascination away. He had removed his suit jacket and, apparently, his gentleness when prodding. The way he had sounded when quizzing his friend was colder and held none of his lackluster warmth.

Rainier seemed oblivious when he replied from the sink in the kitchen, "She was doing a bit better today, so a friend took her out for a walk." Even if all he received was a grunt from his partner, it mattered not to the man of Spierté. He kindly gestured to the table next to the bed, but Cyril just dropped his weight onto the dingy mattress. He seemed heavy, as if burdened by something that related to the very thing on which he sat, which perplexed Skylar, whether or not she let it show.

She took the offered seat graciously and thanked her host. He smiled in recognition of her politeness before snapping the reins on their halted conversation. "I can't believe the queen came to help us herself."

"Why is that?" Skylar blurted out before she had the chance to think.

Rainier looked surprised once again. "It's just … I hope we aren't taking up too much of your valuable time." He had cleaned himself up as much as he could at the sink, but there was evident dirt in the dried cracks in his skin. His hair was fastened against his head in an intensely braided pattern, but it too housed a great amount of dust. Still, his genuine hospitality blinded the queen to any imperfections in his appearance.

"That's exactly what your partner said," she replied, looking over at Cyril and his faint scowl. "You two are the ones most inconvenienced by this situation—my time is devoted to helping you in any way that I can." She assured the two businessmen with a nod.

Sighing with abundant relief, Rainier sank back into his chair. "Thank you so much, Your Majesty. We really appreciate this," he said.

"You're most welcome."

"Well now, with the queen on our side, it's unlikely we'll have any more problems for the next little while," remarked Cyril somewhat pessimistically. He found a comfortable pose resting on the heels of his palms and loosened his tight lips into yet another sly grin.

"How are you planning on dealing with the soldiers at Otornot Keep, if you don't mind sharing?" asked Rainier bashfully.

Skylar ignored his considerate addition and went into her resolution. "My plan is to speak with these men and try to help them empathize with the people of the islands while I attempt to understand them. I don't want to dismiss them and let them continue feeling the resentment that they do; their hatred has been brought to my attention, and I want to do something to try to change it."

Rainier wore a face that indicated the level of awe and the deep-seated feelings of hope he had for her claim. "I see" was all he managed to articulate as her words washed over him. Judging by his reaction,

Rainier was one who likely championed her cause of tolerance and acceptance among all.

"Right? Isn't she a female Xerus?" mused Cyril aloud. He stroked his scratchy facial hair as he smirked cheekily, no matter how the queen let on about her feelings toward the peculiar observation.

"I don't know if I should be offended by you referring to Xerus as vain enough to marry someone just like him or if I should think you're complimenting me whenever you say that." Skylar playfully sneered at her accuser.

"I'm sure he means that in the most flattering way. Right, Cyril?" Rainier prompted him as vaguely as he could, but the way he spoke through grinding teeth gave away his irritation with his friend. Cyril seemingly recognized that he was indeed pressing his luck when he shrugged in response. To ease the queen's feelings, the more respectful of the business partners added, "Xerus is a great king. One I am proud to serve."

"I'm sure he would appreciate hearing you say so." Skylar smiled, for she knew his sentiments were felt by many Varon K'aiians. She felt complimented by words such as these on behalf of her absent mate.

"Yeah, yeah, he's just a big tough guy who has a soft spot for stuffed animals and kids."

"Cyril!" Rainier scolded him blatantly this time.

"Stuffed animals?" She couldn't think of asking about his remark regarding children at that moment. Besides, she was thrown for a loop at the thought that Xerus would allow the beasts of the world to be stuffed and placed around the castle like some sort of trophy collection. She hadn't even known he was a hunter. Such pieces of information were vital to a proud beast master such as herself.

"Oh yeah—you didn't know?" How sinister Cyril sounded. "We all went to visit my hometown once, and the king found himself the cutest li'l' caribou he had ever seen." He said the last part in a childish voice, seemingly to disarm Skylar further. Sure enough, it did.

There was a live caribou in Yukaih Castle? An infant one at that? She had been there for half a year and had never come across such a creature. Was the king keeping things from the queen? Something as silly as an animal companion? That seemed highly unlikely, regardless of Cyril's intriguing words.

With a sneaky grin, he finally revealed all without waiting for a response. "It's this stuffed caribou doll that you can use as a neck pillow—it's called Caribooboo. Some crazy old lady had a crush on your hubby apparently and made it for him. Guess where he keeps it?"

"Where?"

"He hid it away somewhere in that crypt of an office of his."

Skylar could not believe what she was hearing. Mighty, formidable, irrefutably just Xerus possessed a comforting plush known as Caribooboo? Such a simple fact somehow turned her world on its head in a flash.

She found herself hollering with laughter. It was the most damning, forthcoming piece of information she had ever learned about her husband. A darker part of her cursed him for never sharing such a delicious secret with her himself, even if she knew there was not a chance on Ordell's green earth that he would ever volunteer telling anyone such a thing. That must have been part of the reason Raibeart was only allowed to teach her for one hour each session—he had to keep one of his friends and damnatory enemies near at all times to guarantee his silence.

How amusingly absurd.

"You're lucky Xerus is a friend of yours and extremely kind. Otherwise, I might have to find myself a new business partner." Frowning as best as he could while fighting laughter from deep in his chest, Rainier looked slightly ridiculous as he tried to condemn Cyril.

Cyril waved off his remark easily enough. "Oh, come on, Rainier. Don't pretend you're not about to burst."

"Perhaps we should return to the subject at hand." Skylar did her best to speak through her simmering fit, hoping to keep their host from feeling as though he were one small chuckle away from imprisonment.

"Yes." Rainier jumped on board with her offer immediately. "We should talk about our route and when we plan to leave. I imagine we'll have to take the long way around again, through the Marina Path and Sailbrooke."

"About that ..."

"Huh?" asked one businessman to the other.

Cyril donned his previous scowl again, staring down at the floor as he contemplated his next addition to their conversation. Troubled by some internal trifle, he took some time to collect his thoughts before facing Rainier, to whom he declared, "I think it's best if Skylar and I do this on our own."

"What! Cyril, how could you even suggest that? We're partners; this is just as much my problem as it is yours." While speaking, the once calm man was compelled to stand from his chair.

The transformation she witnessed in both men felt ritualistic, as if the argument regarding their fealty as partners was a hatchet yet to be buried. To suggest that she accompany him—effectively in a partnership much like the one he was denying temporarily—was assuredly a blow to their esteemed relationship. It was striking how somber she felt in watching their budding bout begin.

"Rainier." Cyril punctuated his name with a great deal of seriousness. "This whole thing could turn violent; as great as Skylar's plan is, neither one of us can guarantee they won't try to attack us for me tattling on them. If you could fight, I wouldn't need to worry. Besides, with Vérène feeling better, don't you want to spend time with her? Just wait here for us to come back, and we'll set out for Terrinal together once this whole mess gets sorted out. Mmkay?"

"Cyril." His partner sounded as though he understood when he gently spoke his name. Feelings from different ends of his being washed across the Spierté man's face, reflective of the city and its far reaches all over the world. Regardless of the multitude he felt, Rainier stuck with his obvious outrage and surprised them both by making his way to the door. He looked back at the man he called his partner for but an instant before he mumbled something about needing to see to something in town and departed.

It was awkward for a considerable amount of time as Skylar sat with Cyril in his moment of brief abandonment. His following statement did not help matters. "Gee, no matter how much I try, I just can't seem to do the right thing."

"Your intentions were well founded." It was the only thing the royal-in-training could think to say.

Cyril accepted her kindness with a nod, even though it was something she had been obliged to offer him in terms of comfort as the only other person in his presence. A dark shadow fell upon the room with the setting sun, taking away its previously welcome warmth, which only darkened the poor man's features further. It didn't take much longer for the transpired disagreement to compel him to rise as well; without a word, Cyril sighed, seemingly with all the breath he held, and made his way out of the house to follow his friend.

After the door slammed behind him, Skylar closed her eyes in a frail attempt to shut out the flagrancy she had just witnessed. Being left in Rainier's home was slightly uncomfortable, but she did not let it phase her. Their squabble was about much more than Otornot Keep, Cyril's concern for his civil friend, or the discrimination she had left Yukaih Castle to help vanquish. There was a loose thread in their weave of comradery, and the plainest irritation had unraveled much more than either had bargained for.

Opening her eyes, the queen couldn't help but think to herself, *Are all partnerships so easily trumped by unspoken feelings?* The two men were much friendlier with each other than she was with her mate, yet a single show of interpretive care had been taken so incorrectly that it resulted in a mess needing to be cleaned before Cyril's and her journey could move onward.

The debacle felt interpretive in a different sense, reminding Skylar of the suspicious beliefs she held as to how her own partnership with Xerus had fallen apart months ago during the events of one fateful outing together.

Forcing her into ceasing her melancholic thoughts, the sudden sound of a plains flute echoed from somewhere in the room. Startled, she quickly pinpointed the source of the noise: Cyril's suit jacket pocket. *What on Varon K'aii?* She had never heard such a strange variation of a flute before—and with no one around her to play the instrument. It didn't register as a natural melody; it was almost as if it had been manufactured by way of technology she had only ever heard about. It persisted for a short passage and then cut out in its seventh repetition of the same three notes repeatedly playing. Just when she believed she was free from its torment, the familiar tune started up again.

Equally curious as she was bothered, Skylar stood and looked over the jacket Cyril had laid unceremoniously on the bed. There was indeed something resting inside, with a cylindrical shape reminiscent of a flute. She had no reason to think the noise was coming from anywhere else and pulled it from the pocket without concern for its ownership in order to study the device. It had a wooden finish on its body, but it looked to be a painted styling. Confused and displeased with the consistency of the sound, she shook the device in her hand in hopes of discovering some secret it held.

Surprisingly, her jerky motions split the instrument into two halves vertically, revealing a complicated internal setup. The queen prayed she had not just damaged a citizen's property. There were buttons on one half of the device and a glowing rectangular piece on the other, which was flashing in time with the noise the device made. She noticed the symbol of a blocky black feather.

Skylar saw a button matching the strange depiction on the screen and hit it, hoping to end her torture.

"Hello?" A prominent voice burst into the room.

Though startled once again, Skylar recognized the speaker, no matter how scratchy he sounded. She brought the device to her ear with caution, concerned about whether or not she was handling it correctly, both grateful and disappointed that no one was present to see her through this. "Hello?" she answered.

"Skylar?" said the voice on the other side of the strange device. She was somehow speaking to her husband.

"Xerus?"

"What are you doing with Cyril's totem?" He sounded just as puzzled as she felt when answering his summons on the recently revealed totem.

Facing the stairs that descended to the door, she explained, "He stepped out for the time being. We are in Spierté at the moment."

It seemed he was unaware of Rainier's existence, for he asked, "Whatever for?"

"Cyril's business partner lives in this city, and they needed to discuss some important matters." The story of why she stood alone in a home that was not her own wasn't hers to share. She could only imagine how the king might perceive her explanation if she offered it or what sort of words he might have to say. If Xerus was anything, he was a wonderful problem solver, but this was not a problem in which he held any influence.

Their marriage was a nagging issue he should devote his time to instead.

"I see," said Xerus.

For a second, her heart leaped upward in her chest; she feared he'd somehow heard the childish whining she held inside.

Thankfully, he diverted the conversation to focus on her in other ways. "Are you somewhere comfortable while you wait?"

"Yes, I am," Skylar said.

She sensed his relief through the muffled static that channeled his voice. "Good. I called because I wanted to warn you two of upcoming weather reports."

"Weather reports?"

"Yes. You both departed so quickly that the people of the Goodlit Summit saw more of you than Raibeart or I did before you set out on your journey."

Skylar opened her mouth to apologize but was silenced by his onslaught.

"We weren't sure which path you were taking to Otornot Keep, but we have reason for concern for all three of your possible options. Have you decided which road you will be taking?"

"No, not yet. However, Rainier suggested going by way of the Marina Path." She recalled her host's advice just before Xerus had the chance to speak again. The map of Varon K'aii was still fresh in her mind from her lessons with Raibeart, serving as an aid as she kept pace with her mate while he deliberated possible travel plans with her via this bizarre talking device.

Papers shuffled on the other side of the connection while Xerus reported to her, "The Marina Path will be flooding from an extreme rainfall in the next day or so. Depending on when you choose to depart, I suggest you take caution."

His ending remark irked her. "Of course."

"Otherwise, it is merely the more burdensome path."

"Unless you consider that it is the only path that will have us on the right side of Otornot Keep when we arrive," Skylar said softly. She was well aware of the many cities and landscapes they would encounter while traveling the outer edge of Varon K'aii to reach their goal, and were it not for her objective in her trip, she would gladly relish in every moment.

There was a pause on the line. "You could enter from the other side and speak with those in charge first; you will need to determine who it was Cyril spoke to before approaching anyone with the intention of reform. Going the other way around would also allow Cyril and his partner to enter Terrinal and begin negotiations that were previously delayed."

His experience as king had Skylar in awe, and she was suddenly thankful that the technological device in her hands prevented him from seeing her reaction. "That is very true." She had not a clue what else she could say.

"It would seem that your best bet is to travel to Nàmheil by boat."

"And then sail for Terrinal from there." Admittedly, he had an excellent point. The third option most likely involved going through the Vicis Plain, which would only have been a possibility had they exited the Goodlit Summit on the opposite side. They were unlikely to wander back into the royal city only to venture through the murky and forbidden land. It almost seemed as if she were cheating by having the outside help of weather reports in determining their path, but it was helpful to know that her luscious mane of hair would be spared the downpour if they took Rivage Passage to its docks and moved forth from there.

"Yes." Xerus confirmed such obvious information without the need to do so.

When he failed to say more, Skylar stood in for him. "Thank you for telling us this. It has saved us from catching a cold, I'm sure."

A grumble from the other end implied that he might have taken her lightheartedness as derision. "Being sick while traveling would only make your job that much more challenging."

"It would," she agreed in order to pacify him, hoping to rectify his interpretation.

She would never know if she had done her job; he never replied to her miniscule remark. Skylar wondered if she had somehow lost the ability to communicate with him through some malfunction of the device in her hands when he didn't respond.

Finally, he added, "I also called to inform you I might not be in the Goodlit Summit when you return."

Surprisingly, Skylar's heart sank. "Oh?"

"Raibeart and I were both called to meet with another country that plans to support the amphitheater in roughly a week's time; should you return after I depart, I will first travel to Summerside to meet with Emery Mor and then sail to the construction site for the amphitheater to speak with the Luminaries and view the progress of their work."

"I see." It was her turn to use the disconnected phrase on him; Xerus was busy whether she was inside his castle or not, yet for some reason, she felt dissatisfied to know that she would not be welcomed home by him or her teacher but only by servants and the military officers she would most likely spend all her time with.

The amphitheater was a major development in the world, beyond the needs of just the continent that her husband governed, as it was the first step toward unifying every single country across the seas. Until she had left the Nazuré people, she hadn't been aware, let alone dared to imagine, there was life beyond the land on which she was born. Though the project was still in the preliminary stages, Raibeart had heavily implied that it would change the way of life for all different walks of people, including ones they had yet to meet. The concept had sounded overwhelming to Skylar at the time, but she was slowly coming to terms with the notion and was mostly willing herself to accept the reality thrust upon her now that she was being educated and forced to open her eyes to more than the ground before the horizon line.

After all, she would need something of great importance to distract herself from an empty bedchamber when she returned home—something he was surely used to from the years he'd lived in Yukaih Castle without her. He might find renewed comfort in being by his lonesome once again.

"Again." She spoke up after clearing her throat. "Thank you for informing me."

"You're welcome," her husband bluntly replied.

Every fiber of her being told her to study the talking device one more time to discover how to end their chat and put a stop to the most uncomfortable conversation they had ever endured. Skylar felt as though the distance and the technology that allowed them to speak while so far apart hindered their conversation, because she couldn't tell if he cared at all for their separation to last longer than anticipated. Her world had revolved around him for the past six months, and the possibility of having the castle under her control for even a small while should have been invigorating and exciting to the queen-in-training.

Instead, she felt frightened for some unspeakable reason.

Despite the voices inside that willed her to be strong and persevere through her depressing low, Skylar steadied herself as she chose her parting words carefully. "I do have a request of you, though."

"A request?" Xerus sputtered in a way that sounded as if he hadn't sputtered at all.

Typical. Skylar smiled to herself. "Yes. I hope you don't mind."

It was her husband's turn to clear his throat. The heavy sound cracked in her ear. "Not at all. Please, tell me what it is you would like to ask."

She dared not imagine that there was eagerness in his tone, for it might lead her to ruin when she returned to an empty home. Her grin grew wider as she thought of what she wanted to say. She almost had to abort from her decision to speak further to the king of Varon K'aii due to the fit she was sure to have following her giddy words. However, being Skylar, she dared not back down from her opposition of her mate under any circumstance, so bravely, she half whispered, "I would hope that in my absence, you take your precious Caribooboo to bed with you so that you will have something else to help you sleep at night."

Then she snapped the device closed and fell onto the bed, howling due to a complete loss of control.

CHAPTER 4

"I'm glad you managed to make amends with Rainier before we left." Skylar decided to start their first conversation of the day as they walked along the dusty road of the Rivage Passage. She spoke with a gentle smile on her face, hoping Cyril would sense her honesty as strongly as she provided it. They had set out early that morning after spending the night in Spierté; the titian coloring of the sky was disobliging in awakening their tired minds, and a few brave monsters had set to challenge them in groups the size of half a dozen. Holding a friendly chat wasn't too trying of a feat compared to all else they had faced so early in the morn.

Cyril arched an eyebrow at her as he combed his fingers through his hair weakly. "He got what I was saying when he calmed down enough to listen." That was all he had to say about the matter, as indicated by the grandiose yawn succeeding his words.

Not one to pry, Skylar nodded and faced forward as they marched, until a second topic popped into her mind. "Oh," she squeaked, "I forgot to tell you something."

"Hm? And what's that?"

"After you left to speak with Rainier, your device in your pocket made some noises."

Cyril seemed to behave reflexively as he reached for his totem. Peeking over the width of his arm, the queen tried to watch as her partner seemed to scroll through some sort of list titled "Call Log." "Oh yeah?" His response sound mindless and distracted.

"I answered it," Skylar said.

"Whoa, you what?" Her revelation seemed to bother her traveling companion as he looked away from his device and revealed to her his wide eyes. "Your Majesty—"

"Please." She almost begged with her tone. "Call my Skylar."

Cyril winced before carrying on. "Okay, Skylar, you can't just go around answering people's totems like that. It's not really the nice thing to do. It would have been really bad for me if that was someone wanting to talk business or—"

"It was Xerus."

"Oh, never mind then. But the no-answering rule still stands." Cyril clarified his scolding's aim before stuffing his totem into his pants' back pocket, as if its snug placement atop his bottom kept it safe from her clutches.

She found it amusing that he felt so protective of such a noisy invention; the connection with his business could justify his newly chosen concealment, but the way he frowned—almost childlike, more so than anything else he had said or done—made her feel less apologetic than she likely should have.

"What did Xerus want, pray tell? And didn't he buy you a totem of your own?"

His whiny hissing rivaled the cry of the wild jaculus monsters they had narrowly bypassed many times along the highroad. "I have never seen a totem such as that before in my life."

"How is that possible with all the advancements in technology we have nowadays? I guess it makes sense that the tribes aren't up to date with totems and whatnot, but that doesn't make sense. He's a king—Xerus could buy you every totem in the world and then some." He dared not admit it, but her lack of preceding knowledge softened his whimpering.

Skylar thought for a moment and then said, "I suppose there is no need to have one to communicate with when, well, this trip of ours is the first time I've left Yukaih Castle since I married him."

"Really?" Cyril's shock was duly noted.

She nodded. "Yes. I've been within walking distance of him for the last few months, so we wouldn't need to use these devices of yours to speak." Just as it wasn't her place to share with Xerus how Cyril and Rainier had fought, it was even less proper—and highly unwanted—for her to tell her traveling companion that a lack of communication also prevented the need for a totem. She had now learned that her husband owned one. The thought of her possessing a totem must never have crossed his mind for the reasons she had surmised.

"Not only that." Cyril snorted as he tacked on to her conjecture. "He hates totems more than anyone I know."

"He does?" Now it was her turn to face him wide-eyed.

His infamous smirk returned as he waved a hand around. "Oh yeah. If it weren't for the fact that they help people, he probably would have bought the world's supply just to get rid of them."

Huh. What an interesting piece of information. "I see." A giggle escaped her for a single instance. "Then it was probably due to Raibeart's insistence that he warned us about the weather."

"He called to give us a weather report? Seriously? Gee, what a sweetheart he is." Cyril made sure to sound as if he had been wooed by the kind gesture.

Skylar almost cracked her whip on his toes for mocking her mate's generous intelligence.

After all, his call had resulted in the protection of her hair and its flawless style from an oncoming torrent.

"If we had taken Rainier's route, we would have been flooded in the Marina Path." The report she had received sounded somewhat predictable when she spoke it aloud, given the name of the path.

A strong hand on her upper back—missing her hair as it rested in its comfortable pose over her shoulder—led her away from a sneaking freybug so they could continue speaking. "So that's why you chose to get covered by sand and dirt in this desert."

"A little dirt never hurt anyone." Skylar uttered the cliché with a touch of excitement. There wasn't any dirt, sand, or dust in Yukaih Castle; she had almost forgotten what pebbles under her boots felt like compared to the marvelous tiles and carpets she had grown accustomed to as of late.

In light of Cyril's smirk shrinking into a grin, she felt his concurrence of thought before he spoke. "I couldn't agree more." He sounded more at ease, as though he had forgotten what he had scolded his queen about earlier in their chat as he patted her shoulder amicably—until a pair of jackalopes bombarded them and caused him to stumble in his stride.

◆ ◆ ◆ ◆ ◆ ◆

Their arrival at the Rivage Docks was pleasant though brief, as Cyril showed her how to arrange passage across the sea easily. They boarded the impressive ship immediately and set out without delay. The sea breeze was noticeably different from the winds that carried flecks of earth out in the mountain terrain from which Skylar hailed; the moisture it offered felt constantly refreshing and clean as she deeply breathed in its freshness to prevent herself from becoming sick over the railing.

Thankfully, Cyril was wise enough to stand a few inches away. "I take it you haven't had the chance to grow any sea legs," he quipped, a touch of sympathy behind his voice. He stared down at her huddled position off to the side of the ship's deck, rubbing the back of his head in an act of uncertainty regarding how to assist her.

"No." She couldn't bear to shake her head, so she was forced to voice her answer. Skylar hoped he would understand what she had murmured into her knees—she was not lifting her head until they reached the shore. "How long is this boat ride?"

His response didn't sound promising. "Uh, why don't we talk about something else instead? Like how great Nàmheil is!" His thinly veiled attempt at distracting her from her swirling nausea wasn't promising either. Still, if he could manage to make her feel a fraction better, she couldn't fault him for trying.

"Oh?" Skylar said.

Cyril stalled, and she almost found the strength to lift her head and lightly glare. When he managed to concoct some sort of highlight of their destination, it was basic at best. "My buddy Emery is from there."

Her eyebrows pinched in the middle of her forehead as she wondered if she knew who he meant. "Emery Mor?"

"Yeah, the Luminary-to-be. She works at Credit now, but she started off wanting to be an archeologist in li'l' Nàmheil."

It was indeed an interesting facet about the otherwise elementary town. Emery, like Cyril, had a prominent past with Xerus and Raibeart, if she could see through the fog of her sickness and recall such things correctly. There was an undeniable trend in the companions her husband kept, excluding the young woman whose hometown she hoped to reach soon.

"So did you prefer traveling with men mostly?" Her question only sounded incriminating due to the uneasiness in her stomach. Unfortunately, Cyril seemed to take it in such a way as he panicked over her possible suspicions.

"What? No, no! We also had Dalya—Emery's best friend. She goes around to all three of the islands and gets to tell people where to travel to, so I doubt we'll see her anytime soon, sadly enough. But she is real. Really! Come on. Could lady-killers like Raibeart and I be on an all-guys team?"

Skylar never gave her answer, as thinking of Cyril's squirming made her feel a smidgen better than his silly attempt at conversation.

⧫⧫⧫⧫

She could have kissed the ground, but those who might have recognized her would assume she was a weak-willed or insane queen. It was difficult to compose herself enough to even depart from the ship, but she did so with as much finesse as she could muster. The ride from one port to the next felt much more exhausting than escaping the challenging eye of any of the beasts along the Rivage Passage.

She had another ship ride to look forward to when they headed off to Terrinal.

Trying her hardest not to think beyond the ground currently resting beneath her feet, Skylar found a miniscule reprieve with the small isle. It felt barely modern, yet a prospective Luminary had been raised in such a city. Perhaps basic roots were something she shared with the fabled Emery Mor. Her desire to meet the young intellect had not waned, and entering into Nàmheil, she felt as if she was given a tiny quick picture of the woman's life.

The cobblestone streets were just as lovely as the traditional style of the buildings, and olden hospitality was reflected in the kind citizens who greeted them but never imposed. What distinguished the town of Nàmheil were the stilts on which its houses rested. Skylar could easily imagine rough waters threatening the sustainability of the community, which helped her understand the logic behind the locals' decision to raise their homes above sea level; the staggered archipelago that filled the gap between each half of the continent most likely left the people of its only hospitable island in dire straits during times of crisis. Regardless of the challenges, there were still people living on such a dangerous portion of land, which was respectable in the eyes of the queen.

With Cyril in the lead, they wandered up the slight slope in the midst of the small town. The community was small even while occupying the entire island; the staggered archipelago that filled the gap between each half of the continent housed no other city on any of its islands, which was a testament of the people who lived off the land, surely. The lumber houses were strong; the scent of Nàmheil was heavily reminiscent of a sturdy forest. It was a quaint place to tour, but Skylar could not comprehend why they were doing so, for however briefly they were.

"Cyril," Skylar called out from a pace behind, "what are we doing? Aren't we supposed to board a ship to Terrinal?" She was disappointed in herself for being so weak to the sea and for letting it show in her manner of speaking.

Without looking back at her, Cyril explained, "I thought we could check out the apothecary here to see if there's anything we can do about your seasickness."

Perhaps her pride made her believe he sounded cheeky. His gesture was a charitable one, regardless of how he disclosed his intention. The beast master was grateful for his kindness; she could imagine the medicine she might receive as her weapon in conquering the beast that was the open water.

As they passed the hanging sign of what she presumed to be the apothecary's storehouse he'd spoken of, Skylar glanced at the designating placard as it gently swayed, and she couldn't help but take notice of what it said: the storehouse belonged to the Mor family.

Just as she became aware of its ownership, the doors opened before them. Instantly, her typically sluggish companion stood tall as a short gasp escaped him. "Hey, Emery!"

"Cyril? What are you doing here?"

"I could ask you the same thing." Cyril sounded excited as he walked forward to meet his friend. His tall frame was blocking Skylar from seeing the esteemed young woman, and she had no choice but to move around him in order to appear before the unsuspecting Luminary-to-be.

"I just came by the storehouse to—oh? Who's this?" The hazel eyes of Emery Mor blinked at Skylar.

The queen studied her quickly, taking in the rather short stature of someone proclaimed to exceed the high expectations of the world-changing reform that was the Luminary position. Above all else, she noticed the young girl's gentleness, which stemmed from her knowledge of many subjects, and saw what made others speak so fondly of Emery.

The queen was uncertain if Cyril held any expectations of their relationship, until he spoke rather impatiently. "Huh? Are you saying you two haven't met?"

So as not to face further questions, Skylar decided to manage her own introduction this time. "It is very nice to meet you, Miss Mor. I'm Skylar. I have heard many wonderful things about you and the work you are doing."

Recognition twinkled evidently in Emery's eyes as swiftly as a crack of Skylar's whip, embarrassment shining through her typically olive-tinted cheeks at having to meet the queen in such an informal manner. "Wow, it's very nice to meet you too, Your Majesty."

"Uh-uh," Cyril said with a wag of his finger. "It's only Skylar here. We're kinda on a secret mission right now, so we need to keep everything incognito."

"Oh, I see. Then just hi, I guess." Emery smiled with uncertainty. "Can I at least ask what brought you to Nàmheil? I doubt Cyril is your acting tour guide of Varon K'aii, unless you only want to see bars and other ways to waste your money, none of which are here."

"Ow, Em, how you wound me."

Neither female paid the injured man any mind as they continued on with their conversation. "Actually, we were on our way to Terrinal, but unfortunately, I don't seem to get along well with the sea. Cyril wanted to bring me to see the local apothecary to ask for a medicine that could help me."

Emery turned contemplative at once, likely running through the inventory of her family's storehouse in her mind. "I think I have just what you need; we will need to be a bit sneaky before we head out."

"Uh, we?" Cyril said as the three of them began to climb the steps toward the Mors' apothecary as if attempting to locate a secret entrance.

Skylar imagined that Emery was being mindful of any customers patiently waiting inside for treatment, intending to procure a medicine for her without delay. Even so, their jaunt toward the top of the stilted building lasted longer than expected as they climbed to the second floor. She felt like a thief as the trio stepped mindfully on their way to the greenhouse-like room above the clinic, her hands latching on to the railing at an odd angle due to the uneven land it was built upon. With a sigh of relief, the queen happily slipped inside their destination as discreetly as possible, feeling much more accomplished than she most likely should have.

Rows of floor-to-ceiling shelves greeted them, filled with many different vials and jars. She immediately noted that only half of the second level was designed like a greenhouse; the rest of the structure wore a standard roof, no doubt to shield the items that were not fond of sunlight. As Skylar sifted carefully through many different medications around the space with her eyes, Emery stepped off to her right as she clarified the plan she'd devised. "I was actually heading to Terrinal myself." Her precision in avoiding the papers and books sloppily strewn across the floor showed expertise.

"But when I last spoke to Xerus, he said you were meeting with him to discuss the trip to the amphitheater by the end of the week," Skylar said.

"I am," Emery huffed, tossing back her pure-black hair, which was cut short in a style unique to the queen, who held such pride over her long ponytail. Just as the Luminary-in-training happened upon the medicine she had been searching for, it was noticeable how she quickly tried to reclaim her dignity by adjusting her shorts before continuing. "But since I needed to stop by the cathedral in Terrinal before then, I thought I'd drop in to see my parents while I was, well, around, in a sense."

The businessman stood much more competently as he digested his friend's words. "Enjoyed your visit?"

"It was a bit better than expected," Emery said.

Feeling as though she were intruding by hearing such a cryptic conversation, Skylar stepped forward and held out her hands for the pills the apothecaries' daughter had located and prescribed. "We'd love to have you join us, Miss Mor," she said pleasantly while receiving the needed medication to survive the trip the three of them would face. "If all else fails, I'm sure a stimulating conversation with you would help me survive the boat ride."

She could feel Cyril's unimpressed expression on the back of her head. Before he could manage a snide retort, the girl scolded Skylar in a different way: "Please, call me Emery."

"Very well." Her request was something Skylar could abide to, given how she related to informality.

Needing to take nothing else, the slightly larger traveling party exited the small building and made their way to Nàmheil's port. Boarding the seaworthy vessel felt like an accomplishment, given the queen's unfounded fear. The provided pills made her feel unsteady—more so than any waves ever could have—but in a lulling sense. If not for the strange jab she thought she heard Cyril make in suggesting that she ride a creature of the sea the rest of the way, Skylar would have believed she had governed her senses successfully while they sailed the rest of their way across the waters.

✦✦✦✦✦

Xerus had never seen Skylar so enthused by anything in his life, including their time shared in their younger years. Sitting across from her inside their carriage on the way to their hot springs getaway allowed him to take in her appearance and soak in her enthusiasm that radiated as she sat ideally, almost as if she were unaware of—or perhaps, for once, unconcerned about—her not-so-reserved demeanor.

She continued to wear her proud castle clothes, looking stunning in the tailored attire she had designed with the hired seamstress to represent both of her families that she honored when portraying her role as queen. The warrior woman from the scorching mountains wore summery clothes, as she opposed the declining temperature in the frigid peaks she now called home; a short black skirt that bore the wing pattern of her worshipped deity, Essentia, was gently shielded by a wrap that rose into the buckle underneath her bust and descended down in a light-bearing crest. Her torso was mostly bare in the length between her bottom half and the belt she secured under her sleeveless shirt.

Thankfully, her chosen weapon, her formidable whip, wasn't fastened to her person during their special day.

The collar of the shirt she had made rested just below her chin, as if covering her chest entirely compensated for her otherwise exposed skin everywhere else on her body. Her outfit was impractical for battle, even if she wore some sort of feminine combative boots on her feet, yet he found it to be regal in its own right. It reflected where she came from while dressing her much like a queen—however strongly she failed to recognize the vast difference in climate between the two worlds she represented.

Then, of course, never to be forgotten was her esteemed mane.

The blonde hair on her head managed to change its shade to orange just above her emerald eyes and in the substantial strands found in the braid that wrapped around the length of it. She treasured her hair much as an animal would care for its own appearance, only his wife splendored in treating her golden locks with the greatest care humans could manage. It was the only type of extravagance she had ever taken after moving into his castle—their castle. It was theirs now, even if it only bore the fortification of his designs.

Perhaps this trip of theirs could aid him in broaching the conversation he'd been meaning to have with her.

"You seem to be quite excited about this," Xerus observed openly, wondering if she would lock her frenzy away or continue to demonstrate it in the slightest gestures she made.

By the look in her eyes, he was pleased to see she would choose the former. Xerus saw his wife studying him and knew she was ascertaining his purpose in stating such a thing, but finding no grievance allowed her to continue to behave freely.

"There is much to be excited about."

"Indeed," he agreed wholeheartedly, "we will have a great deal of time to enjoy the hot springs, and I have arranged for us to have the entire facility to ourselves."

"Ourselves? Was no one else staying there?"

Her suspicion was well warranted, he assumed. However, was he not allowed to be extravagant in his own right if he so chose to be, especially when doing so in an exigent attempt to shower his wife with gifts that spoke for his silent, deeply embedded affection?

Quickly, Xerus lifted a hand in the air to ease her. "No one was inconvenienced by our trip. I promise."

"Good," Skylar said before she turned her attention to the window and the scenery that passed beyond it. Her eyes jumped rapidly to keep pace with the goings-on outside the single glass pane responsible for keeping them from interacting with the outside world.

Inside the carriage, for the rest of the night and into the morning, there was no outside world for either of them.

For the first time in a long time, Xerus only had to focus on himself and one other person, his wife of a few fast-passing weeks.

"Were you?"

His question startled them both, but he prayed internally that his surprise didn't show, all the while squinting in a rash moment of anger at his own folly. When curious, he was insatiable—Skylar was the most mysterious creature he had ever encountered. Now he had asked a strange question without proper provocation; without the world distracting him, he had already lost his ability to handle himself. How unnerving.

"Was I what?" Her confusion was understandable.

"Were you inconvenienced by my asking you to go on this trip? Or are you inconvenienced in any way now?" He wanted to tell her that she had nothing to fear in being honest with him, but hearing how the thought sounded inside his mind made him seem much less authoritative than he cared to be at the beginning of their up-and-coming adventure. He needed to learn as quickly as possible how to speak to his wife and channel what had inspired the slight glimpse of proper conversation they had shared last night.

She gave him enough time to consider such things with her enormous pause before replying, "I am never inconvenienced by you, Xerus." She was formal, yet he immediately sensed the tone of obviousness behind her words; she was telling him that such an answer was surely a well-determined fact between them. And he supposed it would be, considering how she had sacrificed every night's sleep since her arrival in the Goodlit Summit to guarantee that he slept as well.

He fought a smile and instead channeled it into his reply. "Are you so sure?" he said, verging on a tease. "I believe that is the exact opposite of how you thought of me after our last battle in the coliseum."

Her eyes sparkled as she retorted, "That was because you cheated."

"Cheated?"

"You threatened my hair." As if recalling the horror, she held her mane just so she could embrace it and offer consolation after the reminder of such a horrific incident. It was all he could do not to see her slight frown as a source of amusement—and for Skylar, a frown was simply not smiling at all—so he took to the offense.

They spent their carriage ride blissfully unaware of the passage of time.

CHAPTER 5

"All right, kiddies, say goodbye to Uncle Cyril for now."

"Huh? But we just got here," Emery said. No sooner had they taken their first steps into the glorious city of Terrinal than the businessman was ready to leave them to their own devices. They had barely made their way past the pronounced river that cut through the city, much less glimpsed the waterfall that fell onto the land leading to the Vicis Plain, yet their traveling entourage was within sight of declining in number.

To further showcase his determination in deserting them, Cyril walked with wider steps as he departed. "I'll catch up with you guys later—at the cathedral, right?"

"I guess," Emery said with a careless gesture. It was obvious she was familiar with the older man's behavior, as she quickly resumed her normal facade and turned to face the queen she had been saddled with. "Is that all right with you?"

"Of course," Skylar said, "if you won't find me troublesome."

"Not at all." Emery proceeded to lead her along the artistic roads of the city.

Skylar couldn't contain herself; she nearly squealed as she kept her eyes on the river. "How lovely. I never tire of seeing this city." The whispers she had once heard as an inexperienced babe could never compare to the breathtaking vision she was able to witness as a burgeoning world traveler. Everything looked as if it had been kissed by the promise of a beautiful future, as if Essentia herself had provided life to every quintessence of nature, cozy home, and blinking star in the bounteous night sky.

Raised to honor the deity of peace, Skylar's tribe never failed to teach of the essential darkness, which was necessary for one to appreciate the raw privilege of Essentia's power. They were never made to fear it—awareness was key in facing darkness in its many varieties. However, in Terrinal, the darkness of night housed the city in a way that highlighted the beauty only found in its luminescent allure once the daylight had been swept away by the chilling evening breeze.

Almost equally enticing was Emery's way of conversing. "Never tire? You've been here before, Skylar?"

"Yes." She nodded, breathless. "You could say that Xerus brought me here on a prewedding honeymoon." "I've never heard of anything like that before." Emery sounded as dubious as she must have felt, given the queen's peculiar description of her previous travels.

Perhaps another reason for Skylar's adoration of the city was its preexisting place in her heart, established when her mate offered her a small dowry by whisking her away for a stroll about Terrinal during a late hour all those months ago.

Protective of Xerus in her own right, Skylar smiled at the commentary. "It was merely a gesture he used to win me over, and I gave it a silly name. Xerus knew I wanted to come here." When Emery merely continued to stare with her spirited hazel eyes, she shared a tad more. "Ever since I told him in our younger years."

"Oh. I wasn't aware that you two knew each other before, well …" The young archaeologist turned researcher couldn't find a way within her massive mind to speak of the queen of Varon K'aii's arranged marriage as something more romantic than what it was.

"I moved into the castle?" The young woman needn't suffer so; Skylar decided to conclude her thought in a circuitous way.

Emery's smile as she led them into the central plaza only seconds behind their departed friend showed her appreciation, along with the way she backtracked. "Yeah. But you two are royalty—I suppose you could create your own traditions if you wanted."

She shared this view on the matter. "That he could. His decrees are never so creative—perhaps he'll start a trend." It was entirely possible, given how he moved people from across the world to come together in spite of their once divided purchase; if he shook the planet over diplomatic matters, who was to say he couldn't reform marital traditions?

Emery chuckled. "Who knows? Though no one might pay attention to the way a brazen hedonist, such as Van Austiant, spends his time."

Skylar nearly tripped over her own feet when she heard his ancient name consorted with such uncharacteristic titles. "Pardon?" It was all she could do not to stutter.

"At least," Emery said, clumsily trying immediately to pacify the wife of the man she had just touched upon, "I imagine he was dressed as Van when he brought you here. That was how he explained it to us; he becomes Van when he interacts with the tribes so they don't feel as if he has forgotten what it's like to not live in a modern-day society like the people in the cities do. Or maybe that's how I understood it. It's like he has two personas to suit who he's interacting with. That could be dangerous, but he sees it as considerate most likely."

After hearing Emery ramble on in an attempt to explain her husband's elusive ways, Skylar knew she could empathize with some of her intentions. Ignoring the fact that her assumption had been incorrect, as Skylar distinctly remembered her husband's armored back gleaming slightly under the moonlit night while they wandered Terrinal's pathways during their prehoneymoon excursion, the logic her friend had presented agreed with her. She gazed down at her own warrior's attire replacing her six-month-standing adornment of royal garb and realized she had behaved just as he had when suggesting the change in her appearance before her departure. Though she presently did not dress like a queen, it had never crossed her mind to give herself a false identity—not that she was as world-renowned as King Xerus.

Still. Brazen? Hedonist? One of those titles was more suited for her husband than the other, and it was surely not the one that could involve intimacy, however fleeting. It wasn't necessarily the banners he attached to his name that nearly struck her down—it was the name he used that had stilled her for an instant in her stride.

When was the last time she had had the chance to call him Van?

The last time they had fought and parted ways in the Spierté, she realized.

Unless threatening a girl's hair truly was a sign of affection for the young hedonist-in-the-making, she'd sooner deny the existence of Xerus's Caribooboo before believing him to be a debaucher.

"I suppose he's been too busy as of late to play Van." She glanced at the plaza one last time, eyeing the gorgeous display of an astutely designed key in its center and catching sight of Cyril's back as she looked about, before passing through into the plaza on quick feet.

"I'm sure married life keeps him very busy." Emery tried once more to soothe any possibly ruffled feathers between them, unknowingly willing her to feel the illusionary rise in her back the way a beast would show its defensive state.

However, Skylar was not one to drag out any awkward feelings. She allowed herself to become distracted by the blue radiance of the building before them. "Is this the cathedral?" Having barely left the plaza in her first visit to Terrinal, she had only ever caught a glimpse of the large structure from the steps of the inn. In her eyes, it was the most recluse building in the city, as its curved build shielded some of it from the radiant natural light of the night. For surely prolific reasons, the building had been made to resemble one's mind being offered up to Ordell and the deities in a pair of sturdy hands, with the hopes of receiving their imparted wisdom. If that was the original architect's intention, then it made a great deal of sense that Xerus had relocated the school to the Viskretta Center in order to respect the religious purpose of a building labeled as the cathedral.

It paired well with the scape of the city overall, but the deeply azure build clashed with the xanthous glow drastically once the nighttime befell, in her opinion.

She wondered what color the new Van Austiant wore. If she likened her hair to the light of the moon and stars, what colored glow did Van—let alone Xerus—possess, and would it ever become harmonious with hers?

Though she was dressed in her tribal armor, the renewed sense of disconnect she felt with the king managed to sneak its way beneath her skin. So distracted was she that Skylar could not marvel at the spherical shape of the cathedral, even if it was something that always enchanted the woman who'd lived in tents her entire life. The pair wandered into the holiest place in the land after the hefty door's hinges alerted those inside of their presence. At once, her senses were overcome by incense that smelled so strongly she believed the haze was bound to metamorphose into a physical entity at any moment and become a self-proclaimed deity of odor and piety.

As one who had grown up worshipping Essentia and honed the belief that the deity representing peace was ever present with her people, Skylar was accustomed to the notion of being accompanied by something one was not meant to see with the naked eye.

However, the power of the incense was something beyond even her comprehension.

The queen maintained her composure as she greeted those they passed while making their way to Emery's old study. To her surprise, none of the clergy paid much attention to either of their presences as they strolled along the right side of the pews and easily made their way into the hidden stairwell. They climbed the wooden steps in order to reach the second level, which stood beneath the dome-like glass ceiling of the cathedral. The moon was in the hallway with them up until they located their destination and entered the dusty room.

With no true purpose, Skylar decided to remain silent, positioning herself in the corner of the room with the least variety of texts in the hopes that she might have a moment to herself and bask in a single instance of inaction.

"Speak of the devil." Emery laughed as she shook her head, eyeing the screen of her totem with amusement. Her humor was most likely connected to the lack of actual conversation they had shared between their entry into the Universal Cathedral and the moment in which her totem had surprised her with notification of a call. Having a welcome reason to break from her review of her predecessor's literature, the brilliant researcher took a step back from the computer desk and lifted the totem to her ear. "Hello there, Xerus. Everything all right?"

At Emery's side, Skylar pretended she hadn't heard the king of

Varon K'aii's name. She had been easily fascinated by the beautiful city of Terrinal—even while standing aimlessly in a small office within such an established building as the cathedral—and as per usual, her husband had managed to effortlessly steal her attention away from the grandiose historic design and teeming brilliance of such a unique place. While most of her being yearned to mindlessly explore and take in the cultural capital of the continent, a disruptive nagging festered within, slowly burying her desires and taking their place at the forefront of her being.

Her seemingly simple talk with Emery in regard to her husband had stolen her mind away unjustly.

The young researcher's voice managed to do so again when she repeated the most peculiar remark. "You want to talk to Skylar? Oh, Cyril went to work out a deal in the market as soon as we got here. We're in Terrinal now, yeah. No, it's no problem. Hang on a second. Ah, yeah, that might be best. Sure, I'll take her to buy one once I finish up here. One second, okay?" Then Emery offered up her totem to her, completely unaware of how uncertain Skylar was to answer the call, let alone how the concept of such a strange device still managed to unnerve her.

After all, it would prove difficult to continue processing all she had learned on her own without interference from the man in question himself.

"Xerus." She greeted him the same way she would have if she had gone to reclaim him from his study.

In synchronization, he replied, "Skylar."

She felt Emery's eyes come and go as she returned to the stocked desk, now without further distraction. Mindfully, Skylar stepped toward the door and into the hallway beyond the office. The prominent smell of incense assaulted her the moment she stepped out, and the scent nearly made her sneeze. Surely the clergy who cared for the cathedral had been burning the fragrance for years, and it now was as if the scent had infused itself into the walls. Even from the second floor of the crypt at the back end of the building, there was no way to be free from the wafting aroma. Thankfully, the queen managed to adapt quickly and was able to endure the strength of the devotional balm with ease. While speaking with a respectful whisper, she asked, "Is there something you needed?"

"I called to hear of any progress you had made," he said, and she was sure the captain general's handiwork had inspired the king to make contact with his queen. "Emery said you have reached Terrinal; that's quite a distance to travel in such a short time."

"Is it?" Skylar said with slight indignation. Though the length of the day and her belligerent bout of seasickness had distorted her perception of time, she could imagine that it was only now nearing the end of her second day of travel; had they gone by way of Spierté, as was the original plan, she surmised that their arrival in Sailbrooke would have been a great deal more impressive by such a late hour.

Xerus grunted on the other end of the totem. "I was surprised to learn that Emery is now accompanying you as well. Cyril explained that you experienced seasickness when traveling between the Seahavens."

How could he? The man she'd assumed to be her sprightly equal had exposed her weakness to the one person she would have most liked to keep it hidden from. Was this the former mercenary's revenge for her slight remark in Nàmheil about his conversational skills? She realized she might need to increase her firepower if she was to keep toe-to-toe with Cyril.

"I learned that it is not my favorite way to travel, no." Skylar was ladylike in her shyness upon revealing such a personal detail. Resting against the wall of the room in which Emery still resided, she felt as if she would need some form of support to stand strong throughout this conversation.

"Good to know. I take it you will reach Otornot Keep tomorrow?" Xerus brushed past his miniscule implication of kindness with his requirement of information.

Again, her mental map flashed before her eyes. "That is my plan. However …"

"What is it?"

"I haven't yet spoken with Cyril since we arrived; if he hasn't concluded his business here, I wouldn't want to rush him."

Xerus silenced her concern immediately. "I doubt he could

conduct a great deal of business without his partner being present for any mediation. What Cyril needs to consider his top priority is being allowed passage through Otornot Keep; he will need to prearrange his time accordingly for both his goal and for you. Remember that."

The king made a valid point yet again. As much as she wanted to remain sensitive to Cyril and Rainier's fruition in Terrinal, both of them had business to conduct at the keep, and delaying their objective for any reason would prove to be foolish on both of their parts. Thinking about their shared scenario from that regard made Skylar feel a tad more foolish than she already did. Her sensitivity to one who had betrayed her made her appear much too gentile before her husband. It would seem her traveling companion had one too many incidents to answer for.

Sulking in her transparent way, the queen of the land sighed away from the totem device she held before returning to speak in her ordinary voice. "You're right. I will remind him of our plans when I meet with him later tonight."

"Very well." That was all Xerus had to say on the matter. There was a faint sound of accomplishment in his tone—perhaps for convincing her of his reasoning with little to no pull—but she conceded to it.

"How are things at the castle? Are you preparing for your trip to Summerside?" Though said excursion was not something she felt excitement for, it was a way to convince him to speak of something beyond her. Ultimately, that was what she needed.

"It is not without difficulty. The amphitheater is a project I have spearheaded, yet I require the aid of other countries across the world. As much as I would like to believe other world leaders see the need for international peace as insistently as I do, there is no word yet on who I might encounter upon my arrival." The passion in his voice was aggressive and definite in its displeasure at the turn of events in his overseas outing; the type of work that had consumed his life was being thwarted by those who held alternate opinions and their own ideals and fears, which were not necessarily facets that could be defeated like an opponent in a duel. Xerus was as brilliant as he was physically strong. Both intelligence and physical strength were viable assets to his character, although one was much more aggressive and therefore much faster at achieving the results he required. However, even he had secret desires that must have felt stifling when left unfulfilled.

Skylar sympathetically cooed, "Your country refused to change before, and you saw to it relentlessly."

"Yes." He dragged the word out. "Which is why we scheduled to meet so quickly. None of the other dignitaries I have spoken to have reported any sort of public rebellion to the amphitheater's construction in quite some time, and Cyril's concerns at Otornot Keep are the only discriminatory act I've heard word of, which you are handling yourself; it is best that we take advantage of the silence and plan our next course of action."

"Which would be?" she asked bravely. Inquiring about his line of work was admittedly intriguing, yet the queen had never done so. Her worry of being coddled or possibly outright rejected had prevented her from ever speaking out in such a way before. However, he had already volunteered to her a great deal of intelligence—surely it was safe to probe for further information.

Xerus too seemed to feel comforted enough by their talk to reveal all his intentions. "Nothing has been decided as of yet. I do, however, wish to create a traveling forum composed of those who are willing to speak out against the prejudice that lingers after the unification of Varon K'aii. Perhaps if we hear the concerns of those who are against it, or even undecided, we can understand how to better handle their inclinations."

It was a sound idea in her mind, most likely because it mimicked her current adventure, almost as if she were his trial run before the conference. Skylar wondered if he was merely calling to hear reports of her time abroad so that he could surmise if his possible forum held a chance for success.

But it wasn't the possible lack of concern for her own well-being that made her overtly curious and willed her to voice a thought that had nearly buried itself inside her once again. If he could be so forthcoming, why couldn't she?

"Would Van be joining the traveling forum?"

A sharp loss of breath hissed through the totem. Had she scared him because she had learned of the usage of his discarded name in order to see the world through a commoner's eyes? It had been admittedly stirring even for her to speak the name. But now that she knew of his fronted identity and how it related strongly to the memories that had tethered them in the slightest while over a decade apart, it would have driven her mad had she allowed this opportunity to discuss it to pass her by.

With a crackle, Xerus said, "Who told you?" The gruff way he asked set her on an edge she hadn't noticed she was near.

"Why?"

Skylar could only imagine how tense he might be on the opposite end of the line. He was wise in many ways, as displayed in his skillful avoidance of the last couple of lines of dialogue shared. "That name was lost to me the moment I left the Austiant tribe; I use it as my civilian identity because of that reason. No one knows who Van is, and I hope it will continue to be that way."

The powerful accusation ripped through her more than anything he had ever done. Refusing to tell her of his covert workings in the past six months of their marriage was worrisome enough, but to wordlessly, implicitly accuse her of divulging his secrets to anyone for any design of a cause was an offense she had never imagined she would face from him.

"I understand, Your Majesty. I won't tell a soul." The words felt as if they tried their darnedest to strangle her on their way out. Speaking felt as if it required more effort than it was worth at the moment, and she wondered what proper protocol was in ending a call, given that her singular past experience had involved hanging up due to the wisecrack she had made.

How she'd love to repeat that act, with different motivation.

Suddenly, a sloth-like voice she had recently come to know called out from the nearby stairwell, "Hey, Emery! Skylar? You guys still here?" Behind his bellowing tone, there was a distinct chirping that was impossible to decipher due to its noticeably lower volume. Regardless of his accompaniment, Cyril had arrived to report on his exploits and, hopefully, plan ahead for the final leg of their mission tomorrow. It was the perfect reason Skylar needed to end the distasteful conversation.

"Please excuse me, Your Majesty, but Cyril has returned. I must go."

"I see. Goodbye, then."

"Goodbye." She could not tell if she heard the other end terminate the call before she had the chance to say her farewell. The end to their chat was truly lackluster, considering how distracted she was. However, a repetitive click-clack noise drumming its way toward her on the tiled floor of the cathedral drew her attention away from the unpleasant call regardless. From her stance in the dimly lit hall, Skylar did her best to ascertain who was making such a noisy, hastened arrival. Surely it wasn't the bulky businessman.

Charging at her was a spry young lady with a look of fierce determination encompassing her face and entire being. She wore a long harbor-blue poncho that gave her the look of some sort of royalty or war hero charging forward with the most righteous of intents. Closer and closer the strange woman advanced.

Emery opened the door to the office she occupied, effectively stopping the girl in her path.

Those present froze, while Cyril strolled up behind the messy gathering with a hearty chuckle shamelessly spilling forth from his sleazy smile. The door that formed a makeshift barricade rattled as the person behind sounded as if she were slowly sinking to the ground. Finally, when the woman did appear, she groaned with great annoyance and equal bashfulness. "Aw, Emery! How mean! You made me look so ridiculous!"

"Well, maybe you shouldn't run at people like your hair is on fire." Emery spoke freely, immediately implicating her familiarity with the undaunted girl. No doubt she made the remark about her head in reference to the striking blonde hair the girl had, with the vibrant cerise shift in color near its ends and swirled into her locks. Had the queen just encountered another female who treasured her hair as much as she did?

"Look who I found," Cyril said, missing his timing by a large margin. The way he tussled his own dark locks with his gloved hand guaranteed that it was not her traveling companion of whom he was thinking. "Small world, right? It's like we're all waltzing into each other's lives all over again."

"I'd say. What are you doing here, Dalya?" said Emery as she moved to shut the door that had been brutally assaulted by the established attacker.

Hadn't Cyril spoken of someone named Dalya while Skylar was being tossed about on the open waters? She'd have to let their conversation refresh her memory.

Dalya fixed her attire with speedy hands, from her massive wrap to her one-piece outfit underneath, which was dyed an enchanting gray from its neckline to the cut off of her shorts and had a pure white middle holding her waist. "I came here to do my review on Terrinal, specifically on the cathedral."

"Why am I not surprised?" teased Cyril, winking at the apparent reviewer, who offered a puffed pout in response.

She turned to face Emery and the original question once again. "There was a man here who was giving me the scoop on the history of this place and the waterfall, and he even started to tell me about your time here, Em."

"You could have just asked me if you wanted to know more about it," Emery said as she placed a hand on her hip. She seemed to be prematurely exhausted by Dalya's presence, yet it was not an exhaustion brought on by true annoyance.

"But it's not really a tribute if I get your perspective; I wanted to hear what other professionals had to say about it. A good writer always tries to understand all points of view and learn something along the way. Besides, I want to save my first real interview with you for when you become the Luminary at the amphitheater. Who better to give me a tour than you?" So confident in her admission was she that the proud traveling writer pointed her notetaking pen at her comate as if she had just knighted her with the privilege.

Emery chuckled before giving her dear friend a smile of gentle gratitude. "Well, thanks, Dalya."

"No problem." It was then that Dalya's bright purple eyes drifted toward the other female in their disorganized quartet, displaying the natural wonder Skylar had already begun to associate with her character. "Oh, I'm sorry. Here I am, just blabbing on about my work, when I haven't even introduced myself yet to your friend. Hi! I'm Dalya Napaphe."

The queen was somewhat fascinated to see what type of reaction would follow her response. "Hello. It's nice to meet you, Dalya. I'm Skylar."

Her eyes went wide. Indeed, the young travel agent of sorts seemed to automatically bring down her pen and reveal a readied notepad from an unknown location on her person. Her gasp was as lengthy as it was noisy, even if her enthusiasm was sweet in a rowdy sort of way.

Was there no other person in all the worlds named Skylar? Because this reaction, however charming when acted out by Dalya in all her avid glory, was beginning to outstay its welcome.

Chapter 6

How she loathed it.

Her new totem was silent in her hand, brilliantly gleaming in its color of stunning coral outlined by a shade of green that matched her eyes, so Skylar knew she had no reason to glare at the device purchased by her husband. After her husband's instructions to Emery to assist her in attaining her own calling device for a means of communication—although he had given the order before the shameful end to their horrid talk—the trio of comrades had whisked her away toward a three-story building known as the Feathered Staff in the plaza and forced her against her will to come into possession of the technological affliction.

She might have been demure, but Skylar could yell loudly enough to summon her husband from the other side of the Goodlit Summit if she saw fit to do so. She was first and foremost a beast master. Beyond this journey, her totem would prove to be feckless.

Still, something lighthearted arose within her as Cyril, Emery, and even the newly acquainted Dalya exchanged contact information with her, along with providing her with the king's and captain general's digits. The discarnate ties made by way of sharing such information felt oddly advanced for means of bonding with people she had known for, at most, two days. For someone who had been raised with everyone she knew as a child, upon leaping into this world of modernization, the queen came to learn quickly that she needed to apply a higher standard to her worldly education upon her return home so as not to continue to look the fool every time someone brought her totem into conversation.

She wondered if she could ever behave amicably with her newly attained device.

That was the story of her life, as she saw it.

Sitting at a table in the bar with her friends on the lower level of the building, Skylar pretended not to be bothered by her lack of comprehension of the purchased totem and lifted her gaze to rejoin the conversation taking place. With two or so beers flowing through Cyril so early on in the night, he spoke of the success of his impromptu conference with evident joy. "Yeah, the guy was really nice about it. Said we could sit down to talk with him at our earliest availability." He sounded proud to be conducting bargains that involved obvious professional speech.

"Wow, that's so great, Cyril," Dalya said, swiping her finger along her cheek at the saucy remains from her burger. The redness around her mouth indicated that she had gone awhile without anyone pointing out the mess she was making. Thankfully, her clothes appeared to be spared of any resulting stains.

Emery, sitting across from her childhood friend, nodded proudly. "Having business in Terrinal is going to be really good for you guys. The plaza is always busy; you'll get a lot of decent exposure."

The giddy businessman waved his fish-cake-stabbed fork in the air as he said, "That's why we're doing it." Then he, much like the young reporter, carelessly gobbled up a piece of fish without consideration for the possible bones.

With a complacent smile, Skylar piped up. "So you've finished with your business matters here?"

"Uh, yeah"—he needed to swallow before finishing his train of thought—"I promised Rainier I would wait to do all the big stuff with him."

"Awesome! Does that mean you guys have some free time now? Maybe we could all go visit Kivah and Weswin! I haven't had a break from work in a long time. It'd be really nice to see them since we're all together now anyway. And Sailbrooke isn't too far from here. Whaddya say?" Dalya was animated as she pitched her idea to the table. Given that she was underage, she hadn't touched a drop of alcohol, yet her presence seemed to burst at the thought of the group reuniting, as if she were under some ulterior influence. Skylar knew she would come to adore the young lady, and every passing moment seemed to only raise her affinity for her.

"Fine by me." Emery sounded excited but displayed a milder reaction. "It's sort of on my way. I could spare some time to see them."

Cyril exchanged a look with the queen that hinted at his disfavor for the conversation's sobering turn. As the writer celebrated in her seat, her oldest friend in her presence by years of age seemed thoroughly disappointed to be the one to dampen her mood. Putting down his fork and midrisen mug, he kindly declined the offer. "Sorry, guys, but the queen and I are actually in the middle of something. We'll have to see the little monsters another time."

"Oh." Dalya sounded heartbroken as she looked to Skylar for a gentler explanation. "Are you sure you can't make it? It'd be so much fun to go there all together."

"Dalya." Emery scolded her with a hand in her hair and a sigh on her lips.

Feeling sorry for the poor woman, Skylar thought of their journey's path. In actuality, with Cyril or not, she had intended to take the longer route home in order to view the far side of the continent. There was a certain city that had been teasing her ever since the redirection of her travel plans—even if she had to eventually make her way through the Torrential Ingress, which acted as her mane's natural enemy. Sailbrooke sounded interesting in its own right, and meeting with Lady Mahina informally might prove profitable for her in both a political and personal sense.

Traveling by boat would happen for her eventually if she was avoiding the alternate route through Vicis Plain; at least the voyage between Voulair Port and the Marina Anchorage would be over and done with in one fell swoop, unlike her stop-and-go trip through Nàmheil.

However, beyond her carefree, speculative plans for the future, it was the matter of tomorrow's confrontation that held superiority over all else. If Emery and Dalya were headed to Sailbrooke, they would indeed pass through Otornot Keep, and neither Cyril nor the queen wanted to involve them in their secret assignment. In fact, it would most likely be best that they depart after the other two had long gone, so as not to interfere with the possible stability of Otornot Keep after their handling of the matter.

"I'm sorry, dear." Skylar pacified her new friend as best as she could. "But we have something we must see to first."

Emery arched an eyebrow at her wording, a thought dawning on her. "It must be really serious."

"Oh yeah? Cyril said something about you two being on a secret mission," Dalya recalled, terminating the secrecy she'd spoken of. All eyes turned to the man she mentioned; one gaze was curious, another was piqued, and the middle green glare showed bland disfavor for his babbling ways.

With a distilled laugh, Cyril resigned to the mixed scrutiny. A large fish cake peeked through his teeth as he managed to say, "If it's fine by the queen, I don't mind sharing."

The Nàmheil-born kin then focused on Skylar, who had yet to remove her disapproving eyes from the man seated across the table. There was nothing wrong with revealing their intent to the two companions in the privacy of their arranged hotel room—she was merely unappreciative of the responsibility of determining their right to know. It was something a queen should grow accustom to, she supposed.

She stood from her seat and addressed them all with a smile. "Let's speak upstairs before the man from the market you spoke to asks to know about your secret mission too."

"I was only willing to tell him if he sealed the deal with me on the spot." He was obviously teasing her, removing himself from the table with a playful tsk. "No such luck, I'm afraid."

Skylar couldn't help it—she both rolled her eyes and laughed to herself quietly. Together as a group, they paid the bill for their dinner and rode the elevator up to the highest floor. The distance from the other tourists and citizens within the city of Terrinal somehow felt safer. They were more secluded than some might have deemed necessary, though it felt highly appropriate for what they were about to discuss. The room only had two large beds, but it went unspoken how the pairs would be divvied, given the experience her comrades had with their previous travels together.

"Now." Skylar sighed as she stroked her blonde hair thoughtfully. "Shall you begin, or shall I?"

Cyril sat on the end of his chosen cot and shook his head. "Doesn't matter to me."

The queen nodded and then began. "Tomorrow Cyril and I plan to travel to Otornot Keep so that we may deal with an issue he had with some of the guards there."

"An issue?" Emery eyed her bedmate, the arch in her eyebrow returning as she stared. She received a shrug in reply; Cyril's relaxed persona was chipping away under the weight of some semblance of humility he bore. He was so focused on his own mortification that he failed to see the real upset his friends felt in relation to the description they'd been given.

"Some guys weren't so nice to Rainier and me—well, me, really. They wouldn't let us through—"

"Because you're from Hierony?" said Dalya, likely able to ascertain the truth due to his reaction and her time spent between the islands.

"So I decided to get back at them by telling their boss's boss's boss how much of a pain in the ass they were. Now I've got the queen coming down from her castle in the mountains to give them a piece of her mind. They're in trouble now." Only those who were attuned with him or possessed the ability to read others could had told he was trying to mask his embarrassment. Those same people would never have dreamed to call him out on said feelings.

The famed researcher rubbed her chin as she spoke to the queen. "I see. That's a huge undertaking on your part. Depending on what happens, you could be risking the respect of the soldiers by simply showing up there. In the worst possible outcome, there might be a rebellion, with the prejudiced members of your military stationed there going up in arms over your surprise pro-islanders movement."

"I doubt us going there would cause that much of a fuss." Cyril waved off the realist's predictions. "Nothing I do could start up a movement."

Ever optimistic, Dalya said weakly, "At least you'd know which soldiers are against the peace talks." Her smile looked strained. Her point rang true despite her lackluster delivery.

Neither of his previous companion's words seemed to assuage him; Cyril stood up suddenly and shook his head with great momentum. "Guys, relax. Skylar has a plan, and from just listening to her explain it back at Yukaih Castle, I knew we'd be all right. Have a little faith in us, would ya? Don't wanna offend the queen with all that rebellion talk."

"You're right; we're sorry, Skylar." Emery apologized for both of them instantaneously.

Though Skylar tried to placate them gently, there still hung an uneasiness in the air. No one spoke a word for a moment or two as the previous conversation and established backlash of the mission replayed in their minds. It was unrealistic to believe that her summons of the discriminatory soldiers would be met with high levels of eagerness to change. Had she bitten off more than she could chew? As her first diplomatic outing, had she damned herself—and, in turn, Cyril and all other citizens of Hierony and Viskretta—by boldly taking on such an important task?

No, she was never one to second-guess; as long as her purpose was moral and sound, she would thrive in her first lone act as queen.

The honey-colored lighting in their shared hotel room inspired her to try to warm their hearts. "I do have a plan, one that I hope will work with not only these men but also anyone who is against the peace talks in the future. As long as we balance our determination to succeed with our humanity, everything will be all right in the end."

Her conviction was met with strong responses of encouragement, including smiles and nods. Though Emery was not entirely a naysayer, Skylar seemed to have moved her to the point of agreement, and that alone was a small victory in her eyes. Immediately, she felt much more relaxed in the hotel suite, and in response, her shoulders loosened their upheld posture.

Dalya, on the other hand, jumped up with seemingly a massive amount of energy. "All right!" she exclaimed with her fists planted firmly on her willowy hips. "I've decided! I have to help you take care of this; I want to go with you to Otornot Keep tomorrow."

"I'm sorry?" Skylar was taken aback, stunned by the reporter's willingness to jump into a political fray.

Cyril seemed just as unprepared as she was. "Dalya, you're a travel agent, not a peace maker, and we aren't stopping in for a visit; this is a big deal."

The young woman almost sounded offended as she spat, "I know it is! This has nothing to do with me or my job. I was born in Nàmheil on Varon K'aii, and then I moved to Hierony for work—I've seen the good and bad of both sides. This is a great opportunity to try to bridge the gap between all of the islands, so who better to be a part of this than me?"

"Nice choice of words, there," Cyril said in jest. It was as if he were trying to atone for angering her so.

Emery, however weak in her delivery, said, "But, Dalya—"

Again, she silenced any protests with her overwhelming spirit. "And don't pretend you don't want to go too, Emery!"

Try as she might, the poor Luminary-to-be was unable to successfully deny her childhood friend's awareness of her desire to help. Emery sighed again at Dalya's antics, pretending to be burdened by her uncanny insight. "Fine," she murmured at first, but then she channeled the spunky woman's vitality as she confirmed Dalya's assertion. "I do want to help you guys any way that I can."

Skylar, filled with gratefulness and awe, could do nothing more than deny them. "As much as I would like to say yes, I can't risk any casualties. Especially not the famous Emery Mor."

A whiny protest from the noisiest person at the table was ignored easily enough as the conversation carried on. "But Dalya made a good point: having Varon K'aiians who have gone over and started lives on the islands may help your cause," Emery said. Given her time studying at the Viskretta Center, the researcher had seamlessly validated both of the Nàmheilians' reasoning to join the queen's cause. The hand not resting on her chin offered itself in an open-palmed gesture of informality.

"Yeah, yeah!" Dalya leaped up and down, seemingly renewed in her exuberance by the unexpected praise.

Cyril then joined in with an overtly sweet voice. "Plus, Dalya and Emery both know how to handle themselves should things go south. Not that I think it'll come to that! But this isn't the same thing as Rainier—if they need to, they can take care of themselves."

"So what do you say? Can we go with you?" pleaded the bouncing young lady from her stance a few inches away from Skylar's face.

What was she thinking? Could she agree to this? Their points were sound, but nothing they said devalued her concerns. Perhaps the begging eyes of a certain young lady and the expectant gaze of their two awaiting comrades caused her to cave. For whatever reason, she felt too weak-willed to deny them something so foolishly dangerous, given that it would allow them to complete Dalya's earlier request of traveling to Sailbrooke together, not that any of them seemed aware of it now. Her selfishness in holding on to them might become a problem for her.

Quoting her husband, Skylar surrendered to them all. "Very well." It was as if she had granted them each a wish, considering the celebration that followed.

<hr />

How she despised it.

Her totem was nothing but a troublesome mess of a trap, hitching her to Xerus from anywhere in the world during her single breath of freedom. Living inside his walls had been a vigorous adjustment for her, and having her lifelong dream of traveling the land realized— especially with the newly forged capability of reaching out to their newly acquired islands coming into play—and then swiftly squandered by her husband's constant connectivity to her made Skylar feel like a beast on a leash.

For a beast master, that was a hollowing feeling indeed.

Her chosen device was gorgeous in terms of technological beauty; it wasn't the design that had affronted her integrity. Being able to call or text her mate, as it was explained to her, felt much more debilitating than keeping in contact with anyone else in her totem's address book. Their recent fight might have had something to do with her unwillingness to contact him and inform him of her new digits, but she was not so dimwitted as to believe that her growing resentment could no longer be tamped down by her ingrained sunny disposition in life.

Why must she only sit inside the extravagant igloo that was her noble home, studying her life away? Even though she enjoyed caring for others and found it to be sufficient cause for happiness, why did it feel as if no one wanted to hear of her worries and concerns? Why was her husband's partnership with her such a headache-inducing farce? Were people not supposed to long for home when traveling a ways away, instead of savoring every second they had to themselves?

Skylar shook her head. No, she was not so frail as to genuinely think these questions plagued her. None of them ever had. In fact, allowing them to form in her mind for even an instant was more bothersome to her than whatever had caused her melancholy. True, she was becoming more like the jaculus Rainier had caged next to his home in Spierté, but that did not mean she had grown to hate Yukaih Castle.

No, what she hated was the totem in her hand, which preyed on her individuality during the fleeting chance she had to appreciate it. She was poorly associating all her experiences in order to justify her avoidance of messaging her husband. An angry hum fluttered past her lips suddenly, and she smacked her hands over them a moment later. In the dead of the night, with slumbering party members so near, it was rude of her, even though it had been unintentional.

That did not stop Dalya from rousing at her side, however. "Skylar?" she mumbled, sounding sleepy.

"I'm so sorry," the queen said in her most fervent whisper. "I didn't mean to wake you."

"No, it's fine. It's kinda late, isn't it? Have you gone to sleep yet? We've got a big day ahead of us tomorrow."

Skylar sulked to herself. "I know."

The blankets kept them both hidden in different ways; Dalya was snuggled up to her nose with the plush coverage, curled up in a perfect circle, which forced the queen to sleep in a pose reminiscent of the king and his straight-laced resting state. She couldn't think of getting comfortable when she couldn't think beyond her woes.

When Dalya maneuvered herself to rest high on her hands, a half-lidded stare bearing down on Skylar's sleepless face, the young lady surprised her as she said, "Hey, why don't we go for a walk?" It sounded more like a statement than a question.

"What?" asked the surprised royal in a voice of regular volume.

Without official acceptance, Dalya lifted herself from the bed—after fighting with the entanglement of her sheets—and stood, slipping on her shoes and throwing on her massive poncho. She ignored all protests as she toddled over to the door, lifting a lone finger to her lips. "Come on. Let's go before we wake them up."

Unable to argue with the possible risk of disturbing their comrades, who were fortunate enough to be sound asleep, Skylar slid into her boots and tiptoed toward the door. Once again, she traveled via elevator and wandered into the lobby with the dozy travel agent at her side. They snuck past the hotel doors and down the staircase and turned the corner in order to stroll along the expansive bridge leading toward the outskirts of the city. A glow of azure enchanted them as they walked the path, and Skylar couldn't believe she'd almost left the city without even gazing upon the legendary waterfall once.

They approached close enough to feel the spray of the rushing river falling into the depths of the canyon that led to the Vicis Plain. In both the sunny light of the day and the haunting luster of the evening, it was said that a paranormal-like fog hovered over the terrain and made it nearly impossible to witness its expansive glory. Dalya stationed herself along the railing at its sides, her back resting against it, as she looked over the queen. "Is something bothering you?" She sounded much more alert now; the fresh breeze along the river next to them surely possessed the power to awaken anyone.

Skylar refrained from sighing. "Nothing that should cause you to worry, Dalya." She wanted to go on to state that she'd have preferred the young woman continue sleeping, even if it was her own carelessness that had stirred her. In fact, she would have loved to confide a great deal of things to her new friend, but the middle of the night was not the time to do so.

The day before their trip to Otornot Keep also seemed an inappropriate time.

"Come on, Skylar. If there's something you want to say, I'm the best person to say it to," she said. Then realization struck her. "I promise I won't try to twist your arm this time. Honest!"

The queen giggled politely. "That's very kind of you."

"So go on then—don't hold anything back! Sharing is caring, although I'm not sure if that applies to this conversation," Dalya mumbled to herself, perhaps unable to fully regain working capacities of all her faculties at such a late hour.

While Skylar observed her confusion, it was impossible to deny the purity in her attempt to assist Skylar with any of her unspoken troubles. The white blonde of her hair seemed to glow under the light of the moon as if naturally highlighting her immaculacy. Whether due to women's intuition, her ownership of a kind soul, or a combination of the two, Dalya had risen from her bed and brought her outside without provocation to try to ease her of some of her distress. The gesture was heartfelt, however unpredictable it was.

Again, Skylar found herself relinquishing to her recently acquired friend. "I suppose I'm just adjusting to this journey I'm on."

Dalya nodded, struggling to understand. "It's a lot of responsibility. I can only imagine what you must be going through, having to deal with people like that when you're their boss."

"It's not the mission itself that has me like this." Her brow furrowed. Why was explaining herself so challenging? Had she ever had difficulty speaking of her inner workings before?

"Oh? Then what is it? What's got you so sad? Or mad maybe?"

Composing herself, Skylar straightened and said, "I'm not sure. Being away from the summit for the first time since moving there has me—"

"In a tizzy?"

"I suppose so."

"I see. Hey, Skylar? What's it like being married to Xerus?"

The sudden emergence of a question with her name was titillating until it resulted in such a personal follow-up.

"P-pardon?" The stutter was beyond her control, as was her startled expression. How bold it was of the young lady to ask such a thing, no matter how likely it was of her to do so, given her talkative nature.

As if sensing the queen's thoughts, Dalya immediately clarified. "Sorry. Was that too much? I was just wondering how he is as a husband, not just a king."

The two titles refused to be separate entities in Skylar's eyes. Her husband was the king, and his role strongly impacted their relationship as those who had been betrothed. She was constantly aware that their only time together was in his study, during the walk down the long corridor, and in the few seconds before they both fell asleep; it had always felt as though she were more of a wife than a queen, while he was nothing more than a king whom she served.

That might have been the problem that had instigated her troubles as of late.

He obeyed her, did he not? When she'd first begun retrieving him from his holed-away study, he could have dismissed her and commanded that she leave him be. In his own way, his silent acceptance of her presence might have been the extent of Xerus's ability to exhibit affection. Still, that didn't feel like a strong enough excuse to defend his actions on their one-night honeymoon at the hot springs, nor did it explain his reclusive behavior in the months since then. Xerus never made a motion to work on their relationship as a married couple, as mates, and that steamed her.

Nevertheless, she stayed.

Just as he could have shooed her away, she could have disappeared in the night or formally ended their affianced alliance. Skylar was just as resilient as Xerus was, but she had a more delicate manner, one that didn't trample on the feelings of others; it had always cynically amazed her how he could show such compassion to every citizen in the world aside from the one shackled to him for life. It was possible that he was surviving their association with honor even though he had realized he'd been mistaken in choosing her above all other applicants he must have been faced with.

Perhaps Van Austiant the hedonist had had a repertoire of future-queen applicants.

The thought made her laugh to herself, giving her a moment of humor in an otherwise dismal state. No, she knew it was incorrect to assume he was suffering through their marriage. Xerus had traveled to the mountains that housed her tribe many times to wager a bargain with her as well as the tribal chief, guaranteeing that he won her over as much as he achieved his goal of uniting the tribes with the rest of Varon K'aii. He was also a rigorous fool—he would not admit defeat after a few mishaps in a mere six months of what could be wedded bliss. If she was to be his queen, neither would she.

A hand waving before her eyes startled her into escaping her thoughts.

"Hello in there!"

"Sorry, dear," Skylar cooed. "I was distracted."

"Was it something I said? Sorry if it felt like I was prying; maybe Emery is right—I do talk too much." Dalya was earnest in her regret and willingly offered to retract her unknowingly thought-provoking question.

"No, it's all right. Your talking helped me to realize something," admitted the queen easily. It wasn't every day that such realizations were unearthed, as evidenced by the six months that had passed her by. She had known Dalya for a substantially shorter amount of time, and the altruistic woman had brought her to a bridge and helped guide her toward a more enlightening place to rest her weary mind. "But to answer your question, he is as troublesome as a husband as you would imagine."

To her credit, Dalya appeared surprised. "Is he? He was so calm all the time when we worked with him in the past. I thought he'd be like a big house cat, just waiting to be petted and pampered by you any chance he got!"

Skylar would have loved to know what had given her that impression. The young woman's words registered, and her eyes grew even wider.

"Oh, please don't tell him I said that! He'd never allow me to set foot into the Goodlit Summit, let alone review it, if he thought I might pitch him like that to my readers."

"You have my word," Skylar said. After all, she wanted to save that image in her mind for herself.

"Good. So are you feeling better now? Even a little bit?" asked Dalya. She sounded somewhat pained, as if the anticipation of a negative answer might crush her.

Skylar surmised that it most likely had to do with the poor woman's desire for sleep. Quickly, she motioned toward the inn. "Yes, I am. Very much so, actually. Thank you for your help, Dalya. Now let's get you back to bed. Shall we?"

Dispelling Dalya's claims that the queen was appeasing her, Skylar led them back into the hotel and up the elevator and ushered them into the silent suite, only disturbed for a moment by Cyril grunting like an owlursus in his sleep. The women shared a volumeless snicker as they discarded their shoes once again and returned to their bedding. Without a moment in between, the reporter collapsed and nearly fainted, losing consciousness with such speed that she almost gave her bedmate reason to worry. A small grunt from the slumbering lady confirmed that there was nothing to fear.

Skylar was once again lying in her bed, straightly posed, eyes upon the ceiling, with her totem still in hand. She hadn't realized that it had remained with her, even after cursing the device as relentlessly as she had. Sleep was attempting to conquer her now too, yet she felt as if she had something she needed to assuredly see to before letting another well-intentioned force overtake her in one day. Focusing on her recently attained knowledge of the totem's workings rather than what she intended to do with it, Skylar typed out her first text: "Hello, Xerus. These are my totem digits. Sincerely, Skylar."

The correspondence was harmless, almost pointless, if not for the need to inform him of her digits. She felt as if the message came across as unnecessarily cold; it felt as if she had written a letter while composing it, but reviewing after sending made her think he might view her as angry or unwilling to share her information with him. That had been her state of mind before her conversation with Dalya; she would have done as she'd originally intended—she'd have refused to notify him until after the completion of her mission—if her feelings had remained in such a state. She had decidedly moved past her petty thoughts and chosen to conduct herself in a way that she would be proud of, not a momentary act of retribution. However, there was no way to assure that her motivations were recognizable to him.

Time seemed to saunter by, flaunting her lack of a response before her like a cruel tease. Skylar could not recall ever seeing her husband's totem and therefore could not determine if he carried it around with him in the late hours of the evening. Would she not have noticed it upon her retrieval of him if he did? She was somewhat disappointed that her first textual exchange would take an intermission—exactly like the exchange of a physical letter, in her opinion—but she had no intention of calling him to alert him of her number. That would be embarrassing; she understood that much.

She decided it was best to return the device to the charger and officially turn in.

Suddenly, the jingle that grated on her nerves went off, encased by the palm of her hand.

Hastily, she tore open her totem. Following the instructions she found in her clouded, tired mind, Skylar opened the feather-looking notification that hailed to her from the main screen and carefully read over the text awaiting her: "Good evening, Skylar. I have saved your digits in my contacts. Thank you."

The message sounded just like him; the textual tone suited her mate perfectly, she found. She rolled her eyes with a thoroughly amused grin at the realization that the king and his queen could most likely continue their relationship as if they had never parted if he managed to sound ever present in these conversations of theirs. Confirming her suspicion, he sent her one other message shortly after: "It would seem you are sending me off to bed when you are not even here. I hope you plan to do the same."

Chapter 7

In all its glory, the authoritarian Otornot Keep stood before them. From the west-gate entrance, Skylar could only imagine how massive the structure was inside and how far and long she'd have to walk if she planned to stroll through its entirety. It was a shame that witnessing its staying power was coupled with a distaste for the upcoming confrontation. Hoping to solve their valid issue before the noon hour, the queen took one step beyond her party members and declared to the guards, "I would like to speak with your commander, please."

The unsuspecting soldiers were most likely blinking at her through their helmets' visors. One of them found the nerve to ask, "Our commander? Why would you want to do that? You haven't even told us why you want to pass through here." To them, the four travelers must have seemed like any other passersby. Their confusion was understandable.

"I am Queen Skylar," she announced for the sole purpose of clarification. "I have come here today to discuss a matter of great importance with the man in charge of this facility." In that moment, she realized that preparing herself beforehand with the names of the officers of the fort might have proven useful; she could only hope her wording assured the men that she was not to be taken lightly.

The bright shine of the sun beat down upon them the way it should have, considering the slow rise it had made while they hiked along the man-made trail through the region of the Telltale Echo Valley. The rawness of the elements in which the fort sat made the encounter feel much like a standoff; the earth surrounding the military stronghold looked as if it had been carved out by way of force; the breeze merely caressed them, offering little to no relief; and the warmth that wafted from the sky sat upon them without remorse.

It was the perfect environment for Skylar to begin working.

Her emerald eyes were kind as they stared, hoping to pierce through the soldiers' helmets as well as their hesitation. They were not surprised by her arrival, merely uncertain what could be the cause she spoke of. Nevertheless, they obeyed her in a tardy fashion as one of the two men offered to see them inside. Skylar immediately turned to face her companions, a hefty breath filling her lungs. "Ready?" she asked.

They all indicated that they were.

Fearing if her own behavior was unprofessional would have felt foolish in light of the gossiping guards who preceded them inside Otornot Keep. The metal gates that acted as the doors to the facility dragged themselves over the earth, effectively deafening Skylar momentarily, before the noise pollution inside the elongated building began to buzz in her ears like insects basking in the summer febricity. Being unable to decipher what the secretive chat pertained to felt unimportant when she spied something surprising and amazing.

The Nazuré-raised woman had not expected to see members of the K'aiiniw tribe during her journey, yet their distinctive red cloaks were impossible to ignore as a handful of their family members rested against the wall. Was it foolish of her to assume they were there to help fortify the structure, given that was what they were infamous for in the tribal world? The handful of people from the Irragwa tribe seemed to be unfazed as they meditated just a few steps away across the massive hall. As someone who'd lived her life in the mountains, it had been astonishing to witness the different cultures of the modern societies of Varon K'aii and bear witness to people from different tribes existing in the same space as all other travelers from across the country was extraordinary. Had she not had other responsibilities to attend to, she would have stopped by each of their small camps in the facility to offer a quick hello.

The guards were quick with their steps as they led the group into a room that bore a sign above its doorway: Stronghold 02. The room was distinct in its flushed interior tones, which were in no way relative to the muddy palate of the building. Perhaps they chose the room as a show of decorum when offering to meet with a queen. However, she couldn't help but whisper about its absurdity, imitating the guards she had momentarily thought of as improper. "Am I the only one who sees this room as strange?"

"Oh yeah, totally." Dalya nodded behind a raised hand. "It feels as if they're gonna experiment on us or something!"

"Ah, I hate it here. Why'd they havta lock us up like this? What, we're not good enough to talk to on the main floor or something?" Cyril complained, arms crossed over his chest.

Emery's eyebrows rose. "It's probably the only place not full of weaponry and soldiers. And speaking down here might be more soundproof."

All eyes followed the curved staircase that led to an upper deck. Skylar could only imagine what the summoned commander assumed to be the motivation behind her surprise drop-in. Though no one seemed interested in making small talk due to their unease, all voiced concerns held their own legitimacy and rang within the minds of all who were locked inside stronghold 02.

Eyes still locked upon the stairs, they were finally met with the sight of the commander when the iron door opened, and their host stepped inside. The man, dressed in crimson attire lightly reminiscent of Xerus's, marched down the stairway without removing his birdlike gaze from the lot of them. He displayed no form of judgment, but it was unlikely that someone of his stature wasn't assessing them mentally as he approached. The style of his hair embraced its untamable ways, the dark azure shade both counteracting and complementing, appearing much like a storm cloud above his gray-blue eyes.

The only disarrangement in his presentation of himself was the tattoo he bore on the left side of his face: the characters for the name of Âyâs in the native alphabet were carved vertically over his eye.

Skylar's assessment of the man was that he looked like a humorless felon turned militiaman.

"Queen Skylar, welcome to Otornot Keep," boomed the baritone from the descending man as he came to stand before them. After a cordial bow, he introduced himself properly. "I am Commander Vergil. It's nice to finally meet you."

Skylar nodded in acknowledgment. "Thank you. These are my companions, Cyril, Dalya, and Emery." She purposely refrained from including titles in hopes of keeping the man's wariness under control, as long as he didn't recognize Dr. Mor on his own. If his careful nod in her comrade's direction was any indication, he did.

"I was told you have a specific reason for coming here today." The statement was blunt and provocative; Commander Vergil was planning to address the queen's query quickly, likely disbelieving she could have any truly earth-shattering business with him. Her lack of notoriety was suddenly a burden to her.

Unfazed, Skylar returned his brusque manner. "Yes, I do. A few days ago, I was informed that some of the guards at the east gate were uncooperative, to say the least."

Her oblique wording tugged the corners of the commander's lips downward. "Uncooperative?"

"It went a little something like this." Cyril jumped in, taking some of the heat for himself. More carefully than she had ever heard him speak before, the businessman channeled his professional finesse and repeated his experience to Vergil without the usual admonition he held. Fully outlining the conversation as he recalled it, keeping his anger in line when speaking of the most conflicting part, and explaining his reasoning for going to fetch the king's aid, he was the perfect presenter of his case.

Still, Commander Vergil never loosened his lips or lifted his frown. He paid close attention to the story and used his body language to demonstrate his attentiveness. Nevertheless, when all was said and done in way of a recapture, he immediately remarked, "I see. But what does any of this have to do with you coming all the way out here?" Green met blue as the queen welcomed his glare.

"Well—"

He silenced Cyril with disregard. "If there was an issue, I could have been contacted and asked to handle these men right away. I don't understand why the queen came all the way from the Goodlit Summit in place of her husband to do my job."

As cruel as he was, Skylar was impressed that he dared to speak to her in such a way. After all, she was there to hear out the complaints and resilience of the men who'd wronged Cyril, so surely she could handle their beastly leader. In retrospect, she realized she might not have known how to deal with him otherwise.

Skylar remained resolute as she explained, "I wanted to come here for myself because of the type of issue that it is. The ongoing process of peace between Varon K'aii and the islands we recently welcomed into our fold is a bigger matter than the experience Cyril had here. I didn't want to see the men fired; I want to try communicating with them."

"That's why we're here too." Emery stepped forward to position herself next to the queen, hoping to support her. "As someone who's helped protect and serve all the lands—"

"We wanted to help them see that people from Viskretta or Hierony aren't so mean and scary." Dalya concluded her friend's confession. From behind her, Skylar noticed Cyril stare at the young writer for a fleeting moment when she arose to speak of defending the outer islands. He mumbled something too before facing the vigilant Vergil yet again.

"Whatever the reason," the commander growled, trying to avoid scoffing at their warranted claim, "this situation didn't require the queen and her entourage coming here to take over my job as their commanding officer."

There could have been a lack of respect in his response. He could have viewed Skylar as a queen hell-bent on parading her power around the continent who had found enough cause to do so with the discriminatory story. He might not even have believed the identified discrimination to be all that concerning and might have viewed their claims as willful and futile. However, as the renowned beast master she'd been prior to accepting her royal title, Skylar knew there was another reason for his outright refusal.

Commander Vergil was the alpha of Otornot Keep; he was territorial.

If he truly had been a monster, she could have knocked him down and tamed him into submitting to her cause. If she'd been dealing with a beast instead of a man, there would have been ways to procure his compliance. Sadly, he was a person, and she needed to learn the ways of political ventures in the human world. This conversation could not be guided by the crack of her beloved whip, and that meant thinking on her feet—a talent she was most proud of in the face of an enemy when on the battlefield—was to be her choice weaponry for successfully leading Vergil to her collegial waters.

"Commander." She started by using his title to collect his attention and soothe his riled disfavor. "I do not want to take over your job."

"No?" spat Vergil. His hands rested upon his hips as he moved to stand with his legs farther apart. Even his body spoke of his animalistic behavior. Perhaps men and beasts weren't so foreign in relation to one another.

"I asked to speak with you first, didn't I? I wanted to hear your thoughts and ask for your permission before proceeding with these men. As you're their commanding officer, I thought you would like to know how they have been behaving when on shift. At the same time, I came here to ask for your help. Will you allow me to take advantage of their misgivings? What I do or do not achieve today depends on whether or not you allow me to speak with them."

"Then why did you bring so many people with you?" the commander asked, tossing his head toward her traveling party. His questioning of her noble cause had shifted from her disrespect toward his authority to her numbers—her negotiating submission looked to be winning him over. Like an open palm under the chin of a beast, he was testing her honesty in approaching him with her commitment to the greater good.

Skylar went on, undeterred. "It is as Emery and Dalya said: I thought having those who have experienced all three lands accompany me may help the soldiers better understand who they are discriminating against."

"We don't want to be a bother. If it's easier, we can sit this one out," Dalya suggested. Her empathy toward Skylar's verbal duel came in the form of a determined yet slightly unnerved gesture. Standing a pace ahead of her, Emery nodded in agreement with her proposal.

Then they were left to wonder as Commander Vergil silently reviewed their claims. He was unmoving, almost frozen, while studying them; if not for his breathing, they might have had cause for concern. It was best not to compromise with him any further, for fear of appearing weak-kneed and allowing him his time to concoct his own battle strategy. The austere look upon his face hinted at his inward retreat, giving the queen reason to feel as though her hope was not lost just yet.

After a passing moment, the man-beast proclaimed, "If I was going to let you speak to them, I'd do it here. You and Dr. Mor could stay, but Cyril and Dalya would have to move outside."

"Aw." Dalya sniveled sadly, hanging her head in regret.

Cyril, on the other hand, shrugged away his disappointment. "Fine by me. Not all that thrilled on seeing those guys again anyway."

"Cyril! That's the opposite of the attitude we're fighting for here," said Dalya. It seemed that scolding him was all she'd been doing with him since they reunited; leaving them alone together might prove to be dangerous.

Smirking, the nonchalant man went on. "Maybe when they show signs of improvement, I'll change my mind." On that note, he moved his arms behind his head and lightly swayed, showing his dislodge from the conversation effectively.

Commander Vergil returned his focus to Emery and Skylar. "I will escort these two upstairs and then return with the soldiers who were on guard at the east gate at the time of the incident. But remember, I can bring them to you, and I can stand by what you say, but you can't force people to change from a simple conversation."

Skylar watched the man's tense back as he left, trying her hardest not to grin. He was right in stating the stubbornness of man, but he had been blind to her own subtle manipulation. Could he not see that she had changed his view—however small in comparison—in less time than that?

◆◆◆◆◆

Less than an hour passed before the first of the men stomped his foot in protest of what he referred to as unfair treatment, to their surprise. A second discriminatory guard joined his cause, but the remainder of the quartet had much less animosity than the first two toward islanders, it seemed. After exploding with hatred, the outlandish soldier fought tooth and nail to end the conversation in regard to his beliefs and view of the so-called outsider population.

When denied his request, the man resigned. Shortly after, his prominent ally followed suit.

In awe, Skylar could only watch as the two stomped their way up the staircase while Commander Vergil demanded that they return their armor and exit the facility immediately. It was evident in his aggressive response to their spontaneous desertion that he was astonished by their willingness to behave against the code soldiers were sworn to upon recruitment: protecting any and all walks of life was the purpose for serving and living. The stationed commanding officer, upon seeing his soldiers' conduct in their resistance to unification and acceptance, was visibly offended at having had them serve under him.

After handling the other two soldiers with reprimand and immovable antipathy, Commander Vergil demanded that the two remaining guards—though they were much less hateful than their departed ex-companions—speak to Skylar and Emery and divulge their reasoning behind their distasteful ways. Then he left stronghold 02 to confirm that the discharged men did as he had asked.

In the hour or so following, Skylar learned a great deal of things. The soldiers sounded unaware of their reasons at first for their acted-upon prejudice, so Emery introduced a new approach by way of explaining the functionality of the Viskretta Center at which she studied. Nothing seemed to register with them in the beginning of the lecture, and Emery admitted to wishing she had prepared a proper presentation to further illustrate her points. However, when she recounted the first time she'd stepped off the boat and looked out at the desolate landscape, a chord of pity strummed within them.

Cyril most likely wouldn't have reacted positively to their response, but it was a start. Skylar then took over to explain how the peace talks were thwarted by people such as themselves, including both Varon K'aiians and islanders who felt as they did. The mutual sense of fear and contempt shared among the three territories shocked the soldiers; they wondered what the people of Viskretta or Hierony had to hate them for, when they provided them with healthier crops and owned a much larger, more bountiful land.

Emery responded by explaining that the Viskretta Center was where she was studying all the different lore and cultural histories of every single tribe and city on all three lands. Highlighting the esteemed qualities of each was her way of stating how Varon K'aiians and the islanders could prove useful to each other and how different perspectives led to greater awareness and triumphs, paraphrasing Dalya's reasoning for interviewing other people for her reviews of different cities during their chat the night before. This seemed to further guide the men out of their hideaway holes of discrimination as they pondered her meaning.

However, the queen hoped they would see Viskretta and Hierony as more than just profitable ventures—entire populations of people were housed on the islands just a short boat ride away. Skylar cut in to attempt appealing to their humanity by asking them to place themselves in the shoes of someone who was not from Varon K'aii yet was brave enough to approach Otornot Keep, where the awareness for caution and distrust was quite strong, to try to make a living for him- or herself. She felt so impassioned that she mentioned the upcoming peace talk at the end of the week that her husband was attending, focusing on the efforts being made by the rulers of all the realms of the world in order to lead by example, realms that were even more contrasting to theirs.

The soldiers then both volunteered to be a part of King Xerus's entourage when he made the trip through Summerside.

The soldiers claimed that neither one could be moved to change by mere words. They wanted to try to follow in King Xerus's footsteps—and exhibit the same amount of bravery as the daring world travelers—by testing themselves in the role of escorts. It was a monumental response, especially considering the quitting act it followed. Nothing had proceeded as she had anticipated; the situation had evolved in a way she could not have foreseen, but she greatly appreciated the outcome. Skylar promised she would speak to both her husband and Commander Vergil in regard to their hiring before allowing them to part ways.

She was in a state of unbelievable bliss as Emery congratulated her while leading them up the winding staircase and returning them to a hopefully less discriminatory world.

Cyril and Dalya, who seemed to be in the midst of a delightful conversation when they emerged, halted their talk at once and rushed forward to learn of the outcome. Dr. Mor took over the retelling of events, just as she had during the talk itself, allowing Skylar to remain quiet while processing the accomplishment she had achieved in her quest to Otornot Keep.

Then Skylar excused herself politely, for all she wanted to do in that moment was take advantage of her brand-new totem and call her husband.

It rang and rang before the baritone she preferred most in the entire world said her name: "Skylar."

"Xerus." She couldn't help it—she knew she sounded as giddy as she felt.

"How was your meeting at Otornot Keep? Are you there still? Or have you only just arrived?" It seemed her excited tone of voice had alerted her unsuspecting mate of possible trouble or concerns. It was all she could do not to laugh.

"It just finished," she said with a low voice, "and it went beyond my comprehension."

Her wording guaranteed his investment in her call. "How so?"

Skylar sighed before revealing all to him. "Commander Vergil was against our involvement at first, but he agreed to Emery and I joining him in confronting the soldiers."

"You managed to have Commander Vergil consent to your ways?" Xerus asked, sounding as shocked as he did sullen. What did he have to be disappointed about?

"I did."

"He is quite the domineering man, especially in concerns to his own soldiers." The king chose to inform her of his opinion of the commanding officer a great deal after the fact. It was ironic that he was warning her in her dealing with such a man, when it had been more pleasant speaking to him than conversing with the men to follow.

Skylar said, "I found him to be quite agreeable."

A huff shot through her totem's receiver. "I see. It would appear that you are quite persuasive then. Perhaps you should be the one attending the conference at the amphitheater, with such reputable skill."

"Oh no," she said immediately. "I wouldn't go so far as to assume I could take your place."

Xerus paused, as if he felt the impact of her indirect compliment before she realized she had given it. "I take it, by your tone, that your mission was concluded successfully as well?"

Preparing to disclose the unhappiness in her report, the queen modified her voice to give way to the upcoming disappointment she had to share. "Sadly, no. Two of the four soldiers did not appreciate speaking to us; they quit and left without looking back."

"And the other two? What of them?" Xerus said, bypassing the shame she felt in driving two men to disown their livelihood instead of convincing them of peace.

"They asked to be a part of your entourage when you head to the amphitheater."

Xerus sounded all-knowing when he said, "Did they now?"

Skylar nodded, though she knew her husband could not see her. "It was unrealistic to assume that merely speaking with them could open their eyes entirely, but they do want to see other parts of the world for themselves while boarding the boat at Summerside with you."

Again, he said, "I see." Only now, he left her to hang in a moment of silence. For quite some time, the queen wondered what the king truly thought of her efforts, but it seemed he was more interested in her own personal reflection when he posed his opinion for her: "So your mission was a true success then."

"I believe it was." How she wished she had said that with more conviction. She had wanted to share her proud exploits with Xerus the moment she had the chance, but recounting them for him now made her hear that she had indeed failed half of her intended target group. It was impossible to control the soldiers and force them to comply, so she in no way had made them quit for refusing to abide by customary courtesy, but it did not feel as if she had truly succeeded—she had faced her first political battle and could not entirely tell if she had won or lost.

As if he were attuned with his wife, Xerus assured her, "Though two men did leave their posts today, it may prove to be a venture gained when one considers the number of citizens of Viskretta and Hierony, along with potential worldwide travelers who can now safely pass through Otornot Keep under the watch of their hopefully competent replacements. And in inspiring two of the previous aggressors into taking a step toward congeniality, when they had gone so far as to deny Cyril and Rainier their right to pass through what is known as our largest safe haven, you have committed an undeniable act of justice. Well done, Skylar."

Had he complimented her? Had he gone into a small rant in order to protect her pride and solidify her awareness of what she had managed to change that day? Never before had he spoken so many words to her in such a sweet manner. A warmth passed over her similar to that of the sunbeams she had welcomed when outside, as if his words were encasing her in their promise. Before she knew what she was doing, Skylar was smiling.

"Thank you for saying so." Again, her truest emotion shone through into her words.

"You're very welcome."

Dare she think he might be feeling the same way as she?

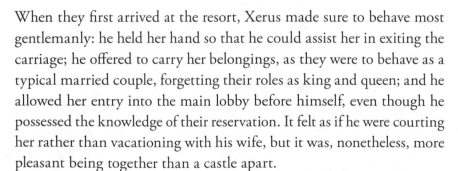

When they first arrived at the resort, Xerus made sure to behave most gentlemanly: he held her hand so that he could assist her in exiting the carriage; he offered to carry her belongings, as they were to behave as a typical married couple, forgetting their roles as king and queen; and he allowed her entry into the main lobby before himself, even though he possessed the knowledge of their reservation. It felt as if he were courting her rather than vacationing with his wife, but it was, nonetheless, more pleasant being together than a castle apart.

He took great care in thanking the owners of the resort for their willingness to comply with his hasty demand of them. The kind elderly couple laughed at his overtly polite ways and assured him it was no trouble to pay homage to the king they so happily served. Xerus tried to inform them that he was not the king as he stayed the night—he was a mere man, a husband hoping to savor the gracious company of his wife—but it did not seem to be a fact they would accept.

Skylar found something amusing while they were checked in and then led to their suite, curiously enough. For the whole length of the stroll from the front desk to their temporary bedroom's front door, she wore a slight smile on her face. With matching eyes of feminine mirth, Xerus genuinely believed he had taken a step in the right direction by asking Raibeart to assist him in orchestrating the spontaneous trip.

"My." Skylar's awed voice was more appealing to the king as they entered the room, the scenery he had previously witnessed during his last visit radiating beyond the windows otherwise engrossing her. She walked past the woven mats that were to be their common room and made her way to the bow windows that oversaw the expansive mountain range. The weightless way in which she pranced told more of her excitement than the single word she had previously spoken.

Thanking the charitable owners, the king bowed to the older couple, who laughed bashfully at his formal ways, before closing the door behind him. He swept the room with his gaze, taking note of the adorning trinkets and sliding doors that led to their private sleeping quarters, and he found himself pleased with the setting for their single-day getaway.

"Xerus," beckoned his wife, her hand flagging him over from her compressed pose against the window pane. "The view."

"Do you find it acceptable?" In his own youthful albeit taciturn way, he teased her as he obeyed her mindless gesture. Coming to stand just a step behind her, Xerus stared out at the mountain range he had barely had the chance to witness the last time he had visited the resort, due to the battles occurring at that time, which had pulled him away from such luxury.

In a way, he felt as though this were his first time relishing the steamy hot springs.

He was also losing himself in the swept-away gaze of his wife. Skylar looked positively beatific when she turned her gaze to him. Before she could utter a word in response to his tease, she shocked him with one of her own: "Why do we always find ourselves on a mountain?"

Her question nearly edged his usual straightened mouth into a grin. Almost was she fortunate enough to witness the rare occurrence, had she not left her post at the windows and headed toward her luggage. He observed her back as she left his side, and he found himself overcome with relief that there was nothing beyond the door for her to escape to—along the man-made stairs outside their windows were the hot springs they had come to visit, so she had no true cause to escape him whilst they were there.

For once, he had his wife within arm's length for more than just the meager moments before he fell asleep, and he couldn't have been happier with the setup of their impromptu, delayed honeymoon.

Yes, if only she'd turned around then instead of focusing on her suitcase, she might have seen him smiling her way.

CHAPTER 8

"I thank you for giving these two soldiers a chance at redemption," Commander Vergil mumbled, glaring at the two newly recruited escorts of Summerside as they stood stationed at his back. While they had all moved to stand outside of the east gate, the man who ran Otornot Keep saw to offer the queen and her party a proper farewell, attended by those she had graciously hired for such an important event in Varon K'aii's history.

Skylar grinned. "I'm glad we managed to come to an agreement. It may have seemed like a simple conversation, but I'm sure we've made a big difference." She spoke directly to the soldiers then and received bashful thanks from both of them.

"Definitely," Dalya agreed. "With more and more people willing to see the other side of things, I know we'll all be able to get along someday."

Commander Vergil, though much more sullen, concurred with her assessment. "We will do our best to guarantee your confidence in our services."

"Thank you, Commander." The former beast master felt as though she were patting him on the head with the specific way she gave him her praise.

"Your Majesty." The commander and his men bowed to her one last time before returning to their military den. For someone described as domineering, he seemed much more like a wild dog that heeled when shown the respect he deserved. Skylar knew she would have no qualm in calling on Vergil's aid, should she ever see fit to do so in the future.

Once the departing military disappeared behind their large iron door, the four friends turned to face one another to devise their next plan of action. Cyril said, "That turned out pretty well. I can't believe we pulled it off!"

"What are you going to do now?" Emery turned to the queen, wondering where her travels would take her next.

Skylar glanced toward Dalya as she harmlessly taunted, "Now I have no clear plan. With Otornot Keep effectively taken care of, I only need to arrange my return trip to the Goodlit Summit."

The easily excitable woman saw the teasing glint in her eye before she had managed to finish speaking, and she let out a gasp that strengthened as her mouth widened inordinately. Dalya's self-control over her easily excitable nature suddenly popped. "Does that mean we can all go to Sailbrooke together?"

"Why not?" said the businessman with a sigh, calculating in his ways while behaving blasé. "I can just call Rainier on the way and head back to Spierté tomorrow."

"I'm still down for going. It would feel wrong not to see Kivah and Weswin now," Emery confessed.

Dalya's head bobbled in agreement. "All we need is Raibeart, and the gang would be back together again!"

"I hope I will be a suitable substitute," Skylar quipped.

Immediately, Cyril said, "Trust me, Your Majesty, you're much easier on the eyes than the old man. You'll hear no complaints from me."

Emery rolled her eyes as she led them off the premises and onto Aesop's Stroll. "Just let Xerus hear you talking about his wife like that. Wasn't it you who once challenged him to a contest measuring your muscles for the position of leader on one of our missions? And didn't he win, saying—"

Cyril opted out of the rest of the remembrance of his playful, shameful contest with the king. Skylar was highly disappointed to think she might never hear the end of what was surely an outstanding tale.

The snarls of beasts and the cracking of Skylar's whip were interrupted by the ring of a totem, followed by a familiar jovial voice.

"Are those the sounds of battle I hear?"

"Are you on your totem while we're fighting?" Cyril gawked at such absurdity. Though distracted, he did his best to defend himself against a massive army of baby wolpertingers. With their little wings and paws, the entire herd of the wolflike creatures swarmed the group as they made their way to Sailbrooke, though it was impossible to ignore the way the entire lot of them flocked toward the businessman.

Meanwhile, as she waved her totem in the air, Dalya smiled apologetically as she did her best to stifle a giggle, saying, "Say hi to Raibeart, everyone!"

"Are you serious? Dalya!"

"It's only been a few days since we last spoke, and he's already forgotten me? Aye, what a rude man he is," jested Raibeart as he chuckled on the other side of the call.

Feeling the need to explain herself, Dalya looked to Skylar as the queen beckoned to a few of the miniature creatures with an open palm extended. "It really didn't seem fair that he couldn't come along. Aren't totems great?"

Skylar hadn't ceased in disliking them, but her feelings had grown a tad kinder toward the technology that was her transportable talking device. However, all the queen could do was greet her teacher before chirping to the wolpertingers who deemed her worthy of their attention. "Hello, Raibeart."

"We are in the middle of something!" exclaimed Emery, exasperated. She leaped over whining monsters and looked to be running away from a fight rather than simply avoiding them or perhaps playing with the curious litter. Skylar could only surmise that they were all about a month or so old.

The captain general—unaware that the enemy they faced were adorable chimera-like wolf pups—seemed unconcerned by their plight. "I'm sure speaking with me is no hindrance, what with your mighty battling skills."

His charm was not successful in winning Cyril over. "Laying it on a little thick there, gramps!"

"Dalya tells me you all are planning to stop by Sailbrooke to visit Kivah and Weswin." As if sensing the lack of humor his prior companions felt at long last, Raibeart cut to the chase when speaking inquisitively of their new destination. "I do so wish I could join you."

"Then come on down! If you can make it here to help us get rid of these wolfinswingers, even better!" said Cyril, likely unaware of how poor his substitute name for their monster foes sounded.

Skylar could only shake her head with slight disappointment at the dip in his cleverness, all while stroking the spine of one of the wolpertingers who had accepted her. A second approached her and, in the blink of an eye, clamped down on her hand with its baby teeth. Skylar felt her instincts hone in on the possible indents in her skin, staring at the wolpertinger's muzzle as she waited to see it cease its gnawing. She knew that as it was a wild animal, she had to concern herself with its perception of biting whether she was to ever see this particular herd again or not. Keeping that in mind, she decided to offer one finger to the gentle creature in her lap and allow it to sniff her offered skin.

In its calmed state, the sleepy wolpertinger examined her finger with its senses before it licked the tip. It was understandable for the monsters to behave curiously with the humans they had encountered, and Skylar hoped their interaction could assist the herd in responding to any other people they would meet later on in life. The previously coerced pup began to add its teeth into its assessment of her finger, and Skylar gently praised it with a light hum from deep within her throat. She received three curious stares from the wolpertingers that surrounded her, but she focused her gaze on the one in her lap.

When the third one decided to join in with their odd gathering, it found Skylar's forearm and immediately began to playfully nibble repeatedly along the side. Again, she rewarded the young one with her attention through a firm gaze and purring praise. There were a few notes of sudden pain, but the pain wasn't anything Skylar was unfamiliar with. In fact, the chamrosh she'd once raised—with a beak powerful enough to skin her arm as a mere afterthought—had left many scars on her body in abstract designs. A pup's playful bite was not able to compare.

The feisty wolpertinger, however, wished to feel equal in terms of receiving her attention. Slowly but surely, it backed off her arm without clamping its jaw shut. Instead, it brought out its tongue and dragged the scratchy surface over where it had left its teething marks. She waited still, aware that the instinctive monster would know that its officiousness was not the same as an apology. Cyril had fallen to the ground and looked to be drowning underneath the momentum of the swarming pack, Emery had taken to standing on top of a nearby rock in order to take advantage of the pups' inability to fly, and the former beast master curled her lips in to avoid emitting any sort of amusing sound when witnessing the average person's ability to handle the monsters of the land.

Dalya giggled in her place, letting the sound echo into the totem. "You're more than welcome to join us."

"I Ieh, wish I could. Sadly, the demands of a captain general are much more powerful than the whims of an old man."

The queen rolled her eyes, sarcastically contemplating when she had first become familiarized with that particular sentiment.

"I'm sorry, Raibeart." Dalya sounded genuinely sad to know he could not make the trip. "I really wish we could see you."

Raibeart brightened instantly. "Well, you are more than welcome to join Queen Skylar in her return home. I would be more than happy to receive you here at the castle."

With a simple toss of glances around the group, it was easy to ascertain that none of them could guarantee appeasing their eldest member. Skylar paid close attention to her comrades and wondered what it must have felt like to be unable to meet with old friends. With the need to resume business, progress in research, or perhaps report and compose another review, the bosom buddies who had spent many hours together long ago could no longer sacrifice their time as they chose. It seemed that even those stationed beneath a captain general had unavoidable responsibilities.

The silence did not go unnoticed, as evident by Raibeart's addition. "If not then, whenever you have time to spare."

"Definitely! You can expect to see me soon, okay, Raibeart?" said Dalya, though her response sounded almost like a friendly warning.

A familiar laugh sounded. "I'll be eagerly awaiting your arrival."

"Mine too." Emery piped up. She sounded committed to the promise she had thusly made, even while the expression on her face demonstrated that she was internally calculating her escape from the miniature pack's fascination.

With a begrudging grin peeking out among the riled forms of an even larger cluster of wolpertingers, even Cyril granted his presence. "And mine."

"Oh no, Cyril." Raibeart denied him outright. "I couldn't imagine taking up any more of your time. You seem to be so busy; I wouldn't want to distract you."

Immediately, the middle-aged man groaned with his head tossed back, his voice wailing in volume so that it could reach the skies, hopefully summoning some divine being to take pity on his soul. Instead, it was the wolpertingers who heard him and decided to take action, yapping away as they leaped all over him with a great deal of excitement. From beneath their furry bodies, a painful cry escaped them to say, "Why does it seem like everyone is having fun at my expense lately?"

❖❖❖❖❖

"I can't wait to see the looks on Kivah's and Weswin's faces when they see us," Dalya said as they made their way through the gateway connecting Aesop's Stroll and the outer entrance of Sailbrooke.

The mighty walls surrounding the clustered city were referred to as the Star Fort, if Skylar recalled correctly. She regarded the height of the fortification with silent awe as they wandered into the town, amazed by the walls that rivaled the height of the hill that held Spierté's coliseum. Yet behind such a man-made barricade were the most demure homes she had ever seen. Overpopulated and somewhat aged though the city was, a distinct charm resonated from the mere architecture. The structures resembled cottages more so than homes; Sailbrooke appeared to be much less developed than Terrinal yet had locked itself away from the world behind an eight-pointed stone barrier.

Perhaps it was because of the cultural strife that had occurred between the tourists and the church in Terrinal that the people of Sailbrooke found the motivation to keep their fortress stationed around their city even after the passing of the war.

Lagging behind at the back of the group, Cyril was much less impressed than the queen, as indicated by the way he inhaled the caressing winds and wondered aloud, "Is school out for the day already?"

"If not, it should be soon," Emery said thoughtfully.

Skylar had little to contribute to the conversation, given that her only school-like experience came in the form of Raibeart's haphazard scheduling for his teachings. Growing up in a tribe had allowed her to focus more on hunter-gatherer pursuits, whereas reading and formal speech had never been part of her instinctive curriculum. Thankfully, she'd been raised in a place where she was trusted to walk along her own path in life as long as she always had a bright light guiding her on her way.

Who would have guessed there was such a beacon buried in the snow-covered mountains surrounding the Goodlit Summit?

"Well, come on." Dalya instigated a clumsy run, charging forth as she shouted out, "We have to get to the school before it lets out! Otherwise, we won't be able to surprise them when they get home!"

"Dalya?" Two sweet, curious voices came from behind the group.

One by one, the four travelers turned to see who had addressed their grand marshal as they paraded down the road. There, in matching pairs of dignified uniforms, stood two young teens Skylar assumed were the twins they had come to visit.

"Oh, hey, Kivah. Hi, Weswin," Emery said. Her greeting was casual compared to her childhood friend's rampant enthusiasm in her surprise.

"The little princes!" exclaimed Cyril like a proud father. "How've you been? You surprised to see us?"

"Cyril." Weswin blushed, pouting as he shook his rage-encasing fists close to his chin. "Don't call us that! It sounds so creepy coming from you."

"But it suits you so well," said the businessman, who had apparently decided on a strong refusal to the young man's understandable request.

Before the angered twin could argue with his callous joke, the one known as Kivah suddenly refocused his attention and noticed the two females who were also present on the street with them. "Dalya. And wow, is that Queen Skylar? What are you—"

"Uh-oh." The tone in Cyril's voice immediately became spooked upon Kivah's unintentional revelation of the formerly incognito royal. The response of passersby was like a domino effect; in every direction, people had heard the revelation of the queen's presence in the city. The rising sense of awareness caused tingles to run along Skylar's skin in a way she'd never felt before. Whispers abounded, and she knew at once that she had been spotted. It felt somewhat nerve-racking to have so many eyes intent on staring.

With acute awareness, their disrupted parade's grand marshal concocted a thorough, well-devised strategy to avoid the forming crowds. Screeching in a panicked whisper, she explained, "We can't go to the twins' house like this! We're gonna have to visit Lady Mahina and ask her to hide us for now. Come on. Let's get out of here!"

As discreetly as they could possibly run, the six of them dashed their way to the female dignitary's home, hoping she would have sympathy for the queen and her traveling companions.

❖❖❖❖❖

"I'm so sorry!" Kivah apologized for the umpteenth time.

Standing next to him was his brother, Weswin, who hid his face in his hands as he channeled his twin's embarrassment and regret.

"I should have been more careful," Kivah said. Both boys hid their faces under the bobs of caramel hair on their heads, too ashamed to face the queen after the blunder in town.

Cutting in before anyone else could speak, Lady Mahina moved to sit next to her young guests and patted their shoulders gently. "It was an accident, you two. The queen is perfectly fine, isn't she?" Though her claim was true, the setup of the dining hall's table felt much like that of an elongated conference-style discussion, based on how they had been made to sit around for tea and sweets. Kivah, seated in the far corner of the back couch, must have felt as though all present had their eyes on him, staring while resting after their race to find shelter in the manor after his revelation.

"He didn't mean it! It was an accident. Honest!" howled Weswin with great concern for Kivah's possible reprimand, it seemed. Given that Weswin was not the one who had identified the queen to the public, it was intriguing to witness just how much of his brother's emotions he took on himself.

"It's all right." Skylar attempted to soothe the worried duo. "You didn't know I was moving about in secret. It wasn't your fault, Kivah. Please."

His sad chocolate-brown eyes peeked up at the friends gathered around him, easily mimicked by Weswin, who took a prominent step forward in case the extended branch of kindness was an illusion. Even so, the honesty of her words seemed to register with Kivah as he moved to sit with a straightened posture.

Lady Mahina chose to move right along. "Well, regardless of how you arrived, it's nice to see you all again." The others welcomed her blatant attempt at viewing their gathering with comedy. She smiled so widely that her own navy eyes nearly disappeared behind her cheeks.

"You too, Mahina. Oh, Raibeart says hi from the summit." To emphasize this, Dalya waved at the mistress from across the dining room table. Luckily, the act only required one of her hands, as the other had already taken hold of one of the plated pastries before her. Next to the hungry young lady, Cyril had similarly taken eager hold of his offered teacup.

"Hi back," Mahina said brightly. "Is there something important you all needed to discuss with me, or did you come by for a surprise visit?"

"We were hoping to surprise Kivah and Weswin as they got home from school, but—"

Emery's explanation of their casual endeavor failed to register with the queen as she felt her totem aggressively shake underneath her armor. Weswin, who stood on the opposite side of the table, noticed the sound, and she showed him an apologetic expression. After curiously retrieving her totem, she tossed it open with great expectation as to whom was trying to get her attention presently.

It was Xerus: "I heard that you called. Is everything all right?"

What on Varon K'aii? He had texted her because of a call on someone's totem? She hadn't even been the one who rang the castle. If he was referring to their group conversation with Captain General Raibeart, it was the spunky travel agent who had made contact with him. Skylar found it abnormal that her husband would message her over such a slight action committed by another in her party. She wasn't offended, but since when had he become so invested in their interactions?

"Right, Skylar?"

Oh dear. She was being summoned. Tossing her head high above her totem's screen, the queen met many pairs of expectant eyes wondering what her thoughts were on the matter that had escaped her attention. She was so hazed by her distraction that she could not even pinpoint who had said her name.

As nonsensical as it was, the queen replied, "Absolutely."

She watched as everyone once again looked to Kivah and his sheepish disposition. Though he had reverted to his shy ways, it was Weswin who stated, "Well, if the queen says it's all good, then it's all good."

"That's what we've been trying to tell you. No harm done, Kivah." Emery made her attempt at quelling the persisting concerns of the young boy. Considering this was a conversation that had resurfaced beyond her count, the queen took her ostensible opportunity to reply to the king: "Everything is fine. Dalya was the one who called. How are you?"

She snapped her totem shut, thinking she should put the blasted thing on its silent mode rather than letting it vibrate, as Emery had shown her. However, the thought was vanquished when she tuned in to hear Lady Mahina speak of their unknowing first acquaintance with one another: "At Yukaih Castle just a few days ago. You came into the great hall because some friend of the king's had arrived."

Her desire to involve herself in the conversation had been a pressing one, and the inclusion of a memory she was meant to recall forced her hand to do so. Even as her totem rattled in her hand once again, she conquered her mind and tried to place the woman as Cyril claimed, "That friend was me."

"Oh!" Skylar exclaimed louder than intended. "Yes, I remember now. You congratulated me once again on my marriage. I believe I saw you at the ceremony months ago."

"You remember? We only spoke for a moment, so I wouldn't have been surprised if you had been much too busy on your wedding day to remember me. Well, that and I unfortunately could not spend the evening in the city," said Lady Mahina as she adjusted her outfit, as if embarrassed for the social fumble. "I cannot recall why now, but I believe I had something to attend to here in Sailbrooke."

Skylar smiled gently. "Do not fret, Lady Mahina. I promise you I—oh, is that chanting?" Her mood shifted as the queen impolitely diverted from their conversation to take note of the low rumbling of voices from outside of the manor. The purpose of the gathered people wasn't clear, and their presence resulted in nothing more than a rather unpleasant noise buzzing about from just beyond the lawn. Surely the guards stationed throughout the property would not need to act if they were confronted by such a group, should they remain peaceable in their actions.

"It's nothing new, I'm afraid. Please don't let them bother you. Some of my brother's most devout followers have yet to adapt to my new role and continue to find any excuse to gather outside my home. Let's resume our conversation. Shall we?" said the mistress of Sailbrooke shyly. Her tone had been honest, but her eyes allowed her guests to witness the sadness she held behind them. Skylar regained her manners quickly and knew that it was not her place to ask.

Weswin was not as reserved, it seemed. "Do you think they're here today because they know the queen is here? Not everyone likes that Xerus is the king, right?"

"Weswin!" Dalya was quick to admonish the young man. Cyril was just as disappointed and made it known that he was not in favor of the question by ruffling his auburn locks. The question was immediately forgotten as the angrier twin turned to his brother for help; the quieter twin was trying to avoid conflict while sipping his tea.

Hoping to break away from tension and supply the room with something else to discuss, Emery instigated another topic of discussion she could comprehend. "How has Sailbrooke been otherwise? Are the people still debating the termination of the cannons in the fort walls?"

As Lady Mahina garnered the focus, Skylar decided to quickly peek at the message she had received while swapping compliments of wardrobe: "Busy, as I've told you before."

After going out of his way to contact her, that was all he had to say? Unappreciative of his contemptuous tone, she decided she would not let him surface from their text-talk without providing her with some sort of gratifying dialogue. The queen chose to use her undisclosed power of information to enlist his talent with words: "I recently learned something interesting. Would you care to enlighten me?"

She was proud of herself for constructing such a message to him. A smirk played out on her features as she chimed in to the conversation taking place with her own talent for speech. "We managed to make a positive change at Otornot Keep, yes. It was indeed an ordeal but a successful one."

Lady Mahina seemed thoughtful as she digested what the queen had admitted. "Hm, well, I hope I too may be successful with my people. We are such a peaceful city usually. Speaking of which, if you plan to stay the night in Sailbrooke, you're more than welcome to do so here, and then you can leave at dawn. You're more likely to sneak out undetected that way. What do you say?"

The others would need to pan out their sleeping arrangements; a text had come in from Xerus: "I would be more than happy to. You may ask me anything."

Whatever she had done, Skylar had set him off before she'd played her sly hand the way she had. Now he was rising to any challenge she set before him. It was exhilarating to know she could behave so carelessly and free-spiritedly with the man titled as her mate in such a way. She wrote, "There was mention of a competition between yourself and Cyril once, measuring muscles? A competition implies a winner, does it not?"

"Please, I insist. After everything you all have done for me and this city, let alone Varon K'aii, I would be more than happy to have you stay the night." Lady Mahina enacted her authority in a way that wasn't authoritative at all; she was merely suggesting through the power of stating her desires in a candid fashion. It would be a hardship to refuse her when she had worked herself into such a state.

Dalya revealed her excitement first, voicing the feelings a bashful-looking Kivah surely shared. "Yay! A big sleepover!"

Without saying so, the remaining members of their traveling party found themselves accepting the offer of lodgings with unfeigned gratitude. Skylar herself reflected their expressions before hurriedly returning to her totem in order to view the anxiously awaited response: "Indeed it does. As you should well know, there is no way I could lose a duel such as that."

A luscious pout overcame the queen's features as she sulked down at the message-bearing screen; she was thoroughly disappointed that he had bested her at her own game.

CHAPTER 9

S kylar felt somewhat sorry for Cyril and Emery; they had gone to bed earlier than the rest of their friends and were cooped up in the bedchamber across the hall, having only the other to keep company with. She could almost guarantee—without ever setting one foot in their doorway—that the two dignitaries, the twins, and the eccentric writer were having a great deal more fun, partaking in quite the slumber party.

It was soothing to have one's hair tended to by another, and Kivah's gentle stroking with a rounded brush through her tresses almost caused the beast master to purr. The young man had been obviously curious about her hair and had shown no shyness in wishing to toy with it. He was cautious in his movements and not at all distracted by Weswin, who was a great deal less enthusiastic to play barber to the queen but had refused to leave his brother in another room for a night, as he'd explained in not so many words. Even though his bushy orange hair was short and visibly knotted, surely he wouldn't mind a soft brushing.

Plus, he thoroughly enjoyed resting his head in Her Highness's lap.

"Oh, did that hurt?" asked the voice of her informal beautician over her shoulder.

Skylar opened one of her green eyes and said, "Hm?"

"I thought I caught a knot."

"Oh no, dear," said the happy customer, hoping to quickly encourage him to return to his gratuitous upkeep. "Don't worry."

"Wow, really? I can't tell if your hair is really thick or super strong," said Kivah admiringly as he slowly restarted his task. The speed with which he resumed matched the closing of the queen's eyes—that was, until another slumber partygoer called for her attention.

"It is very lovely," Lady Mahina said with a hint of wonderment, sitting a stone's throw away on the carpeted floor. As she was holding a large platter of assorted fruits and a complementary dip in her hand, it was evident she had just returned from her personal trek to the kitchen to supply them with a late-night snack. It was a task likely inspired by her own hunger, given that she had descended the stairs in her chosen pajamas of blush capris and a simple tee.

Dalya, who was in the process of shutting the suite's door behind her, couldn't help but include herself once aware of the discussion topic. "Does everyone in your family have hair like that?"

Skylar's gifted bedtime appearance had her beautiful white-and-rouge locks tied into a bun atop of her head. The oversize shirt from Kivah bore a flowered circle design diagonally along her side, which corresponded well with the way the collar drooped off her shoulder. Her shorts, which had been offered to her by Mahina, were mismatched in design—a lovely deep purple to her upper half's robin's-egg blue—but all together, the outfit suited her nicely.

Somehow, she had also managed to procure a pair of slipper boots, which had ribbon ties at their backs for no purpose other than to increase the decorative aspect of her appearance; it was as if she didn't feel complete without some kind of footwear, though had she really needed them on her trip to the bathroom, one couldn't help but wonder.

Smiling to herself, Skylar explained, "Yes and no. My tribe is made up of people with blond hair, and we use products of the earth to put the orange dye in our hair." She knew the talkative young ladies were drawn to gaze at her two-toned bangs, and she followed suit in imitating them.

Assimilating with the talk of colors, Kivah gave reason for the queen to feel dismayed as he popped out from behind her. The roomy nightshirt he wore for bed was teal and showcased a white design of what was most likely the crest for his school, and the shorts beneath matched. He looked studious with his curious eyes, but it was talkative Weswin who spoke in place of him. "Wow, Skylar. You're from a tribe?"

"I didn't know that," added the other twin.

Was it uncommon knowledge? There were those who still did not know her by look, but she assumed the gossip of her origins had circled the land infinitely more than she could dream of herself. Realizing she had opened the door to her personal information unconsciously, she felt it was only right to supply the details herself. "Is that so? I assumed everyone knew I lived in the mountains beyond Spierté before moving to the Goodlit Summit."

Lady Mahina looked pensive. "I think we all thought you were from Spierté itself; isn't that where you and Xerus first met?"

A pronounced nod was her answer.

Weswin eyed his queen with uninhibited scrutiny. "Mm, no. I think we all would have remembered seeing someone with a hairstyle like yours."

"When we visited Spierté with His Grace during the war." Kivah finished his brother's thoughts for those present whom he did not share such a strong bond with.

"Wait a moment." Feeling as though the topic had been altered with a near tectonic shift, Skylar rose onto her knees as if she were about to stand. "You two were with Xerus when he was campaigning for unification?" The shock that spilled forth from her words was merely a taste of what sort of energy her aura possessed. To think of the young boys before her being present during one of the most violent moments in Varon K'aii's history was upsetting, to say the least, and her darkened emotions swirled inside, inspired by her husband's supposed sound judgment.

Skylar was so distraught to learn of such an alarming tidbit of history that she did not immediately take note of the panic that befell Mahina's face the moment she asked the question. Damage control appeared to be her primary concern, as she quickly blurted out, "No, no! They meant my brother, Jovost. Sir Jovost Gaellen."

"He was rumored to have been on every front line with Xerus," Dalya said without much tact as she munched on a plump grape. Once more unaware of her surroundings, she remained calm while all other sleepover members were undeniably tense.

Taking a deep breath, Mahina centered herself before responding to the nosy woman, even though her gaze fell upon Skylar instead. "Yes, my brother followed Xerus from the moment he visited the manor and asked him for his help. Really, His Majesty only requested soldiers, but Jovost felt so strongly about the cause that he named me the acting duchess of Sailbrooke so that he could fight for a brighter future for everyone of Varon K'aii. He wanted every single person who set foot on this land to feel just as safe and prosperous as the people protected behind our walls."

When the explanation sounded as though it had accidentally become more personal than originally intended, Skylar lowered herself to sit with her legs tucked beneath her as her nervous energy dissipated. Her lessons from Raibeart regarding the war were usually dry recollections of what she had assumed transpired, and due to courtesy of her teacher's own experiences, she avoided asking for more information; the basic elements of the motivations, strategies, tyranny, and victory were laid out before her on maps of the land draped across large tables, but the personality behind every single calculated move was usually brushed past in order to move on to something else.

How could she not have known that Mahina's own brother served at Xerus's side?

"He sounds like a wonderful person." The queen offered her belated respect to the departed brother of her hostess.

For a moment, she wondered if she had trespassed into uncomfortable territory by not following Raibeart's example of simply pressing forward when touching upon topics pertaining to death. To her surprise, Mahina smiled as though born to do so eternally and kindly replied, "Thank you, Your Majesty. He truly was."

Young but wise, Kivah tried to ease the tension of their sleepover and piped up to add, "Didn't he hate the heat of Spierté, though?"

Dalya pointed at the young boy as if she were waving at him to pause the conversation so that she could speak next. "Yeah! I remember him once saying that he would offer to carry one of Xerus's banners just to get some shade."

Mahina snickered. "I think he asked me to send him a hat once in a letter just to block the sun from his eyes. To be fair, the weather around

Spierté seems to be perpetually hot, even though the Goodlit Summit is only one city away."

"Two—don't forget the fabled Tel Adis," said the writer before digging into the snack tray once again.

Skylar didn't dream of responding to that particular comment.

"I don't know how it is explained in schools," said the queen as she reached across the informal huddle to pluck a grape for herself, "but in the tribal world, we see the weather as a manifestation of the zenith that resides in the land. For example, Relic was rumored to travel the continent in a spiritual form in order to keep the land lush and thriving, wasn't he? After the war happened, it was believed by my people that the Vicis Plain became uninhabitable because he deserted it due to mourning the tribe of his people, since their territory was once in the middle of the battlefield."

"Wow, was it?" Weswin's enthusiasm was evident in the startled gasp that preceded his inquiry.

To once more provide substance to his brother's words, Kivah said, "We don't know where the tribes live necessarily. It isn't taught to us at all, which is probably why the separation between the tribes and the cities is so big."

The queen merely nodded in understanding, the reason behind such a decision soothing the tribal side of her greatly, before Mahina tried to continue the lesson of how the tribes saw the world. "So then do you know why the Goodlit Summit is surrounded in ice? They say Agloolik lives along the Tundra Path, don't they?"

"Yes, he does." Skylar's voice unknowingly spoke of her ability to verify the zenith's existence. "And he represents Syvant, who then manages wisdom and knowledge, which are essential attributes to a king."

The room was momentarily silent in awe, as if it were much more exciting at a slumber party to discuss history and lore more than anything else. Given that she had never experienced such a friendly endeavor, Skylar could only assume she was participating correctly. In an attempt to end the silence, she tried to resume their discussion by switching the focus. "How is it that you learned about the different climates, boys?"

Kivah was prepared to expound such details but was rendered mute by the talkative woman who was tying her white-and-rouge hair back, preparing for bed.

"They are told that Ordell created the clouds to give us water when we need it and nothing more. No offense, Mahina, but the education on certain topics in Sailbrooke is a little closed-minded. Though speaking of different educational systems, I wonder what it's like to learn about these things on the islands, since we have the deities and zeniths here on the mainland and there isn't talk of any in Hierony or Viskretta."

The judging Weswin eyed her suspiciously. "You're worried more about the quality of education in Hierony, right?" He slowly turned to look at Kivah and shared a knowing look.

Dalya glared softly and posed a harsh-sounding question. "What?"

"Nah, nothing!" Weswin lay down once again in Skylar's lap and seemed to be in much higher spirits. "We're not thinking anything."

It was evident that the poor girl who was subjected to such teasing had had her fair share of verbal torture by the twins when her seething generated a terrible amount of illusionary steam from her ears. Instead of tackling the accusation, she implemented one of her own. "Hey! I know what you're getting at! I'm not going to be teased by a couple of kids who have a bunch of secret admirers! Who are you to talk?"

"Oh no, we already know it's the Deyvin triplets—the girls from another town," Kivah revealed simply.

The two royal Varon K'aiians did not see it in such a plain light. It was indeed a more pleasant surprise to the lady of the house, who nearly cheered as she asked, "You mean the daughters of Mayor Deyvin have taken an interest in you two? That's adorable."

"From Summerside?" Skylar added for further clarification. Raibeart had once mentioned how commercial the port city was, so it was not too shocking to learn that children were sent to other cities to receive a proper education if it was deemed affordable and necessary. Nevertheless, it was amazing that the unaware schoolchildren had managed to make such prominent contacts and friends.

Kivah and Weswin nodded in unison. Then the eldest went on. "I was upset about it at first because, well, there was a lot we didn't agree on. Things like procedures for traveling between the cities and how moving the school from Terrinal to Viskretta is beneficial for Varon K'aii overall."

"But when we started to at least listen to them, we realized that we both had ways of looking at things that had potentially good ideas. So we told them to stop being so sneaky and just talk to us out in the open more. Now they're like our, uh, friends kind of." Weswin finished off their story with a proud grin.

The way they spoke seemed almost insightful as to the ways in which those with differences might learn to adhere to one another; the twins had proven to be quite wise in Skylar's eyes. She smiled with them easily, wanting to do so for more than a single cause. After mulling over many mixed emotions inside of herself for a handful of minutes, it was almost refreshing—and, dare she say, enlightening—to hear of someone viewing a possibly debilitating issue with a more positive attitude than she herself had displayed on a few personal occasions. They showed the queen great promise for the future if the youth were speaking of matters among themselves with heads much more level than those of some of the adults beyond them.

"They're actually very smart," Kivah said brightly.

Weswin nodded and eagerly explained, "And we all compete for marks in school." His behavior guaranteed that the young men, however brilliant, were still children at heart.

As pleased as the duo was, Dalya seemed defeated—until she bucked up in an actionless rage and proclaimed, "You have a better relationship with three girls than I do with whomever you're implying! I'm not even allowed to stay at anyone's place when I'm visiting Hierony!"

"Why would you be visiting?" said Weswin, insinuating all over again despite knowing that his unintelligible act was agonizing to the poor woman.

As her so-called friends giggled at the sight of her complete and utter terror, Dalya seemingly did her best not to explode and shake the mouthy twin for all he was worth. Lady Mahina must have sensed that her fuse was reaching its end, for she politely suggested that it might be time for bed. In a small scramble, the group arranged themselves, deciding that, given that it was a slumber party, none of them was opposed to laying out the blankets on the floor and sleeping all together. They arranged their makeshift bedding quickly before lying on the floor, with Kivah and Weswin on the opposite side of the sheets from Dalya as a preliminary caution for one of their lives.

Skylar dozed off with a smile, feeling oddly satisfied to have stayed the night and bonded with the lady of the house, the writer, and the twins. Never before had she felt so comfortable with people she had only been partially acquainted with. *Perhaps there is something to be said for getaways such as these*, she thought.

------◆◆◆◆◆◆------

"Shall you enter the hot springs first," Xerus called to his wife as she sat in her nearly permanent place beside the floor-length window panes, "or shall I? Whichever you prefer."

The light of the afternoon reflected off her lightened strands of hair. She looked to be illuminated, celestial even, when she gave her attention to him. With Skylar still choosing to wear her monarch clothes, the sight only further galvanized his heart to pine. Beat for beat, he made his way to her, feeling bedeviled and finding the experience satisfying.

His wife seemed not to mind his commencement in her direction or the essence of his presence, as she simply said, "Why would we not go together?"

Xerus was thankful he'd reached his destination so as not to appear shocked into stillness by her words. What she was implying involved their naked bodies being hidden only by towels that were just as saturated by the heated waters as he was by her warm glow. And dare he imagine that she thought of such a thing, they were also allowed to enter the hot springs without any coverage at all. Surely his demure wife was thinking of the former option when she dared to suggest such a thing.

"Are you certain?" He formally needed her to clarify what she wanted of him. His naturally serious inclination arose when extracting her truth, as it would indeed be the first sign of intimacy between them.

If the flashbacks to his visit prior—when young Weswin repeatedly attempted to leap off his shoulders into the waters in all his naked glory—were any indication of a woman's usual distaste for sharing bath time with men, Skylar's gesture was indeed a treat.

Suddenly, with her expression of permeated calmness that kept her ever still, Skylar turned away from her enchanting window panes and faced him effortlessly. With a slight tilt of her head, she said in retort, "Are we not married? We share a bed; we can share a hot springs." Her explanation sounded so clear that it caused him to feel inadequate in his trying politeness construed as reservation.

She was, of course, correct. If they had planned to spend their entire vacation apart, why had he bothered organizing one? Though it wasn't how he'd imagined their first act of relative intimacy, it was yet another step in a direction he was excited to pursue. "Very well," he said more softly than he'd known he was capable of. "Let us go in together."

CHAPTER 10

It was breakfast time. With so many of the temporary residents of the manor readying themselves for their new destinations and the journeys that would take place in between, the meal was prepared to be filling and hearty. One by one, they met around the dining room table once again, with Lady Mahina the first to rise, and found themselves awaiting to hear the plans decided on by each guest individually.

The most obvious departure was voiced first, preceded by a satisfying sigh that implied just how much Emery enjoyed every last drop of her morning tea. "Well, I should be heading to Viskietta soon. I've left Ágoston and the others alone for far too long. I was only supposed to be grabbing something from Terrinal and heading right back, after all."

"But you all ended up here." Mahina pointed out the obvious result of her travels, a smile on her face over the rim of her own teacup. "I'm really glad everything worked out this way."

Kivah nodded ardently in the seat next to her. "Of course. It was really nice to see everyone again."

"We had a great time!" exclaimed Weswin. As he leaned toward his brother, he surprised the others with his staying power as Kivah rose from his seat and bid everyone a quick farewell; he lifted his jacket off the back of his chair, fixed his appearance as fast as he could, and then offered a bow before making a break for the front door. The abandoned twin must have read everyone's mind, for he added, "Until he leaves me behind the next day. I hate when Kivah goes to school without me."

Emery delicately explained, "Kivah has an extra morning class at school. Weswin starts an hour after his brother does."

"Don't worry," Lady Mahina said, offering a show of comfort by patting Weswin's shoulder. "You'll be in class together before you know it."

Weswin did not believe a word of her promise, for he murmured, "Not if I know how to tell time."

"Sorry I can't stay and keep you company, Weswin." Dalya apologized for something none had accused her of. Nervous in habit, she fixed her outfit as she went on. "I gotta bring my review of Terrinal to my editor to see if it's ready to go to print. It's my most important piece so far!"

Emery grinned. "At least we can go part of the way together." Her longest-standing friend nodded at her observation.

With the assertion of travel plans emerging at the table, Cyril turned to the queen as he divulged his own, though he spoke at a pitch that allowed all those present to hear of his intentions. "I need to meet up with Rainier as soon as I can, but I could take you back to the summit if you want. Spierté is on the way, no matter which way we go."

"But wouldn't it make the most sense to have Rainier travel to Terrinal and for you to await him there?" suggested Skylar, trying to appear strategic. In actuality, she was merely hoping to have a justified reason to politely refuse his ushering of her to Yukaih Castle, as her plans still felt undecided.

The businessman surely appreciated her shrewd observation. "Oh, good idea. I guess I'm headed backward then. At least I can test out if Commander Vergil managed to hire proper guards since we last saw him." Given that he was referring to the confrontation that had taken place the day before, it was more than likely the task of finding replacement soldiers had been completed long ago.

The queen's lack of a finalized path did not go unnoticed by Lady Mahina, though, who asked, "Then what will you do, Skylar? Will you travel all that way by yourself?"

"No way." Dalya provided a response in her place without question. "She can come with Emery and me to Summerside if she wants. Or just go back the way we came with Cyril." The further along in her suggestion she went, the more it sounded as though her friend was conditioning her to only the two choices she presented her with.

Skylar, having become too distracted by the moment at hand to further enjoy her simple serving of hot cereal stylized with maple whipped cream, which was entirely a shame, spoke whatever came to mind in reply. "Both roads lead to the Goodlit Summit at some point."

"And hey, once Rainier and I are done in Terrinal, I could go all of the way with you."

"Cyril! That's Xerus's wife you're talking to!" said Weswin in the same playful way he had bothered Dalya before sleep had overtaken the slumber party.

"Stuff it," said Cyril with playful animosity in his bland gaze. His target of aggression heeded nothing and giggled evilly while stuffing himself with some lobster-egg delicacy.

The queen graciously bypassed the remark. "Thank you, but …"

She had a choice to make. She could continue her travels with Cyril, slipping through Otornot Keep and back into her favorite city—well, her favorite thus far. If she never explored more of the wonders Varon K'aii housed, she could never know if a different town could take its place. Another consideration was the reaction Commander Vergil might have to her sudden return to the fort; he'd most likely misconceive her normalized and nonpolitical intentions. Those were two solid reasons that made her alternate route seem more appealing.

Returning by way of Summerside would allow her to visit more than her fair share of extra destinations, just as she had wanted to do all along. Viskretta sounded modern and appealing to her sense of progression toward a unified future, and Hierony was Cyril's hometown, which she had yet to learn anything about—she had so much more to see and experience. The mystical Tel Adis she had heard word of in the vaguest sense while living in the mountains was at least the last stop she had to make before returning to her home high up in the mountains. Making her way along the far side of the continent might even provide her with the chance to visit the Nazuré tribe if she felt so inclined. The only true downfall to the plan was the possibility of being discovered and captured by Xerus should he find her along the way, but that would not be the case if she paid a visit to her people.

"I think I'll go to Summerside," she finally decreed.

"Really? That's awesome." Dalya hurrahed with a shot of her arm high in the air. Next to her, Emery agreed with a simpler gesture: a kind, welcoming smile.

Cyril rubbed the back of his neck, taking the indirect rejection of his company in stride. "Ah, I guess this is where we part ways then. Hey, it was fun hanging out with the queen of the land. Even if it felt like I was walking around with a buxom version of His Highness half the time." Or perhaps he wasn't too fond of his lone travels after all.

The distasteful mention of his teasing ways irked Skylar one last time for the sake of their memories. Skylar decided to be just as gracious as he had been in return. "You know, with how often you refer to Xerus, should I be concerned that it wasn't me you wanted to travel with when you came asking for his assistance?"

Cyril's body twitched at the thinly veiled accusation. He lifted his head, a knitted brow resting over his olive-tinted eyes, and stood, prepared to depart in that moment. "And I'll take that as my curtain call. Don't expect an encore!" Waving over his shoulder, he was the second to make his way to the front door and depart.

After an elegant, solid laugh, Skylar decided to call her husband to inform him of what she had determined to be her plan of action. She excused herself from the table; made her way into the hall, which wasn't exactly private, just distant enough to allude to attempted separation and confidentiality; and began to pace mindlessly along five or so floor tiles. When dialing, she took a deep breath to steady any possible nerves. Indeed, her strength to remain firm was evident in the way she took control of the conversation by being the first to speak as soon as she heard him pick up her call. "Xerus."

As always, he answered, "Skylar."

Kindly, in ways of social protocol, she asked, "How are you today?"

"I am well, thank you," said her husband, almost as if their talk were much more casual than it would most likely be. "My meetings with the people are starting soon."

"I see." Skylar nodded as if he somehow could see. "Then I shall need to speak briefly."

Xerus tried to dissuade her hurry. "There is no need. I would like to know how your day has started out to be as well."

Gobbling at the bait he offered like a starved animal, the queen divulged carelessly to the king. "Now that I have completed my original mission, I will be returning to Yukaih Castle. But first, I have decided to accompany Dalya and Emery as they travel to Summerside. I then plan to travel the scenic route, if you will, before coming home." Proudly, she had explained her newfound direction and kept her worry of his negative response from her voice. Her determination now grew tenfold, as she knew she could convince herself to stand her own against him in talks such as these.

"I see." The complimentary phrase was becoming a staple in their progressing conversations, whether or not they actually ascertained the other's meaning or motivation. Then, to her surprise, at her nervous expense, her mate uttered an extraordinary thing. "Though I don't believe any of what you said answered my question."

Had Xerus the king teased her as a husband might? Was she correct in believing Xerus was pestering her in an amicable manner? What on earth had gotten into the water at the summit? Or had Raibeart slipped the king his all-powerful elixir of wine so early in the morning? Indeed, her teacher had told her of a time when he had managed to intoxicate her unsuspecting husband and his usual high tolerance with some fruity spirits. Surely the captain general wouldn't be so cruel as to play such a trick on the king, especially prior to his addressing his citizens' concerns.

Whatever had caused this change in his attitude, Skylar found it delightful.

Her grin was unmistakable as she returned the same sort of enthusiasm. "Oh, I'm sorry. I've enjoyed my breakfast of hot cereal, and I accused Cyril of having a deeper interest in you before he left for Terrinal. Needless to say, I've enjoyed my morning thus far."

A deep, rich, distinct chuckle merged with a sudden crackling down the line, but Skylar assuredly heard his initial reaction to her honest depiction. However, he had to pretend that he had been disturbed by her interactions with one of his supposed friends and said, "I hope he denied you until he ran out of air."

"Until he was out of the manor," she promised.

"Good. So Emery and Dalya are your companions until Summerside, and then you plan to travel the rest of your journey on your own?" Their small game was decidedly finished by his change in topic, but it had been a highly delightful interlude.

Skylar nodded outside of his view once again. "Yes." Something new she had learned about herself as of late—ever since she had been provided with her own totem—was that she tended to groom herself with clear lethargy whilst conducting a call. It was a habit she was perfecting as she spoke to Xerus then and there; her hands positioned her stockings' winged rims properly over her knees and toyed with her hair over the shoulder farthest away from her device.

She needn't pretty herself for the man over the totem; she was just taking the time to preen for her own self-fulfillment.

"If you can spare the time"—unaware of her vain pastime, Xerus carried on without hesitation—"my offer still stands, Skylar."

What a perplexing comment he'd made. "What offer is that?"

"The one to have you join me at the amphitheater. If you'd merely prefer to observe and make your presence known, you are more than welcome to accompany me. I won't be arriving for another day or so, but if you agree to attend, I will leave here as soon as I possibly can. It would most likely suit you best to visit the meeting place that will unite all of the different countries around the world. With Summerside being the most flourishing of our port cities, you should be more than capable of finding a great deal of things to occupy your time while you wait."

His sudden rambling was not lost on her; he continued to push the boundaries of the most words spoken in a single breath in every other verbal chat they'd held. It happened only through their devices—seemingly they were unable to make such contact face-to-face. But it was the words he had spoken to her, not the way he'd said them, that bewitched her.

Xerus had invited her to participate in the development of the amphitheater.

Where on Varon K'aii that idea had come from, she could not say. She also realized she might never know. The cause was irrelevant, though, as its validity was unquestionable. The only matter worth contemplating was her readiness to expose herself to firsthand experiences of participating in the designated plays of back-and-forth politics, should another country's representatives arrive at the same time as them. After handling the situation with Commander Vergil, she knew that her skills with people—though relative to cues that were self-taught for a beast master—were expanding, but was she at a level fit to stand next to King Xerus and demonstrate why he'd chosen her to be his queen?

There was only one way to find out.

"Should you find yourself lost or in need of assistance beforehand," Xerus said in order to propitiate her further, "I could call Mayor Deyvin and ask her to help you transition."

"If anything, I would prefer to speak with her about such matters myself." Skylar knew her answer hadn't been defined, and for some reason she could not explain, even after receiving some of the attention she had secretly longed for, she was grateful he hadn't given her the chance to articulate her once conclusive thoughts.

"Then I shall provide you with her totem digits so that you can call her once you arrive," Xerus said. His tone gave no telltale sign as to whether or not he believed she had formally accepted or how either response she could give made him feel.

For the last time, she offered a nod to him in response before she straightened her pose into the one she'd take if she had her own throne to sit upon. "Thank you. For more than just her totem digits."

"You're welcome."

"I mean that sincerely, Xerus," she whispered to guarantee her gratitude's confidence. Even if she were vague in her own working conclusions, his token of belief in her as his partner meant more to her than she cared to share, especially by way of her totem. If ever there was a time to hint at her adoration, it was in that moment.

And it was a moment stretched out beyond her liking, as the man who had earned it seemed to be stilled, stunned by her kindness. She had half a mind to issue a teasing bout once more, if only to return him to his previous senses, but he thankfully returned not long after and with an act of benevolence of his own. "I hope you will continue to keep me aware of your travels."

Silently, a smile possessed her. "I will."

"Very good," he said with a forced tone of indifference while perfectly describing how he had made her feel.

* * *

Xerus was not one to adorn a towel when he bathed, not even when in the company of his fellow men. He had nothing to hide, and the bogged-down fabric felt like unnecessary weight to care for. No, he appreciated the freedom of movement while soaking in the luxurious hot springs, just as he would in his own bathing quarters.

What shook the earth beneath his feet was the knowledge that his wife apparently felt the same as he.

While he descended the outdoor staircase to the open-air bath, her head of golden tresses received its own bathing under the brilliant beams of the setting sun. So much of their day had already wisped past them, and he had rushed to join her so as not to waste another second. Even if he was made to wear an unfavorable cloth around his hips so as to showcase his characteristic dignity, he wanted to spend every instant with her to appease his personal suffering.

As he stepped onto the rocks surrounding the entrance to the spring and Skylar turned to face him, deserting her position of leaning over its ledge to lose herself in the sunset's comeliness, he saw enough skin along the upper swells of her breasts to know that she had entered the warm waters without any shred of cloth-like decency.

Her eyes seemed to depress as she uttered a meager "Oh."

"I just naturally assumed that we would … If you are not opposed to sharing the bath in that manner, I—"

"You needn't strip down if it makes you uncomfortable," his wife informed him, her decorum found in her words alone, it would seem. "I would need to find a towel for myself, though."

"No." The singular, fervent word was out of his mouth without thought behind it. Skylar was indeed a beauty, and he was not going to request that she conceal herself if she had been led to believe they would cherish their time together without a shred of material between them. If the only entity separating their naked bodies was to be the hot springs' waters, then so be it.

In a single swoop, his large hand gripped the farthest reach of the towel he wore and tossed it aside in a direction he cared not for. He stood before his wife in his most natural state, and it somehow made his already sturdy confidence detonate to know that her eyes could, if they so chose to, explore every detail of his body. Under the warm, waning light like the element he associated her with, Xerus knew he could never replicate how empowering it felt to first expose himself to her with such earnestness.

He made his way into the water, the steam welcoming him as it crawled along his skin to tease him of the rapture taking place beneath the surface of the hot spring. He submerged himself enough to sit upon a ledge much more sunken than hers so that they could come close to resting at the same height. Fiendishly, he pretended to ignore the way Skylar observed his trek into his seat, in the hopes that it might inspire her to continue her blatant recognition of her attraction to the man she had married.

"Are you enjoying the hot spring?" asked Xerus in his personalized style of teasing his wife, knowing that her formidable endurance of the heated vapors was representative of the lands in which she'd been raised.

"I am." Her all-consuming breath of relaxation was a sound so new to his ears that it was as stirring as it was striking. "I'm surprised you didn't request a bottle of alcohol with your bath to better enjoy yourself." She had offered to continue a conversation with him, but when she began futilely rushing splashes of water over her shoulders to allow her entire being to experience the precious warmth, his mind nearly fell into a trap of welcome distraction.

Carefully, Xerus spoke. "I thought we might appreciate our privacy."

Skylar slowed her bathing motions as she brought her emerald eyes to meet his. Something that warmed him in an entirely new fashion compared to the natural spring was sparking, igniting, and traveling between them suddenly. He had admitted to wanting to spend his evening becoming better acquainted with his wife without so much as a peep of interference—he wanted to gain much from this single night's trip. After having a taste of intimacy with their naked states only an inch or two apart and sleeping closer to one another every night for the past few weeks without as much as laying a gentle caress upon one another's body, there was nothing more he wanted than to solidify his place in his wife's life from that moment onward.

"I think we would too."

Her response was soft like the tender strokes of the steam upon his skin. A chill tried to make the mighty King Xerus shudder, but he defeated it with great control over his body. "Good," he replied to her agreement, her first admittance of willingness to let him come inside and discover who the remarkable girl from his childhood had grown into and become. The excitement that thrummed inside his veins was almost too great to bear when she refrained from speaking—like the moment on a battlefield when an expected strike did not take place and the opposition was left wanting and waiting—so he mercilessly transfixed his sight on her profile and studied her much as he would an enemy. Her hair was most likely wrapped into her warrior's loop to protect it from the water's wrath, but it willed him to rise to any occasion she presented him with.

In an attempt to perhaps alert her of his predatory ways, he asked, "This is your first time to a hot springs, is it not?"

"Yes," she said, strumming him, winding him tighter. "I never imagined how much I might come to love it here." It was as if she confessed to the waters that held her, as if she had not yet had the time to properly develop such sentiments for her own husband, who was experiencing growing adoration for her.

His scowl emerged. "Is that so? Perhaps it is due to the heat, which you are most accustomed to."

Skylar's temporary contemplation made him wonder what it was she had to think about—that was, until she brought her hands running over her shoulders to a halt and turned to look at him once more. In an airy voice, she suddenly said, "I'm growing accustomed to the Goodlit Summit's weather."

The personal statement felt as if she were defending herself, as if he had implied something with his last remark that had made her feel as though she had yet to prove her assimilation into his snowy kingdom. It was understandable that such adjustments would take time, yet she seemed willful in her determined reply that she was already finding comfort in an environment that was the exact opposite of the one she had known for nearly thirty years of living.

His first response was to adjust himself so that he could exert solemnity by way of his body and his reply. Nevertheless, his constant awareness of their mutual nakedness kept him from reaching out to her the way he had last night when his fingers were enchanted by the strands of her hair. "I expected some difficulties, yet you almost seem to enjoy the city's cold treatment."

The words rose from a spring of contempt for his own lackluster marital ways deep inside.

While he knew his own uncertainty when dealing with his unexpected self indulgent resentment forced him to continue his studious ways, his wife's imitation was impeccable, as she too seemed unable to tear her stare away from his violet eyes. When she graced him with a fortuitous smile within the blink of an eye, Xerus experienced what he assumed to be an emotional take on the experience of whiplash.

"I believe I can handle the summit."

Her almost youthful spunk had arisen in her; it was just as enchanting as the sunset merely peeking at them now over the horizon line. The lanterns stationed along the rocks were lighting themselves one at a time down the row in an orderly fashion. No matter how she was illuminated—by natural or manufactured glow—Skylar was unquestionably dazzling, especially in terms of what she meant to Xerus. There was no other queen for him.

"I know that you will." He revealed his confidence in a voice that was less vibrant and more mystified; he almost did not recognize his own sound, given its rare reveling of his wife. She, however, saw through his tone and into the meaning of the words he had spoken, and the way she blinked at him symbolized her surprise.

Before he could feel a redness in his cheeks that was not caused by his surroundings' heat, she moved. Slowly, almost slinking, Skylar began to close the gap between them. His heart hammered once and then stilled, only to imitate the pace he'd felt many times before when engaged in a battle that required his heart and soul in the endeavor. Yet he remained still, as if his city's infamous weather cursed him into the form of a frozen statue as his wife positioned herself at his side.

Past the lapping waters, through their eternal heat, a wave of realization rushed across his skin when hers was so close, so barren and near. If he was not composed—if he so much as flinched—their arms would graze, and he could not imagine what would follow such an act, even though he was aware of the instinctive way in which he situated himself to better match any imminent, staggering intimacy with her.

"Skylar," he choked out as the hand that held a fascination with her mane motioned to bring the strands above her face off to the side so that he could see her better, admire her unsheltered features and expression, and ultimately look down into the depths of her soul to discover for himself if she knew what she had caused to arise inside of him.

Skylar answered him with a nearly strangled "Xerus."

With her completion of their personal, consummate ritual, he moved to possess her and conquer her, as he had been bewitched with wanting. With Xerus's intensity coupled with his queen's devastating radiance, they seized one another and razed their aggregate emotions, leaving nothing but their underlying passion to devote itself solely to satiating their undeniable yearning.

Chapter 11

S kylar did not set foot in Summerside, nor did she call the mayor. Her trip with Emery and Dalya was pleasant enough, especially their time combating feral monsters on the Voulair Pathway. Working the muscles in her restless body felt more like a tease—a remembrance of the nearing end to her spectacular adventure—than anything else, but the familiar strain of her near acrobatic maneuvers reminded the queen of a simpler time, when she was free to battle and train beasts of the wild languorously. Without someone to report to, as the leading beast master of the Nazuré tribe, her power was vital and legendary in its effects upon the tribal world; her betrothed title as wife to the king never invigorated her the same way cracking her precious whip did— and she wasn't sure she was capable of ignoring the fear found within such honesty any longer.

In between bouts, the three of them would chat about one arbitrary topic or another. Skylar's favored discussion was the supposed encounter between Emery and Essentia, and it nearly sent her into a state of jocularity. "*The* deity of peace?" She asked for clarification for what felt like an innumerable time.

Emery did not let on if she felt bothered by the constant questioning of her tale, as she appeared to be quite familiar with reiterating stories or facts that others did not believe in. "Yup. It was a surprise for me too. She was very, uh, theatrical."

"Theatrical?" Now it was Dalya's turn to reveal her query.

"Maybe *buoyant* is a better word." The familiar gesture of the researcher's hand hiding itself in her mess of ink-toned hair implied a strange nervousness in recounting the encounter. "She was just very ... How should I put this? Essentia and I did have the chance to have a real conversation, but she whirled around me like a rainbow-colored tornado."

"Oh my." Skylar was forced to put her hand over her weak lips, afraid they would let loose an undignified chuckle.

Even though she seemed put out by revealing such a thing, Emery continued. "She managed to hug me with her wings and protected me when someone tried to cause me harm."

Dalya shrieked, "What! Emery, you never told me any of this! I can't believe you've supposedly met two of the deities now, and you never thought to share!"

That remark was gripping to Skylar; not only was the tale intriguing for someone who had only felt the presence of the pixie-like deity and never laid eyes on her, but Dalya's revelation of Emery's possible connectivity with another metaphysical entity became just as fascinating as the buoyant Essentia.

Sadly, she would never have a chance to learn the secret of Emery's signature affinity to Varon K'aii's deities, as the now thoroughly flustered young woman stopped her strolling pace in order to garner her two traveling companions' full attention. "But I didn't do anything." Emery defended herself apprehensively. "Even though I told her I appreciated the way she sent her zenith to help me, I didn't think it was necessary to—"

Dalya gasped. "Whoa, you met Hildesuin too?"

"That is absolutely astounding!" Skylar marveled, more envious to know that Emery had seen such a fantastic mythical beast than the fact that she'd met a deity.

"Well, no wonder you're studying hard to become a Luminary; you've already got connections! Hey, is it true that Essentia only appears, you know, au naturel?"

A sudden breeze washed over the companions while they stood in silence, making the bashful Emery uncomfortable. Her cheeks permeated with blush, her eyes were wide with immature horror, and her mouth was open without a sound escaping it; there was nothing she could do but reinitiate their travels toward the port. When she walked past the two stunned ladies, the younger one turned to the queen and said, "I guess that's something she'll have to get used to if she's going to be our connection to the deities."

"That," Skylar mused, amused by the turn of events, "or the same curiosity that helps her with her Luminary studies might have helped her discover just how much of Essentia's body truly changes color on a constant basis, as the legends say."

Dalya snorted, alerting their departing friend of the teasing mumblings the two of them shared. "Coming!" Dalya said, seemingly unaware of how inappropriate her reply was while jogging to Emery's side.

Needless to say, the rest of the journey toward the sea was a courteous one.

When they arrived at the Voulair Port, Skylar revealed her intentions, explaining, "I'm going to head to the Marina Anchorage from here."

The queen had been strategic; unaware of her decision until the last instant, she had failed to reveal Xerus's offer to have her meet him in Summerside to either of her newfound friends; that way, they could not be privy to her informal desertion. It wasn't so much that she wanted to jilt her husband at such a prestigious gathering, but rather, she had not yet decided if she should attend something as prominent as a meeting at the amphitheater while it was still in production. It had been a gratuitous gesture from her mate, and she would always think of him highly for extending such a kindness to her; regardless, that did not suddenly give Skylar reason to believe that her newly planted roots at the Goodlit Summit were sturdy enough and nourished enough for her to stand alongside such political stock.

It also did not pass her notice that returning to Yukaih Castle—with or without her husband—meant she would be sitting on her pedestal once again, beautifully posed inside of her monarchial cage just as she had been for the entirety of her marriage. Her sprint around Varon K'aii had come and gone quickly, and it felt almost like a mistake to have the taste of her journey as if parched for adventure only to be hidden away again inside of the tundra now known as her den.

The queen needed to savor her last day or so of her licensed freedom and take in the remaining sights of the land she supposedly governed.

Based on the looks on her departing comrades' faces, they merely took her words at face value and saw nothing in her cover-up. One offered her a nod and wishes of a safe journey, and the other embraced her and nearly terminated the existence of any breath within her being. She stood on the dock and waited, watching Emery and Dalya as they boarded the boat that would take them to Summerside—to where Xerus expected her to be awaiting his arrival—before making her way toward her own vessel.

"Skylar!" shouted Emery from the rail of the ship. "Don't forget to take your seasickness medication before you board your ship!"

That must have been the cause of the upset in her stomach—the thought of traversing the sea. Surely she had no other cause for such a sensation.

◆ ◆ ◆ ◆ ◆

The queen was not destined to visit her original home or the legendary city Tel Adis; instead, she found herself in a place much more awe-inspiring.

The Marina Pathway was indeed a treacherous place, with the bones of defeated enemies and stationed weapons strewn about along its way. As it was the main passage between the Anchorage and Spierté, it was the most dangerous road in all the land. Skylar lived on the opposite side of the coliseum-owning city and had never before witnessed the battlefield that was the pathway, but it was indeed a sight to behold. There were just as many human bones as there were remains of mighty beasts that lived along the route, from the werehyena to the ennedi tiger. Missing from the destruction were most assuredly the bones of the zenith Grootslang, which belonged to the deity Vaoz. Years of testimony to the levels of strength of different tribes before arriving at their final destination had caused a great decay in the fruition of the land, which was something the other male deity, Relic, would surely be disappointed with.

Wandering down such a trail felt foreboding to the queen. She'd had nothing to do with the destruction and somewhat ceremonious funerals, but the spirit of the Marina Pathway housed the unbridled energy of the tribes. Her spine was rattled by a tingle that felt just as nostalgic as it did cautionary, because even without a tournament being held in the near future, encountering another person or even a wild beast could result in a vicious setback in her journey—unless, of course, she was immediately greeted by the sight of a familiar face headed in her direction.

"Sh-Shia?" Skylar stuttered atypically at the surprise of meeting her sister-in-law for the first time—while somewhere that was not the Goodlit Summit or Spierté, no less.

It took the woman with features much like her brother's a moment to focus before she recognized who had called to her; Shia's amber eyes squinted for just a second in the same way Xerus's would have, surveying her surroundings carefully in a way that would have been imperceptible to anyone unversed in the Austiant mannerisms. Once recognition flashed behind the frames of her glasses, the two women met with gracious smiles on their faces. Tidying her robe-like attire, Shia curtsied. "Why, hello. It's very nice to meet you, Skylar."

"You as well," said the queen easily, playing along with her gentle quip. "Aside from our brief moment in the Goodlit Summit a few days ago, I had not seen you since my battle with Xerus in Spierté."

"That would have been twenty years ago or so," Shia said. Her tone was even, yet her expression showed how bothered she was by the dawning awareness of the unfortunate lapse in time.

Touched slightly, Skylar nodded. Then she boldly asked, "What are you doing here?"

"Well, I suppose I could ask you the very same thing," teased her sister-in-law as she motioned to somewhere off to her left. "I came this way to stop by and visit the Austiant tribe before returning to work. I will be away teaching for the next few months, so I thought now was as good a time as any to see how everyone is doing."

"Teaching?" said the queen, curious to learn more about her.

Smiling with a calmness that seemed natural, Shia replied, "I am a professor. I usually offer my services from one school to the next, but

I am currently working on devising a curriculum for the Luminary project at the Viskretta Center. My plan was to take my pupils on a tour of the summit and Spierté and teach them the history of Ordell and the Four Deities, as well as expose them to both the regal and ritualistic sides to the continent. I'll be working with students from Hierony and Viskretta as well, making it my goal to guarantee that my lessons go beyond what they could read in any old book."

"That's a very important position," the queen said quickly, "and a busy one, I bet. Now would surely be the best time to visit your tribe then."

Shia turned to face her lawful sister and smiled softly. "Indeed. Would you like to join me? I'm sure it's only fair that you are allowed to see how our tribe functions." She spoke with great care so as not to allude to the fact that her brother had surely seen the Nazuré people in their natural state many times in his attempt to coerce her into marriage and had therefore given her every right to reacquaint herself with the people of his origins. In Skylar's mind, it would also serve Shia well to have a warrior at her side as she made her way home, since she still seemed to travel without any combative authority.

"That's very considerate of you." Her open praise—which was well warranted, as it seemed to be a genetic trait among the Austiant to be forever compassionate, even if possibly to a fault—ushered in an amiable instant between the women. They shared another set of grins before they initiated a second conversation and took their first few steps toward the awaiting tribe.

Shia took the opportunity to reiterate her previous sentiment as she walked toward a pair of enormous battle axes stationed like another set of memorial weapons. The blades were longer and therefore mostly dangerous at their tips, which was why Skylar was amazed at how the professor before her stepped along their thinnest edges and used the leverage to hoist herself onto a rocky ledge above the pathway; it appeared the Austiant people had designed a secret entryway into their grounds, and though the queen was stunned momentarily with admiration, Shia returned to her original question without missing a beat, even after hoisting her supposedly delicate frame onto a higher surface. "What are you doing all the way out here, Your Majesty?" Before Skylar could hazard an answer, she added, "Are you still on your journey?"

Skylar inhaled sharply before following in her footsteps and replying, "Yes, I am. I wanted to see as much of Varon K'aii as possible before returning home." It did not take her long to lift herself over the rocky wall, however tall it seemed to be. A lopsided forest was the sight that greeted her, one that surely housed the Austiant people in secrecy while travelers made their violent treks into the city. The Nazuré woman initiated their stroll.

"Oh, I see. How resourceful of you. Have you enjoyed yourself? I see that Cyril is no longer with you."

Her shrewd observation was duly noted; Skylar could not have known if her sister-in-law had been previously familiar with her first traveling companion, so it wasn't her admitted knowledge of his name that was noteworthy to the queen. No, it was the fact that Shia remembered something of no consequence to her that showcased the woman's intelligence, memory, and attention to detail.

"I was initially traveling to provide him with some assistance. Now that the matter has been resolved, I chose to take the opportunity to visit Tel Adis. It was a wonderful surprise that I encountered you beforehand." Considering the lighthearted tone of the conversation thus far, Skylar basked in the natural vibe that resonated between them and acted a tad more forthcoming.

Shia did not sound or appear too appreciative of her honesty, as she faintly admonished the queen. "Does Xerus not need you at the Goodlit Summit? Do you have the time to delay your return?"

Immediately, Skylar felt as though she had been scolded for her free spirit. She recognized that those questions were well warranted; before marriage, she had never stalled in her duties as the reigning beast master when she had lived with the Nazuré people. The gentle interrogation only made her insecurities regarding her decision blare within her mind. Even though they were different people entirely, it did nothing to soften the blow when she was faced with an expression akin to that of her husband's, all too familiar in the sense of servitude.

Just as she began to feel unfamiliar to herself with a heavy touch of self-deprecation, Shia seemed to instantaneously become aware of how bluntly she had spoken to royalty, let alone to a newly acquainted member of her undisclosed family. As the shock of her abrasive speech lifted the lids of her eyes, her mouth fell open. "I'm very sorry. I shouldn't have said such a thing."

"It's all right. It's a valid concern," Skylar said, sounding weak to even her own ears. She smiled sweetly albeit flimsily as she hid beneath the shade of the overgrown trees that covered them along their way.

The peaceable air that had encircled them nearly imploded in a desperate struggle to flee the scene. Both embarrassed and equally repentant, their second silence was of a drastically staggered variety compared to the small smiles they had previously exchanged. It felt abhorrent that their first meeting might be tarnished in any form, and Skylar racked her brain almost painfully in search of a neutral topic to discuss safely. Just as proactive, though, Shia's astute mind worked quicker as she suggested, "Perhaps I could practice my lesson for the upcoming field trips on you. If you don't mind, that is."

It seemed suitable, given how juvenile the teacher's audacity had made her feel. "That would be wonderful, thank you." Skylar spoke cordially while graciously accepting the offer. "I'm sure there is a great deal more I could learn about Varon K'aii from a professor of your caliber."

"I hope my students share your attitude," Shia said optimistically. Then she gestured toward a tree that had been visibly butchered by arrows, implying that they should head toward the nearly barkless landmark. Skylar followed her motion and moved with her along the suggested route. She watched as the Austiant woman removed two arrows from the tree and handed one to her before proceeding along the path as if they each hadn't collected one part of a weapon. Humming insects seemed to whisper an unsteady tune, given reason to grow nervous and scurry away. Too intrigued by the protocols of locating such a battle-ready people, Shia nearly missed the beginning of her intended lesson.

"To start, we can discuss the very city you intended to visit today:

Tel Adis was founded by the first tribe that lived off this land, the K'aiiniw, those whom Ordell first created. It is believed that forging the Four Deities to serve alongside it was not enough for our creator, so humans were subsequently conceived so that Ordell had something to care for and nurture." The professor began to bestow upon her the knowledge she would soon provide to children much younger than Skylar, yet it was interesting to be reminded of all that Raibeart and her own tribe had taught her over the course of her own lifetime; the queen's ability to keep pace with the impromptu refresher of her basic understanding of the land unintentionally served as a minor test for herself.

Almost unaware of the woman at her side, Shia carried on. "Originally, the Four Deities were made to be companions to Ordell, and each one of them was bestowed with an amazing power: Syvant would govern wisdom and philosophy; Essentia would cherish the importance of equality and peace across the land; Vaoz was made to be responsible for upholding truth and justice; and Relic would watch over Varon K'aii and guarantee its prosperity and survival."

There was another mention of Essentia, the female spirit who'd visited Emery and whom the Nazuré people tended to favor. Most tribes respected Relic for his earthly duties, and legends spoke of him traveling throughout Varon K'aii; therefore, he was the only deity without a partnered zenith. With Syvant being the one who imparted knowledge to those who prayed in churches or studied in schools, few members of the tribal world looked to her for more than battle strategies when in times of war, a similar fate suffered by Vaoz and his requested assistance for resolving conflicts; it was assumed that this specific requirement for their attention could be attributed to their abandonment of all walks of life during the most troubling time in the history of the land—or at least that was what Skylar had grown up to believe. Would those who lived in guarded cities with exuberant churches and structuralized schools have different perceptions of the senseless violence of that era? She couldn't help but wonder.

"Varon K'aii remained extremely peaceful for quite some time, as the humans prayed to Ordell, and many differences in opinion simply resolved themselves by way of separation and the formation of new tribes. A few centuries would pass before there would be any sort of conflict between the humans that required the assistance of the deities. But since we both reside in the Goodlit Summit, let's see if you know the answer to this question: Do you know the name of the family who first ruled over the city you now call home?" From lecture to quiz, Shia was relentless as she stopped to face her sister-in-law on the rickety bridge on which they were crossing, in order to observe her reaction while answering. It seemed they were not meant to pass through the vast gorge they had stumbled upon until she answered the question—and correctly.

Skylar, not seeing the point of knowing some figurehead's name, answered almost right away, "Was it not Tiriaq?"

Shia shared with her a proud acknowledgment. "Correct. It was the first generation of that tribe who managed to build themselves homes out of the snow in the mountains. Their chief was rumored to be blessed by Ordell for resolving matters peacefully and creating a community in such a hostile environment."

"So it was him?" Skylar murmured to herself accidentally. When she slowly realized her folly, her eyes rose to meet the amber ones that stared at her questioningly. "I'm sorry. I've always wondered if it was the person Raibeart taught me about; he once spoke of a man who was rumored to possess the ability of aurasthesia and who was able to communicate with Relic while he traveled. And the ability was passed down throughout his line, even unto the king Xerus battled when he claimed the summit during the war."

"Really?" Shia began to ponder to herself, just as Skylar had, and thought aloud. "I wonder how useful that ability was to their family. Or how they used it, for that matter."

It was the queen's turn to educate the teacher, it seemed. Excited to share the superstitions of the people she had come to know, Skylar explained, "Many of the citizens of the summit are thankful for Xerus's uprising, given how the last King Tiriaq left them isolated and freezing. They believe that the aurasthesia ability was then passed on to Xerus, and that is why the weather on the mountains has calmed since he became the new king. In their eyes, he must have met with Relic and promised to protect the land, the beasts, and the people."

Though it was not history, it did seem to interest Shia that there was some lore to her estranged brother's conquering. Thoughtfully, she mumbled to herself, "I doubt Xerus needed assistance in communicating with monsters, what with Léonie being a part of his forces."

Suddenly, Skylar's world stopped. Almost breathlessly, she probed. "One moment. Are you saying that Xerus was associated with *the* Léonie, the last of the Relics?"

Seemingly bothered by the obvious detour in their lesson, Shia looked perplexed that the woman before her was unaware of the king's past comrades. "Yes, I am. Léonie devoted herself to Xerus and used her status as a beast master to fight for him. There were many supporters but none as great as Léonie herself, along with Jovost Gaellen from Sailbrooke."

Skylar had learned all there was to know about Jovost the night before; however, Léonie's name echoed in her mind with startled astonishment. How could Xerus have been so familiar with the master of the craft she studied singularly, a passion comparable to his own rejuvenation of Varon K'aii on a much smaller scale, and never once spoken of such a relation before?

It might have had something to do with the substantial distance between them that only felt worthy to scale when they were farther apart than ever before.

"They joined him at separate times," said Shia meekly. Whether she was aware of troubled Skylar's internal disarray or felt she had a right to provide her with the famous and deservedly known history of her brother, she pressed on, both conversationally and physically. "But they both saw purpose and a future in Xerus's plans. They worked tirelessly in order to help him achieve any goal he set his mind to. I met them only once or twice, so I don't have a great deal to teach you, I'm afraid."

Once more, the kinswoman Skylar had once wished to meet dealt her another unwitting, critical blow: Xerus had never invited Shia to visit the castle since he had been wed. The rational side of her troubled mind reasoned that his hectic dealings with governing the land and constructing the amphitheater could have prevented a formal introduction. The emotional portion that had begun to apply considerable pressure to the wall of tolerance she had constructed in order to fend off such beggared sentiment from His Highness could not help but pose a gnawing question: *He was much too busy in the entirety of the past six months?*

Learning of the exuded truth made the cage she imagined herself returning to seem a great deal smaller than ever before.

When still she failed to respond to the generous lessons provided by the history teacher at her side, Skylar realized she needed to remain engaged to seem thoroughly unfazed. "How lucky you were; I had always wanted to speak with Léonie. Becoming a beast master was something the Relic tribe excelled at, and for someone like me, I envied them greatly. Sadly, I know that she is no longer of this world."

"Yes," Shia affirmed grimly.

Her expression appeared much more grief-stricken than expected for someone who claimed to have only met the woman of legend on a couple of occasions. Seeing her in such a state only made the queen feel her unrefined envy heighten, to know that her childhood idol truly stirred a grave sense of loss in those who missed her. "Do you mind if I ask when exactly …"

"How did she pass on, you mean?" said Shia. Then she bolted into an explanation as if she had witnessed the tragedy herself. "It was during the battle in the Vicis Plain. She fought valiantly, as always, truly living up to her reputation, even after months of campaigning with His Highness. The last of the civilized forces who defied his dream to unify the entire continent stood against Xerus and his companions when they arrived at the battlefield, creating the largest clash during his opposition.

"They came in waves, strategically hoping to catch Xerus by surprise and wear down his forces until there was nothing left. Léonie was the greatest challenge due to her size and strength, so she was targeted just as much as Xerus himself. Days passed, and they continued to fight, even as their numbers dwindled down to just the three of them—the king and his greatest supporters.

"It was when Jovost was struck down that Léonie was rumored to have lost her stride; on her way to retrieve his body, she was ambushed. I won't go into details, but it is most likely because of the loss of his most valiant comrades during the battle that Xerus swore off his swords and now only fights with his staff in times of danger. No one will speak of how he managed to come out of the Vicis Plain alive, let alone as the victor, yet here we are, under his rule."

The story washed over her with such awe that she was beside herself with wonderment. Indeed, hearing all that Shia could recount of that fateful day had confirmed Skylar's belief: Léonie truly was someone worthy of her admiration. She could not imagine an instance in which her husband had been pinned down by an enemy—walked closely with death once in his life—yet such a moment had occurred for both him and the most powerful woman to have ever lived. To know that the beast master before her had lost her life for the sake of her husband's dreams and had fought alongside him until the end was absolutely piercing. Though meeting her would be a desire left deficient, it was impossible to ignore the gratitude she felt toward the woman for so much more than ever before.

"I never knew that Xerus was so fortunate to have such companions," admitted Skylar, unashamed in announcing her ignorance of the bonds before hearing of the fatal cataclysm that was the horror of the Vicis Plain. It mattered not if Shia was privileged to how their marriage functioned, for in that moment, she was able to put aside her detrimental feelings, if only to focus on the wonder that was the man she had be connected to—tethered to, in an abstract sense—and yet another one of his prestigious accomplishments.

Inadvertently, Skylar supposed the fact that their marriage had even transpired was an achievement for both of them; she preferred the sunnier outlook over the more menacing one that had been haunting her since leaving Sailbrooke that morning.

Who was she to complain of an eternity with him, when he had accomplished so much for the greater good, not only for his people but also for the benefit of the entire world?

As if sensing her righteous change in disposition, Shia clasped her hands before her lap and smiled. "No matter how lonesome he may be, even Xerus knows that no one can truly be alone forever. With how many people he serves on a daily basis, even he requires some form of companionship from time to time. Though it is mostly for combative and political purposes, you are proof that he has become more aware of the bonds forged between people who are just as empowering as any of his justified causes."

The line that spoke of comradery stood out to Skylar; that was all she'd ever wanted from him—to have guaranteed companionship, to know they relied on one another in a way that was inexplicable and unable to be experienced by any other person. Knowing he was capable of wanting something so personal suddenly reminded the queen of all the sweet notes they had shared recently via text and the caring words articulated throughout their calls via their totems, including the sly gestures made when they had spoken mere hours ago. Yes, if she could triumph over her darkened moods and he could learn to be more forthcoming whenever he could spare the time to see her, perhaps it was not too late for them to try to revive the once promising bond that had led them to be wed.

With enough energy to skip the rest of her way to the Austiant tribe, Skylar smiled. "I'm not so sure," she teased lightly, revealing just how much of her spirit had returned. "I believed he married me for political purposes. And I am skilled in battle too."

Shia blinked over her thin frames before replying, "No doubt you are; I think my brother requires someone with a firmer touch." They laughed momentarily, and then she added, "That woman he worked with before would never have endured his discommodious traits for very long."

"Who?" Another unknown person had come into their conversation as they made their way up onto a small hill. Skylar was curious to know of any and all mysterious allies her husband had.

Shia lit up temporarily in a flash, ready to educate once again. "As foolish as it sounds, she reminded me of the deity Syvant, as the records speak of her: she had the greenest eyes that could only be described as otherworldly, her linguistic ability was quite proficient, and she usually spoke in some form of poetry. I swear on my name that I once witnessed scribbles shift and change on her body. Though I do not encounter him often to this day, I saw her both happily and aggressively speaking to him from time to time."

What a perplexing description, the queen thought. "Aggressively? Why would she do that?" Counseling and receiving counsel were second nature to her husband. Surely he could never have quarreled with anyone, let alone a possible advisory deity.

"I am not sure, given that I did not hear what matters they spoke of. All I can recall is whenever she was around, they would go off together and speak privately. Whether she was a mere fanatic of Syvant or an actual incarnation herself, her holy words were only meant to be heard by the man who was sanctioned to hear them.

"Nevertheless, he always took the time to meet with her, even if she summoned him during a meeting with his allies or his meager hours of sleep. One would assume that her obvious distraction during wartimes would be quite an imposition to Xerus, but it is because he allowed her his time that I truly believe his campaign was assisted by a deity." Shia's elaboration ended with a slight implication of her unfavorable opinion toward her brother's actions in this particular story, only hinting at the faintest graze of distaste.

At her side, Skylar felt conflicted once again. She had assumed there were other female soldiers or allies who endorsed the king's goals and had imagined them to simply act as part of a unit under his guidance and control; the deity who governed wisdom not only had been so kind as to work with the king but also had done so intently and religiously. Shia had specifically used the word *together*—if he had been given the aid of Syvant, then the pair had surely functioned as a devastating twosome hell-bent on their envisioned utopia. She had abandoned the world during the rule of the scion Tiriaq but had found a place of utility at the side of the hopeful king of the future and helped him to manage his strategies.

Together.

When Xerus had accused her of running the risk of revealing Van Austiant's identity over their totems in Terrinal and torn through her with his denunciation, Skylar had assumed she could never have been made to feel so ill from meager words. Now that she had become aware of his previous partner, the likes of a female deity with a power that had been beneficial to the relentless king in his quest for unification and peace, she got the distinct impression that nothing she felt in terms of placid fortitude could ever pacify her within the confines of her marriage ever again.

Ever since that lamentable hot springs trip, Skylar had not thought of Xerus as her active husband; perhaps Shia's revelation finally offered clarification as to why he also refused to view her as a partner, as a wife.

She was not Syvant.

Was that why her zenith guarded Xerus's city?

Skylar let out a sickened laugh as she attempted an imitation of Cyril's distant, blasé expression. "And the war was won."

Shia shook her head, sounding a touch disheartened. "In a way, it was; Syvant has taken to a roaming lifestyle similar to that of Relic, they say. And yes, the fighting has ended. But now there is an even bigger venture to be faced with that amphitheater of his."

He was capable of so much, destruction and pacification. His Highness was undoubtedly more than worthy to rule Varon K'aii, its people, and its future. She had been told he needed companionship, yet he needed no one beyond her usefulness in his championed causes. Raibeart was his new right hand—the captain general who served in the line of duty, all while acting as her teacher—and he had his army. There was nothing else he required—unless he ever needed a celestial being to provide for him thoughtfulness beyond himself, which he could call upon his allied Syvant for.

It was Skylar who was not needed, before their marriage or after the toll of the death bell when they had signed their marriage license.

It was a shame she had seen the truth through conversing with his sister after enduring his farce of a partnership for half a year of her life.

It was intriguing to note that she still felt depressed in knowing she could never convene with the beast master who was her hero, yet she was overcome with regret in realizing that the boy she had always intended to meet once again had evolved into the only man to ever steal away her lighthearted frame of mind, which was the truest essence of Skylar Nazuré.

Without optimism, she functioned solely based upon her desire to thrive. Shia had bent down on their stationed hilltop to dig around in the dirt before the queen politely exclaimed, "He will be able to unify the world just the same, wouldn't you say? That's why he is the unopposed king of Varon K'aii."

"I suppose so." Shia concurred, however suspicious she sounded. With a quirk in her brow, she rose from the ground with an old, disheveled bow in hand. Likely, this bow was meant to coincide with the arrows they had retrieved, and together they would act as some sort of key into entering the compound that was the heavily guarded tribe of the Austiant people.

"Well then." Ignoring her curious glance, Skylar stilled, donning her brightest grin. "Thank you for teaching me everything you have today. I believe you taught me more about Xerus than he ever has himself."

That admission did not seem to surprise the king's sister. Her familiar amber eyes drooped with disappointment, and her eyebrows met and rose in the middle, revealing sadness. As protective of her brother as ever before, Shia spoke low as she bluntly said, "He does not consider himself in concerns to other people, because his role prevents him from being the sole ally to anyone in particular. He is a public servant and always will be."

Nothing she said was incorrect, nor was it groundbreaking to Skylar. "I completely agree."

"Skylar?"

"Yes?" she answered quickly, itching to avoid a visit with his past tribe at the moment, prepared to leave the Marina Pathway as quickly as her feet would carry her.

"Do you remember Van's behavior the night you last saw him in Spierté?" Shia quizzed her once again, only now she posed a question that the beast master knew the answer to unmistakably.

Nodding, she said, "Of course I do. I would not have agreed to marry him if I hadn't remembered the boy who defeated me all those years ago."

"I didn't ask you about the battle you had," said the historian, whose presence resembled a protective monster in defense of a pack member rather than an inquiring teacher. "I am solely referring to the last words you spoke to him before he left with me."

"I said to him the very same words I used to repeat to myself in the face of adversity—I remember," said the queen, no longer appreciative of the scolding she felt she was receiving. She too had transformed into a beast in her own right; her instinct to flee was mystically tugging on her body, trying to lead her toward the Marina Anchorage, which she had a sudden interest in reacquainting herself with.

Privy to her maddening state or not, Shia declared, "I remember them as well. I think you deserve to know that we discussed them briefly before returning to the Austiant tribe that night. No matter what you may think, I truly believe that you impacted Van in a way that has never been replicated since. So no matter how trying Xerus may be, I hope you know that there was a reason he pursued you to be his queen, even after being twenty years apart."

Then her sister-in-law bowed to her once again before turning swiftly and firing the arrow she carried into the woods below the ledge on which they stood. With her backward steps leading her in the direction of an uneven hillside, Skylar felt a jolt travel up her leg as she came to a standstill with Shia, who stood posed with her hand stretched out, expectantly waiting for the second arrow to be returned to her. It was almost dizzying to think of how personally they had spoken without knowing one another aside from appearance and name before their informal history lesson; they certainly could not deny the impressions they now held for one another, and Skylar wanted to understand what Shia thought of her now at a later date.

Though uncertain how she felt about Shia in that moment, the queen still behaved favorably when she placed the idle arrow in her open palm and provided her with some parting words. "No matter his name, I have supported him in any and all endeavors, because I know just how wonderful of a person he is. There does not need to be a reason for me to understand how fortunate I am and to know that he was as wise as he claimed to be when he chose me to marry."

"Where are you off to then?" Shia's voice rose to guarantee that the queen heard her query after she had turned on her heel, single-minded in her own desire to leave the secretive woods.

Skylar simply said, "To meet my husband." Then she charged down the slope of the hill and took a deep inhalation of breath. Yes, she intended to head to Summerside. She still had at least half a day's time to win the race in terms of their separate arrivals, and whether on land or by sea, she knew that every inch traveled toward her destination was necessary to allow her the time to think.

CHAPTER 12

Skylar felt nothing the entire time she rode the ferry back to Summerside. She was so empty inside that she could not articulate what it was she specifically struggled with, let alone comprehend it herself. The medicine Emery had thieved from her parents' clinic proved to be impotent compared to her internal skirmish, which allowed her to retrench the last of the supply. It was not lost on the queen that her choice to venture out on her side quest was the main reason she had to conserve the miniscule remains of her seasickness medication—it was also the sole circumstance for her current state of melancholy.

Perhaps her bohemian-like lifestyle was deserving of the reprimands she had received.

No longer being allowed to live as a freelance Nazuré woman had never felt more difficult to accept than during her boat ride, during which the conversation she had shared with her long-awaited sister-in-law replayed in her mind constantly. Skylar was a queen—she had married into a role she had worked tirelessly to fulfill—yet she knew her behavior had been much less prestigious as of late. It was as if the mere reminder of the shackleless life she used to lead drove her into a state of insanity and transformed her into an unrecognizable delinquent when playing with the fabled insecurities in her heart. She did not like the person who had gone into the woods with Shia that day, nor was she favorable toward the woman who had left in such an undignified haste.

Her protective instincts had pushed her away from the tribe she had secretly wished to see—had she not left when she did, Skylar feared what she might have said to unsuspecting, incognizant Shia. She regretted her infantile decision to flee simply as a result of the unwanted information she had been given in regard to her husband, His Majesty King Xerus.

It was not fair to penalize him for what other people had shared with her; had she not joked about Caribooboo at his expense? She had tried to seize the chance for a foolish revenge when teasing about his muscle-measuring contest. Oddly enough, both selfish quips were made in relation to Cyril. If she enjoyed and took advantage of all she had learned that suited her, she could not punish him for the stories that brilliant Shia had bestowed upon her. Whether or not they affected her was not by Xerus's doing; for that, she had to suffer in silence.

Syvant—the name of the mysterious entity that had managed to forge a much more personal relationship with her husband than Skylar could most likely dream of haunted her with great torment. Why did she feel jealousy over a relationship that was most assuredly finished? It wasn't the faceless spirit that hampered her natural persona of idealism but, rather, the functionality she must have experienced with the king of Varon K'aii.

Would it ever be Skylar's turn to know what such propinquity felt like?

With the glow of the sunset shimmering on the sea out to the darkening horizon, Skylar recalled the single instance of intimacy she'd experienced during her short marriage to Xerus—their romantic encounter at the hot springs. The heaviness in her heart felt like an anchor that meant to drag her into the depths of the sea while the memories of their evening were nearly revived in the fibers of her being as she recalled it all—their reticence, the unashamed nakedness, the inescapable pull, the indescribable jubilation that had felt like a blessing from Essentia herself when such a wave of sensation had washed over her riled body. It had been a spellbinding experience, the first of which she had ever known.

Now it felt much more mythical than anything else, what with that lone act of physical predilection existing between them.

Skylar would have assuredly traded in that singular encounter if it meant she had her husband's respect and commitment of comity.

He was more than capable of relentlessly devoting himself to the most righteous of movements—anything that resulted in the benefit of all his people—yet he could not dedicate himself to her? Though her methods of obtaining the tale of Syvant had been somewhat deceitful, it did not change the fact that he was indeed aware of what it meant to work together with another person—a female, no less. Their partnership had happened. Hers had yet to start.

The sorrow would dissipate eventually, and then she would be faced with her greatest test yet: what to do with all she had been told. Never one to back down from a challenge, Skylar would have to decide how she would approach her husband and their situation—both the unspoken one of the last six months and where they were to head in the future—and all the while keep in mind the dignity of the Goodlit Summit and the Nazuré tribe. Her outward reaction would need to reflect everything she was—past, present, and future—which required much more thought than any decision she had ever made before.

Thank Essentia that Xerus would not be standing before her until tomorrow afternoon.

✦✦✦✦✦

When the ship arrived at Summerside, Skylar immediately picked up on the sounds of busy people shouting, laughing, and haggling. The grandest port of the land was indeed a lively place; some eager young ones nearly bowled her over when departing the ship. After a maternal order for an apology to be issued, the children ran off once again and forced their dear old mother to chase after them into a crowd surrounding a shop that offered a promising sale. The sight, though somewhat troublesome for the older woman, was a tad charming to behold.

The same was true of Summerside itself, in a much more modern sense. Though the island-wide port appeared just as freeing as it did intimidating, the people present captured a sense of excitement in the way they roamed about the impressive island. Given that she had merely stepped foot onto the port, the queen found herself feeling a small thrill about joining the line of civilians.

"Skylar? Ma'am! Is that you?"

She immediately turned to the one who'd so boldly addressed her in public and realized it was none other than one of the soldiers she had worked with in the Yukaih Castle's military. Though he was coated in armor from head to toe, the voice and familiar way in which he ran indicated she was speaking to none other than Burke. He was still a smidge clumsy, it seemed, what with one of his oxford-blue strands of hair peeking out of the veil of his helmet.

"Burke," she said with an elated smile, "how are you doing, darling?"

The solider was caught off guard and nearly skidded to a halt before her. "How did you know it was me?"

Wanting to preserve his pride, Skylar identified him differently than she truthfully had. "Only you called me ma'am instead of Your Majesty."

If a blush could have burned, the veil of Burke's helmet would have melted off his face. He had always been shy and overtly courteous but had always addressed her respectfully in his uncordially way, luckily for him, the queen had found his behavior endearing. She doubted that his commander had shipped him to Summerside due to his inability to conquer his worst habit, but no matter the reason, it had been a shame to see him go.

"Right. I'm sorry, ma'am—I mean, Your Majesty!"

"It's all right, Burke. It looks as though you are doing quite well for yourself since I last saw you," Skylar said, attempting to distract him from his rising embarrassment. Slanting her hips, she vaguely surveyed the brick-laid city again, only now she had the intent of ascertaining how many soldiers were stationed. She saw a fair amount, and it was a positive note for her bashful friend's career that he was one of them.

Burke looked around at the island that he served, speaking cheerfully as he explained, "I've only been here for two or three months now, but I think it's a better fit for me than the Goodlit Summit. No offense or anything, but I feel like I am accomplishing more here."

That assessment was both shocking and admirable. His honesty in surmising his surroundings as a root cause for his poor performance at Yukaih Castle showed a great amount of personal reflection, something she had assumed Burke to be exceptionally capable of. With how closely she worked with the military at her home of a fortress, Skylar could not help but think of some of the weaker soldiers as the runts of her battalions—sheepish Burke had always shown the most promise in her eyes. She supposed that had made her behave somewhat motherly toward him, and she beamed with happiness. "That's wonderful to hear."

Standing at attention, he acknowledged her praise with military-like gratitude. After a moment of maintaining his posture, though, Burke blurted out, "Oh, I heard you met my brother recently."

Skylar paused for a moment in thought. "Your brother?" she repeated, uncertain.

"You went to Otornot Keep recently, didn't you?" Burke said. "My brother is Commander Vergil."

She could not identify the cause of his hesitation, especially considering the concealment of his expression behind his regulated helmet.

In contrast, unprepared Skylar found herself nearly gawking at the revelation, though given her natural elegance, she mostly maintained her expression and therefore wore an unnoticeable measure of shock. "I had no idea," she admitted lamely.

Burke quickly explained, "I didn't really want anyone to know; it might have caused trouble if people knew I was related to *the* Vergil. Since we're completely unalike, I figured I could keep it a secret really easily." That he did, if he'd managed to fool even the queen.

His oxford-blue hair was almost similar to the storm cloud Vergil donned over his head. It angered Skylar that she had not once picked up on their lone similarity. "And you succeeded," said the queen, who was disappointed in her lack of observational skills most comically.

"Even the king himself didn't know about my brother. I think, at least."

"Don't worry, Burke. Your secret is safe with me," she said as she cooled. A loose hand waved away his concerns as she went on. "I enjoyed meeting Commander Vergil. You two must be quite close; I only spoke to him yesterday."

"Oh, he called to tell me that two of his soldiers were supposed to be coming here to escort King Xerus somewhere out to sea. Although …" Burke rarely experienced a thoughtful moment; his delays in speech were always caused by nervousness, which alerted Skylar to something curious.

"Is something wrong?" she immediately inquired.

Burke snapped out of his contemplative state, startled. Nervously, he said, "It's just that, well, King Xerus arrives tomorrow, doesn't he? I haven't heard of any new arrivals yet, and knowing my brother, he would have sent them over as soon as possible so that they could meet with our captain and get a better understanding of their positions here."

"It is a very quick transfer; perhaps there was more to sort through at Otornot Keep first," suggested Skylar, even though she believed every word he said and found the realization to be inquisitive herself.

Burke nodded unconvincingly but tried to warn her of his concerns thereafter. "He called me last night to tell me about the two soldiers he was sending over. I assumed that meant they would be here by this afternoon at the very latest. Knowing Vergil, he would not have stopped working on their transfer until he knew they were in position for tomorrow's conference."

Indeed, that was a sensible response, considering the viewpoint those soldiers had held before being allowed the position of His Highness's guard. Burke's knowledge of his brother's behavior and his valid concerns were also noteworthy, given the fact that he was labeling the behavior of a military commander as unusual in his roundabout way. She herself had described him as a man comparable to Xerus—neither one accepted anything other than perfection in his command's execution.

Though feeling slightly intrusive, Skylar decided she had every right to involve herself and voice the concerns Burke was having to his overseeing officer. "Why not ask Vergil where they are directly? Or perhaps your own commander? Tell them I have arrived here in Summerside and would like to know if the two soldiers sent from

Otornot Keep are in position. I don't need to meet them—I merely would like to hear confirmation before moving out."

"Oh, okay!" exclaimed Burke, impressed by her strategy. Eager to attain the information they both were seeking, the ungainly soldier jogged away, calling back, "I'll be right back, ma'am—I mean, Your Majesty!"

Thankfully, the population of Summerside was too enamored with their personal pursuits to pay much attention to the revelation of their queen. Although she realized her decision to join the king on his voyage meant she no longer needed to conceal her identity, the reflex to see to her continuous concealment felt as though it were engrained.

She nearly started when her eyes locked with those of a young custodian.

For a long while, they maintained their gazes, simply staring at one another as if waiting for the other to turn away first. Though her onlooker appeared to be gentile, he stubbornly remained still, as if he had been offended by the slip her previous trainee had made. Skylar attempted to apologize for any disturbance Burke may have caused, but the man gave her no chance to, as he posed a gentle question: "Excuse me, but are you Xerus's wife?"

The male worker looked to be of an age that barely surpassed Dalya's, appearing slightly more mature due to the uniform of Summerside's recreational staff. His voice sounded just as she had predicted but with a distinguishable edge of sadness. His simple glasses only seemed to magnify his lackluster approach to life. However, despite the dispirited look on his face, he'd managed to find the spontaneity to question her marital status.

Her fingers loose, ready to reach for her whip if given reason to do so, Skylar replied, "Yes, I am. Is there something I can help you with?"

There was no reaction for the first few moments after she openly revealed who she was; the young man stood there observing her longer than proper conversation allowed. "I see," he said finally, though turning his head away made his low volume hard to hear. "I didn't know he got married."

It was unique for a man to appear so concerned with his knowledge of the marital affairs of Varon K'aii's king, even by her standards. There could only be one explanation as to why the solemn custodian from the nation-wide port found her marriage so interesting. "I take it you've met my husband." When his eyes opened wide, she knew she had assumed correctly.

"I did. We met a few times," admitted the custodian, carelessly sweeping the bricks around him as if to distract himself from the thought. A few unkempt strands of his slicked-back hair fell over his forehead as he busied himself with the ground.

Skylar decided to act oblivious to the obvious discomfort the young man was feeling as she boldly said, "Well then, is there some sort of message I could pass along for you?"

For the second time, the young man showed surprise. His trademark seemed to be silent standoffs, and he instigated yet another while concocting some groundbreaking message she could share with her husband next time they spoke. Hopefully, it would serve as a touching icebreaker before they engaged in a much more serious conversation.

The young man mumbled, "Tell him hi for me."

"Hi?" Skylar repeated, somewhat in disbelief of the underwhelming report she had to deliver. "Of course I will. And your name?"

"It doesn't matter," said the young man, seemingly nervous to speak of such a thing.

Reserving her judgment, the queen nodded respectfully as she swore to pass his one-worded message along. "If you're certain."

"Yeah, I am. Bye," he responded bluntly with courtesy before moving along, heading toward the crowd partaking in the sale the mother and her children had raced off to, likely anticipating a great deal of work to be found there.

As if sensing the end of her conversation, Burke returned to her side. Playing the military officiant, Skylar asked briskly, "What have you learned?"

"It's bad! Vergil apparently called here asking for confirmation of their arrival too. He said they left first thing this morning and should have arrived here just before noon. He's trying to get a hold of them right now because my commander told him they aren't his concern until they arrive." Burke seemed to have become a complete mess in the time it had taken him to retrieve his information and return to her; his all-consuming panic not only was the reason he'd been reassigned—moved from the front lines of protecting Yukaih Castle, should it ever require it—but also indicated another blinding difference between the two military brothers.

Yet Skylar knew she would find herself pouting later for not having realized their genealogy.

"Might I make a suggestion?" said a familiar, friendly voice from behind the sulking queen.

She nearly leaped out of her skin when she whirled the upper half of her body around on her hips. When she realized who had surprised her, she almost moved to give her dear friend and teacher a welcomed hug. "Raibeart!" She gasped with excitement.

"Captain General Raibeart!" Burke said in shock.

Indeed, it was none other than Raibeart Dhrio standing behind her, looking amused that he had startled both of them so. Ever gracious and refined, he bowed while wearing the most mischievous of grins. "It's wonderful to see you again, Your Majesty."

"Come now." She stretched her arm and tapped his shoulder in an act of both comradery and admonishment. "There's no need for that. We aren't at the castle."

Burke, on the other hand, could not have been any more formal; standing straighter than when he'd greeted his queen, the young klutz fumbled with his handled weapon before he said, "It's a pleasure to see you again, sir!"

"You as well, soldier. Now, if I heard everything correctly, we have two soldiers unaccounted for. They were part of the group you dealt with, were they not?" When Skylar nodded, the captain general said, "If that's the case, why don't we have our young friend here contact Commander Vergil and let him know that you and I will be seeing to this matter personally?"

"Do you really think that's best?" Skylar said, impressed that the older gentleman was willing to behave proactively in regard to a military placement case. He was not actively involved with their soldiers on a regular basis, what with his prominent involvement with the formation of the amphitheater and its security, and it was surprising to hear of his willingness to take up a mission in such close proximity to his upcoming departure.

Raibeart soothed her worries as he said, "We do not know why these men have yet to arrive, but if it has anything to do with what you discussed, it's best that we remind them of just what they promised to do when they offered to come to Summerside and join Xerus's guard."

"Very true," she admitted in a low mumble, "unless they behaved like the other half of their group." Keeping the details confidential, Skylar hoped the king had informed his captain general of all the happenings she had endured when partaking in her political mission.

"They need to be dealt with nonetheless. Soldier, I need you to get in contact with your brother for us. We will need him to call off any of his dog hunts—wouldn't want to be caught in any crossfire, would we?"

Both the queen and the typically klutzy soldier found themselves gaping at the sly trickster Raibeart, his admission of the brothers' connection nearly bowling them over. As the unsuspecting Burke walled and fiddled with his personal totem in order to call for his captain, Skylar simply shook her head—with everything the captain general knew, it was amazing they had to hunt anyone down.

The raspy chortle that sounded from him as the call took place was unashamed. "Shall we be leaving then?" was all he had to say on the matter before preceding her in their mutual exit.

CHAPTER 13

T hough the dirt crackled beneath their focused steps, neither Skylar nor her newly instated cohort heard anything aside from their conversation, which was much too noisy to notice any other sound.

"You all made traveling sound like quite the experience, so I had Xerus give me leave the night before the conference. I was so excited that I departed just after lunch." Raibeart chortled after concluding the explanation of his sudden appearance with a tale similar to the queen's own pesky enthusiasm. The personalities they housed individually came together in regard to certain compelling traits. For one, they both savored adventure and, occasionally, working at Xerus's expense.

Feigning disappointment, Skylar said, "It's a shame you missed the others, even with such a speedy arrival." As she arched an eyebrow in the captain general's direction, he posed a similar facade toward her. It was not long before they both found themselves inexplicably grinning, regardless of the truthfulness in the words she had spoken.

"The way I see it," said the older gentleman, nearly bubbling in their playful chitchat, "they're the ones who are missing out. Wouldn't you say?"

Skylar's attempt to silence a boisterous giggle, however abrupt it may have been, was futile. The entire circumstance of their conversation was absurd, and it only escalated when she slapped a hand over her mouth at just the right moment to avoid expelling an undignified snort. Even with a guarded fist before his lips, she couldn't help but notice how the pristine Raibeart was unsuccessful in shielding a blatant chuckle of his own. The teacher and student undoubtedly made quite a pair.

They treated their backward voyage toward Otornot Keep much like a stroll in the late evening of a soothing summer's day rather than acting with the crucial focus it deserved, the queen knew. Something about the all-knowing, serene persona of the captain general of Varon K'aii allowed Skylar to feel slightly carefree while trekking along Aesop's Stroll, his presence rejuvenating the experience of wandering along a path she had traveled that very morning. *What a most appropriate description*, she realized: given that it was their first time interacting outside of Yukaih Castle, Raibeart not only maintained his friendship with the queen whom he educated but also put forth little effort to ward off some of the social courtesies that were expected of them and enveloped the two with an aura of bygone friends.

It was just as silly as it was intriguing to note that her best friend was a man twice her age; to truly be defined as *bygone*, he would had to have known her when she was no more than a babe.

With the setting sun grazing the land, indicating the oncoming night and possible difficulty to their quest, Skylar felt they were both presently behaving like children. Deciding to proceed with a fraction more grace, she cleared her throat and said, "Speaking of people who are currently missing, we should focus on the task at hand."

Raibeart straightened at once, pretending to be in deep thought over the matter. "Oh yes, of course."

"Since the soldiers stationed at the Voulair Port said they didn't see our missing soldiers—"

Her companion finished her thought. "And Commander Vergil claims he sent them on their way this morning, we can assume that either they have deserted the cause and perhaps defected to their original beliefs, or something obstructed their journey before they could reach the harbor."

Though she had every intention to focus, surmise, and devise, Skylar could not help but mention a small tidbit that had troubled her since leaving the flustered soldier's side. "Right. You made it clear that you knew about Burke and Vergil's relation back in Summerside."

"Of course," he answered proudly, "I had every right to know, after all. It was because of Vergil's request that Burke was allowed to train at the Goodlit Summit. He hoped that our reigning commander at the castle could—"

"Modify his clumsiness with the most likely success?" said Skylar.

"Yes, exactly." Raibeart nodded, smiling, thankful for her supplied wording.

Sighing, Skylar recalled the times when Burke had appeared lost when enduring scoldings or fretted over his level of competence. A runt indeed he had been compared to many, if not all, of the castle's soldiers, who were perfectly stationed and heavily trained as masters in the unofficial craft of supervising the city and safeguarding the summit. Burke's meager glimpse of fortune came during the off chance that he managed to house his messy hair inside his helmet and appear presentable to his commander. Based on the rebellious curl peeking past the barrier of his visor when they became reacquainted no more than half an hour ago, it seemed he had failed to conquer the habit.

Whoever the captain of Summerside was, he was oddly much more relaxed, which was beneficial to the meek soldier.

"There are things that cannot be changed, no matter how much one may try to make it so," Skylar remarked with a coincidental touch of ease, verging on coming across as too indifferent to Vergil's concern. In her eyes, Burke had no reason to change after procuring a station that tolerated his clumsy ways—he had shown the promise of growth while in Summerside, and therefore, it seemed wrong to make him feel disconcerted in his place as a soldier again.

Raibeart, on the other hand, was immediately taken aback by her response. He leaped into their conversation at once with an alert question. "What makes you say that? Are you referring to the soldiers at Otornot Keep who failed to see our cause? They perhaps lied?"

"Oh no!" His misunderstanding, which was comprehensible, willed Skylar to attempt an immediate diversion to his worried thoughts. "I was referring to people in general, I suppose."

"You suppose?"

It felt as though the older gentleman were baiting her into a dialogue with a topic too vague to give her confidence in addressing his concerns. It was tempting to arch an eyebrow at him and appear as inquisitive as he sounded. Considering they were heading toward Vergil's base on the edge of dusk, the nearly fatigued queen wasn't entirely certain she could deflect such prying eyes and childlike curiosity from the captain general.

Facing the direction in which they wandered, Skylar attempted to steel herself as she clarified. "I was first speaking in regard to poor Burke, but I realized that the statement could hold true for a great deal of things. People especially, since they are always uncontrollable variables."

"I see," Raibeart said in response to her powerful statement concerning a wide berth of philosophy.

What sort of teacher was he? Before she could reveal how aghast she felt, he went on.

"I suppose that's the way a queen must be prepared to appraise any given situation. Though I thought that way when I was in my previous line of work as well. Only back then, I had a less peaceable way of handling myself. It can be a very dissociative mind-set."

The surprising insight into the person that was Raibeart Dhrlo consumed Skylar with intrigue. Imagining the kindhearted captain general interacting with others without patience and consideration— treating them as mere pawns to position and pose to fight for his own aims—was nearly impossible for the devoted queen and friend at his side. It appeared to be a thought that haunted the man of sixty-three years; the bullet-wound scar on his cheekbone had always had the potential to demonize him, she supposed, but his nature was too welcoming, and the windows to his soul were filled with wisdom that spoke of travels and adventures, which he expertly hid as he mulled over the confession he had willingly spoken. Now she felt as though she had unwittingly tricked her dear friend and teacher into addressing matters he might not have been prepared to articulate, especially during the midst of their judicious task.

The pace at which they wandered along Aesop's Stroll did not hold the vital importance that their mission did, but it had given Raibeart the faint impression of a thoughtful stroll, Skylar assumed. After a moment of silence between them—barely noticed amid the noisy sounds of nearby beasts and the rustling winds grazing the grove of trees just steps away—the spirited Raibeart lifted his head to face his companion and simply said, "If there is anything I can teach you, Skylar, please remember this: each individual does indeed hold a will of his or her own, and though that may obstruct you from your goals now and again, do not hold ill will toward those who cannot comply with your plans. It may feel unproductive, but compromising is the quickest way to both securing an end result and broadening your own perspective for future endeavors. There is no real loss in meeting someone halfway."

His advice was duly noted instantaneously, even though he might not ever understand exactly what it helped Skylar to comprehend. Raibeart spoke in larger terms than the queen could currently see— his advice to her in regard to any future royal decree was preceded by the benevolent words that would more than likely help her better understand her husband. His advice applied perfectly to the profound hole she had dug herself into earlier that day. In fact, it was amazing to note that even a trip around the land she ruled—the wonderful world of Varon K'aii, which she had longed to see—could not compare to the teachings of the astute Raibeart, who was a friend always at her side. It did not escape her notice that she could have learned the schooling she had experienced with Cyril, Emery, Dalya, and especially Shia from Xerus himself when stationed at home with him, had she ever been brave enough to simply ask.

Her grin felt foolish as it spread across her face, uplifting her cheeks as she laughed at her instant reaction. Skylar nodded with her typical poise as she committed herself to his teachings. "I understand. If anything, working with beasts who cannot communicate with me without the usage of beast craft has helped to prepare me for this lesson."

"Oh, is that right?" Raibeart said, a smile of his own splashing onto his typical expression of verve.

"Of course. Now that I think about it, men have taught me how to work more effectively with beasts just as beasts have taught me how to manage men."

"Manage, huh? Now, whatever do you mean by that?"

"Come now, Raibeart." The queen nearly pouted as she waved away his question with a comical rebuke. "I cannot divulge such secrets to someone who works so closely with my husband." There was an exchange of sly glances between the two troublemakers, who were separated in age by three full decades yet equally unruly with the best of intentions if given the chance. Easily, the pair shared a hearty laugh, one that rattled their bellies with an unyielding rhythm—until Skylar's gaze snapped toward an approaching jackalope charging toward her instead of staying close to its pack a few feet away. She fully expected it to run circles around her, as other jackalopes had in the past. The creature hopped wildly, as if frantic and unfocused in its charge, eyes wide yet unaware of its surroundings. It suddenly veered off to the queen's left and barreled toward an odd ledge on the trail after a small display of its frightened confusion. Upon seeing its destination, she grew rigid with concern.

"What is it?" Raibeart readied himself for anything when he spotted her unease. He tossed the tartan wrap around his body back from his hip, bringing the scabbard of his dark blade into view in case it was required.

She shook her head once in a sharp motion before explaining, "The jackalopes—do you see them? On that ledge over there. It looks as if they are trying to peek into that opening on Aesop's Stroll. Isn't there supposed to be a hidden area around here, Raibeart?"

Speaking as if he had transformed into an instructor, he replied, "The Byrinque Thicket is a forbidden area for the populace, given its overgrowth and undocumented wildlife."

"The Byrinque Thicket." As she said its name, the Nazuré tribal woman's voice revealed the dawning of her realization. "That's where Essentia's zenith is rumored to be, is it not? If a zenith owns the land, why are the jackalopes of Aesop's Stroll peeking inside its entrance like a bunch of shy schoolchildren?" The odd behavior of the frantic herd urged the beast master to discover the cause of their visible distress. Only by approaching them and temporarily deserting her goal did she suspect herself of stumbling upon a potential clue to her main search.

A bundle of the trees around the edge of the thicket had been halved, but it looked as though the smaller branches were tangled and holding them together. The uneven earth that the jackalopes were sniffing appeared shattered along its crusting top layer. It was not difficult to imagine the quarrel that must have broken out to create such a scene of destruction, especially for a beast master. After all, the beast master turned queen could easily recognize the signs of a weapon's vengeful strike through the splintered trees, given that no such creature along the trail wielded the strength or limbs to do such a thing. The location was curious for such ruinous behavior to take place. *How strange.*

"It wasn't like that when you walked through here with Emery and Dalya, I assume," the captain general said, "which is curious enough on its own."

Skylar faced Raibeart then, her voice low. "Yes?"

The strategist next to her seemed pleased to reveal all as he said, "But considering that the entrance to the Byrinque Thicket is just beyond them—a dark and confusing maze for even the best navigators—I presume we would find ourselves some trouble if we were to investigate further."

"Wonderful," said the queen as she nearly raced to the miniscule stone wall that stood in her way. She leaped over it with a pulsing zeal, prepared to solve the mystery of the missing soldiers and return to Summerside with much to be excited for.

"Excuse me, little ones." Raibeart sidestepped the startled jackalopes with relative ease despite the alarming stampede they traveled in as they rushed out of his way. Skylar, on the other hand, walked directly into the thicket without acknowledging the miniatures beasts. She couldn't keep herself from smiling when she heard the captain general speak to them in such a formal way. The charming moment did not distract her from the lessening visibility she currently faced while progressing forward, and with the same straightforwardness, she took on the role of an unqualified leader as they entered the unknown territory.

It was murky, pungently coated with a swamp-like moisture and the scent of overtly hydrated forestry. Now that night had befallen them, the befuddling maze known as the Byrinque Thicket had become a burden to traverse. With monsters in every area and around every corner, waiting to have the two royals fall prey to the natural traps set up within the forest and become unsteady victims of an attack, it was even more treacherous than Skylar had first imagined. She had heard word, though, that Raibeart's eyesight exceeded that of any other human being. Therefore, it was easy to assess from his lack of complaint and his even pace that the suffocating darkness did not deter him in his quest. Skylar more so relied on her hearing and sense of smell than any other of her senses. It was important to utilize her greatest strengths in a situation such as this in order to potentially locate the missing soldiers.

There was also the element of surprise to consider: had someone taken refuge in the boggy forest, it was best not to announce their own arrival, so they would need to move with stealth of their own and do their best to manage. Skylar made sure to walk ahead of Raibeart by two steps at a time in order to survey the pathways, if only to warn his heavier body of any roots they needed to step over or any changes in direction they would need to make.

"Could you not ask some of the monsters if they saw anyone suspicious?" Raibeart wondered aloud while his voice indicated to Skylar that he was looking around, observing their surroundings through the darkness as best as he could. Ever the strategist, he was right to try to think of the most efficient means to their end goal.

Skylar nodded but then said, "Beasts are just like people. Each has its own personality, regardless of the class it falls under. That is why I must choose carefully who I approach, in case it causes a disturbance."

"A disturbance?" Raibeart, unfamiliar with beast craft, seemed to find her explanation both taxing and fascinating.

"Attempting to corral the wrong monster could spell trouble for us. Since this is an extremely wild territory, we can't assume that just any of them would be willing to help us," the queen said to justify her unseen plan of action. The hissing sounds that indicated life around them surely belonged to the carcolhs, what with their anticipation of an evening meal—a perfect example of a breed they would be wise to avoid.

Passing through the overgrown branches of a weeping tree, Raibeart whispered just behind her shoulder, "Is there a certain type of beast we should be on the lookout for?" They stopped to both contemplate their options and wordlessly mock his choice of words. A few steps afterward, Skylar realized they were being forced to jump over an open ledge, and Raibeart thankfully followed safely behind her. The two quickly questioned one another for any signs of harm, and once they were satisfied with the other's safety, they progressed.

"I wish we could speak with an enfield, but they're pack-oriented, and failing to communicate with them could hurt us more so. Ratatoskr don't always travel in groups, so singling one out wouldn't be too trifling."

"An enfield is much faster than a ratatoskr, though; if the monsters did know of someone hiding in their territory, they'd be able to take us straight to them," Raibeart said, understanding her intentions when outlining the service either monster could supply. "I suppose we could always speak to the alphyns. They are considered the watchers of the thicket."

"An alphyn?" Skylar did her best not to sound too displeased while speaking the monster's name as a viable option as she leaped over another ledge. "Yes, we could ask one of them for assistance. Now, left or right?"

With a throaty chuckle, he replied, "I believe I chose last time; lead the way, Your Majesty." He must have known his cordial politeness would earn him the miniscule pout that Skylar wore in times of discontentment, yet he sounded as though he were blind to her meager suffering. Almost as if out of spite, she decided to traverse under and around a ginormous set of upraised roots, mockingly wondering if his old bones could keep up.

"Are you hoping to locate our prey based on sheer luck then?" she said.

"It was thanks to your keen observational skills that we knew to come here, wasn't it? I put my complete faith in your ability to guide us on our way."

How charming he could be.

"You flatter me." The queen's light touch of sarcasm was firm in its delivery. "Considering you are the one who has been here before. Oh! Raibeart, watch out!"

"Are you all right, Skylar?" Raibeart sounded as though he demanded to know. He squirmed his way free of the tree's underbelly to stand at her side, only to quickly realize what had alarmed her.

They had unluckily stepped directly into a patch of sticky, slimy overgrown plants bearing sap.

Looking to one another in the darkness for some sort of confirmation of their mutual foolishness, both the supposed queen of Varon K'aii and her dear captain general found themselves laughing softly at their own shared expense. They kept their voices low, but that did not safely shield the way their chuckles bombinated in the swamp-like thicket. "Do you still trust me?" Skylar boldly asked while hiding her sprightly smile behind an elegant hand.

"But of course," Raibeart responded without missing a beat, "especially now that you've learned how not to warn your companions of upcoming danger."

"If you say so. Oh, you mean danger such as that?" In time with the pace of their conversation, Skylar was able to once again spot a peculiar happening: just below the nearest cliff edge, a pack of alphyns were panting and hungrily whimpering to themselves. Given the way the noises reverberated, it sounded as though the lot of them were looking over an edge of yet another ledge, only this one seemed to lead to nothingness. The echo confused their minds in ascertaining just how close they were to the massive wolfish creatures.

Concerned, Raibeart nearly started. "That's odd."

"I wonder what they are so taken with over there." As the queen spoke, the pair faced one another again, now with grave expressions of consternation through the blackness: both of them quickly understood that there were too many alphyns conglomerating for the gathering to be considered natural. Given their causes for concern since setting out, it seemed appropriate to deal with the wolfish monsters and their apparent fascination.

They leaped down from their steep height and pulled their weapons free of their binds. Skylar made a high-pitched noise that sounded similar to a leaf whistle in order to garner the monsters' focus. One by one, the alphyns motioned to face the two of them; the outlines of their bodies seemed much larger the closer they came. Before any form of beast craft could be activated, the wild wolves grew restless and moved to attack.

Raibeart raced forward from his two paces behind while Skylar leaped into the oncoming fray. She attempted to count the alphyns before cracking her whip across the frontrunner's paws. As it flinched, she bravely danced her way through the rushing horde in order to slip out behind them. Leaving the temperamental creatures in Raibeart's capable hands momentarily, she needed to discover just what had fascinated the alphyns so.

The objects of interest happened to be their two missing soldiers.

Though only one could be heard, she detected notable sniffling and some hyperventilating from just over the ledge. When she attempted to test how far forward she could step, the side of her bare thigh felt something harsh brush up against it: the barely frayed edges of a thick length of rope. Tied to a tree, the two hired guards were hanging above what appeared to be a deep pit into the thicket's depths. It was concerning to note that she only heard the sounds of one man's fear, considering the number of soldiers they intended to find.

With slight panic, she called out, "Hello? Are you the soldiers from Otornot Keep?"

The sputtering soldier heard her and sounded as though he flailed in desperation. "Queen Skylar!" he cried shamelessly.

"Raibeart!" Skylar barked as she spun around to defend against a swiping paw that had dared to pin her down. Jumping off to her right, she made sure to stand to the side so that she couldn't be knocked over the edge her soldiers were hanging from. "I found them!"

"Argh!" He grunted at the monsters from the opposite side of the fray before replying. "We must rescue them; I will take care of the alphyns if you can—"

"My queen! Wait!" begged the desperate man, refusing to go unheard despite the snarling creatures that dared to threaten Skylar. "We were sent here by the men! The soldiers who deserted us at the keep! They're taking our place with King Xerus! We have to—"

A deeper, harsher, more accusatory roar wailed above their heads and effectively cut out the rest of the captain general's plan.

The panic she felt for Xerus prickled her skin, crawling across her chest and over her heart as if fear could be embodied and possessed the ability to drag its deadly talons along her flesh; the reaction she had to the monstrous cry that warned her of an immediate threat on her life merely caused her body to grow tense as she surveyed the thicket as best as she could.

"Oh! Raibeart!" Just as Skylar screamed his name with a fearful warning, a giant thud shook the ground they stood upon. It rattled them both on their feet and caused the poor soldier whom they hoped to save to experience another reason to fear for his life. Sadly, he had every right to be so horrified.

From the cry that had startled them, Skylar knew the monster they now faced was nothing like the alphyns that had them outmatched in number; the zenith Hildesuin had leaped over one of the many cliff-like elevations in the Byrinque Thicket and landed just behind Raibeart's unsuspecting form. Its noisy clamor sounded as if it could decimate the area that surround them, yet it was not a warning the creature offered. The change in its stance was identified by the sounds that escaped its wide mouth, as was the intention behind its tall pose. Skylar could only watch as one of the zenith's gargantuan hooves rose high above her dear teacher's head. In the blink of an eye, the squealing giant boar prepared to slam down upon him. All Skylar could hope to do was warn him once again of the danger that could befall him as she shouted, "Look out!"

· ·✦✦✦✦·· ·

When he awoke the following morning, Skylar was not at his side. It disappointed him greatly to note that he had not been the first to rise, but most distressing was knowing what it felt like to greet the morning alone in their shared bed. Though that bedroom was temporary—with the plush futon's usage coming to end in a matter of hours, once they checked out of the remarkable hot springs resort—Xerus slowly came to realize that his chagrin that day must have been reminiscent of how his wife surely felt whenever he departed their chambers for work early on in the day without even a word.

Given that they had shared themselves completely the night before, the king believed he had finally reached his wife and discovered for himself a place in her heart.

With that knowledge, he vowed to change the confines of their married life. He could not always commit to her his time, nor could he guarantee routine sessions of his affection, but Xerus felt as though he had experienced an epiphany as he rose. All it had taken was Skylar's willingness to grace him with her tenderness. He sighed as the memories of last night washed over him as if he had fallen into the warm waters all over again and submerged in their tepid embrace and the unmistakable sensations that came when he and Skylar were undone by one another.

"Good morning." His wife, cheery with her sunny demeanor, greeted him from the doorway of their suite's bedchamber.

Casting his eyes on her as if attempting to reel her into him, Xerus noted how her creamy silken robe was tied nicely around her lush body, complementing her just as thoroughly as her prized hair. It occurred to him then that he had not seen her mane unbound once while on this simple vacation, which was a secret shame.

"Did you sleep well?" she asked.

"More than ever before," he admitted as he stretched his arms forward in order to loosen the muscles in his back. The nakedness of his chest now felt much more revealing than when he had walked into the springs nude before her, though the king could not comprehend why. Perhaps it was due to the fact that she was clothed now, while he had disregarded his luggage before taking her to bed. He remembered falling asleep to the sight of her blonde locks just beyond his nose last night—it felt somewhat irksome that she continued to stand so far away from his grasp.

Skylar smiled and nodded, though she refused to approach. "I never imagined I'd witness you sleeping," she said in cheeky recognition of his lengthy slumber.

However endearing it might have been to exchange such pleasantries with her that morn, Xerus couldn't help but feel his brow twitch when he noticed how stagnant she was while trying to offer him a jest. Remaining unfazed, he simply said, "It is indeed a rarity. One I'm afraid you might not ever witness again." Though his quip was much less obvious than hers, he knew Skylar would understand his austere humor. Indeed, she demonstrated such a comprehension when she politely laughed for him—a gesture he expected from one of his citizens who hoped to procure his assistance, not his wife, whom he had shared the evening with on their belated honeymoon.

"Is there something wrong?" Xerus asked for clarification of her comfort for the umpteenth time; he felt as though all he had done the entire trip was guarantee her well-being and satisfaction at every turn, yet Skylar had morphed into the distant creature she had been before they had spoken two nights back, when he had complimented her hair and safely seen a glimpse of the woman who had loved him just a handful of hours ago. What had caused such a change in her that she would refrain from returning to his side?

He feared he'd never know, as his asking merely seemed to help her realize the folly in her appearance. "Oh, I must still be tired." She weakly supplied him with an obtuse explanation before making her way over to her designated side of the futon they had shared. "We had an engrossing evening, after all."

When her green eyes struck against his amber ones like two stones attempting to light a spark, Xerus immediately eased. Perhaps he had been too suspicious of her so soon after such a drastic change in their relationship. The revived fire he felt in regard to his wife, his queen, should not have been so easily tempered by his own lack of experience in the realm of romance. Surely she deserved much more credit than he had given her.

In an apologetic act, he leaned in to offer her a chaste kiss. However, with or without the call of the owner's wife from the hall warning them of their incoming breakfast, Xerus would have failed to kiss his wife all the same. Something flashed behind her eyes when he tried to move close to her once again. Even if he hadn't been privy to her hesitation, the way Skylar fled their temporary bedroom to assist the owner in laying out their meal only made him feel a tad more foolish than he would have naturally.

How dare he doubt his instincts and ignore the warnings, regardless of how small they might be?

As their day carried on, she seemed at odds with herself; from a devastatingly temperate creature to an ethereal lover, Skylar sat across from Xerus in their regal carriage, having reverted rather than advanced in her demeanor toward her confused husband for reasons he could not comprehend. No matter how many times he reflected on their belated honeymoon and the minor escape they'd had from the Goodlit Summit's world of royal duties and decrees, the king found himself at a loss when attempting to ascertain his wife's devolution. That she could go from gazing into his eyes with a wanton fire behind her own to avoiding his stare entirely felt almost like an unjust desertion from the festivities he had strategically prepared for the two of them.

Her fingertips tracing the shape of the muscles in his arms, the way her taut thighs had felt atop of his hips, and the way she'd managed to ignite a fire in his frozen being all felt like distant memories beyond last night. Their splendid time together seemed to be just as far away as the time they'd first met, only now there was a much different battle to be waged between them: a marital dispute was surely on the rise for the postcoital monarchs.

Just as Xerus's typical frown threatened to sink deep into his jaw, the carriage jolted along its path, distracting him momentarily from the displeasure he found sickeningly consuming. When the wheels settled on the road once again, he heard a familiar call: "Xerus."

His head rose in the blink of an eye. With his arms crossed and legs spread wide, the king maintained his authoritative posture as he replied, "Skylar."

"Are you an adventurous man?" she asked, as if the sudden question was well suited in its intrusion of their silence. When his expression refused to budge in its stubborn demonstration of his present dislike for her, his wife showed him the most mischievous grin he had ever seen her adorn before she repeated herself with emphasis: "Are you adventurous?"

"In what way?" Xerus responded with ample caution.

Her emerald eyes closed, no longer sparkling under the miniscule beams that entered the carriage from the poorly concealed window. Though her smile remained, Skylar knowingly stood and moved to position herself in the open expanse between his legs. He gripped her wrists in his tense hands the moment hers rested on his shoulders, for fear that another jump in the road could cause her to tumble. When he looked up in order to take in her expression—perhaps to assume her intentions—those eyes he recalled from the heated night in the hot springs rested above him, glaring down into his soul.

Just as he thought he'd found something lurking behind them, Skylar asked him again, "Are you adventurous, King Xerus? Or do you save your greatest exploits for when you conquer kingdoms?"

CHAPTER 14

Xerus was most cross with his wife, followed by Varon K'aii's captain general.

He had allowed Raibeart's leave for Summerside the day before he had departed himself for the massive port; a promise of confirmation from his friend via text upon his arrival had guaranteed his permission. The latest advances in technology had improved upon the amount of time between the connections of the progressive devices, promising digital interaction within a matter of minutes with whomever one might hope to contact.

The king's totem had received no messages in the past day.

His wife had been traveling for much longer and had diligently kept her word by notifying him of her current destination and future intentions, and they'd even entertained a few promising teases between them—something that had felt like a lost trinket along the clunky chain of their marriage—every step along her journey. He had extended an invitation to have her stand at his side during one of the most prominent moments in their modern history, something that was just as vital to the world as his conquering unification of his own territory. Though his queen had not promised her attendance at the conference, he had justly anticipated some sort of indication of her choice.

His totem did not ring with any sort of notification from her either.

Both of his most trusted and revered allies had supposedly deserted him, and though he hoped their actions held a mutual motivation, they had most assuredly wronged him by keeping him in the dark. What if they were not working together to decisively aggravate him? They had earned his faith in their competence, and he held no fear for their safety; nevertheless, their absence was thoroughly disappointing, especially his wife's, what with the familiarity of her sudden change in poise wherever he was concerned.

Indeed, as Xerus stepped into Summerside's harbor, with many excited civilians gathered to praise him for his arrival and his ongoing efforts for peace, he couldn't help but feel that her presence was rightfully missed next to him as he acknowledged the crowds. His assigned troop of soldiers kept him stationed in the midst of their control while leading him toward his awaiting ship, staying rather close without Skylar being there to space out their positions.

As a king, he had both hosted and attended many forums, but never had he demonstrated to the people of the land that Skylar was his bride. He clenched his fists at his sides and felt the prominent thickness of his wedding band wrapped around his finger. The realization made the king wonder why he had allowed such a failure in his duties as a husband; though he was still considerably new to the position in regard to active duty, if he had learned anything from the past few conversations they had shared via totem, it was the young boy from Spierté who had been handling his role as a husband since their miserable hot springs honeymoon, not the proud king who had sought out her hand in marriage. Perhaps that was the first step on his road to recovery with her—if he was ready to face the challenge of her enigmatic devotion, his first priority once they returned to the Goodlit Summit was to organize a proper spectacle of their coupling to all the citizens they served.

However, his first and foremost priority was to handle his current problem: the deceptive soldiers in his party.

Xerus's instincts were not easily tricked. His sense of awareness had always been potent and never proven wrong in any such instance. It was impossible to ignore the hateful, most likely murderous energy that stemmed from the pair of guards who had rotated into his traveling fleet with the responsibility of leading him onto the newly built vessel, the SR *Nereid*. Determining the target of their rage was easy, what with the organized public manner in which Mayor Deyvin planned to receive him. It was not they alone who caused the king to proceed with such heavy concern, though.

The rising number of auras he felt while boarding the ship meant to take him onto open waters compounded the two traitors' desire to wreak havoc for their king.

Imagining the risk of possible causalities in accordance with his chances to strike, Xerus maintained an irenic expression so as not to alarm those who were unaware of the threat surrounding him. Their malicious intentions needed to be dealt with, and the innocent people who had swarmed him with praise and dedication moments ago deserved to be kept safe. Many customers of the city's shops, which surely attracted more clientele when royalty was scheduled to pass them by, would face a brutal end if the lurking assailants, likely hoping to violently protest the amphitheater's development and the plans to unite the entire world, went wild with their vengeance. If he moved to stop the hateful men and women before they implemented their plans, he could unintentionally initiate uncontrolled hysteria among the people as well as the hidden traducers who would challenge him.

Xerus, powerless as he strolled with the would-be murderers of government officials and unsuspecting civilians, could only hope that Mayor Deyvin was prepared to greet him with readied, credible soldiers of her own. The moment the enemy drew their weapons, he would be allowed to defend both himself and the people of Summerside. Until then, he was left to wait for his turn to play their potentially catastrophic game.

Stepping out onto the *Nereid*, Xerus quickly surveyed the make of the sturdy boat. He made note of the two masts wrapped every which way by ropes supporting many different makes of sails, as well as the different elevations of the massive length of the deck. There were sailors and soldiers decorating the brig from the bow to the stern; he estimated sixty people planned to sail away from the harbor. His amber eyes flashed molten as they ran over the faces of all on board he could see, in an attempt to uncover how many of those present were in fact his enemies: he discovered quickly that close to one-third of the ship's passengers were planning on taking his life into their hands on that fateful day.

It took all his control not to challenge them like the heathen he used to be and dare every single one of them to oppose him in a battle of strength, his rage quarreling with the composure and endurance required of a leader.

The king of Varon K'aii decidedly threw his stare to Summerside's mayor in the hopes that she could intuitively understand the distress warring inside of him. Surrounded by her own ring of guards, the unceremonious Deyvin waddled toward him as she too came aboard. Greeting him with a gruff nod of recognition and a tight smile, the woman who was more than double his age was swift enough to catch the glimpse of his peculiar glare without showing indication of her recognition. "King Xerus," she drawled with a faint hint of a question in her voice, something only one who was familiar with her pattern of speech would have noticed.

"Good afternoon, Mayor Deyvin," Xerus habitually replied before he chose to speak in the predetermined code devised between them for a moment such as this. "It seems we've managed to gather quite a crowd. On such a sunny day too."

The older woman showed her age in a timely way as she answered, "Today is an important day for everyone, not just Varon K'aii. We are lucky the weather is favorable." Her voice hardened near the end of her proclamation. It was clear to Xerus that she understood his implications in their seemingly pointless mention of the apparent elements; the king would be forced to thank Raibeart for this particularly brilliant strategy of secret communications, should the man choose to show his face anytime soon.

Deyvin's warm brown eyes were overcast by a furrowed brow as she took a step back and then another, alerting her own guard party to form a protective stance around her. Her decisive action to close herself off to a frontal attack was immediately understood by not only her nearest soldiers but also those scattered across the ship in a wavelike motion of comprehension.

Though there was a fierce moment of confusion among the *Nereid*'s crew, the two traitorous soldiers who stood directly before their king caught on almost instantly. In the first instant of their recognition of the plot to thwart them, Xerus reached for the compacted staff underneath the plate of armor covering his right hip. He whipped the weapon forward so that it finished its assembly between their heads, and he whispered to them viciously, "Don't move."   After his last battle to obtain the lands of Varon K'aii, he had sworn off his swords in a blatant attempt to avoid taking any more lives. It was a simple guideline to abide by, as the people he had promised to serve had not shown him any form of animosity since his coronation. It would take all his might—every fiber in his being and every ounce of energy he could pour into his reflexes so as to amplify his natural speed—in order to handle the apparent threat before any prejudiced attacker had the chance to endanger a single life.

"Mayor Deyvin," Xerus said.

Immediately, she called out, "Captain! Are you ready to set sail?"

"Yes, ma'am," the uncertain official replied.

"Good." On that note, the helpful mayor nodded to the king and was safely removed from the ship just before it set sail. The cheers of the locals who begged to see him on his way reached Xerus's ears, and his willpower swelled due to the uplifting chorus of their voices. It did well to soothe the aggression inside of him, helping him to overlook his own selfish desire to handle these enemies however he chose to, out of sight from their unsuspecting minds.

The *Nereid* was saturated with tension; the sailors were the only people who were allowed to move while they drifted away from the docks. Every single person on deck who was donned in valiant armor was caught in a deadlock, awaiting the signal to strike, with only Xerus himself able to recognize who was a foe and who would help him defend his cause. With a sharp bite to his bark, he demanded to know, "Why?"

A couple of snickers shared between the men standing before him were the only reply he received.

Rushing past their disrespect, his voice rose in order to reach all those who were presently aboard. "I ask that all of the *Nereid*'s crew who are not required to sail lock yourselves in your cabins below deck, somewhere you will be safe. Do not reemerge until I personally come to retrieve you. By order of your captain."

Again, the man who was meant to oversee the ship simply agreed with the orders of someone who was stationed well above him, only this time, he gave his compliance in the form of an exuberant number of nods. A stampede of twenty or so sailors rushed through the scene of stationary soldiers in order to barricade themselves in every safe corner of the ship. The unsettled captain and a few men remained on the upper deck, guarding the wheel, the guidance of the voyage.

"I am going to assume that you are not the men Commander Vergil intended to send to me." Xerus growled loudly enough for those closest to him to hear. This time, his words were not met with rude chuckles but with a single flinch from one member of the villainous pair. That single action instigated the other into attacking their known target, and a barbarous battle began.

Their lances were drawn and ready to pierce through any viewed weakness in his armor, and Xerus bested them both with agility and force while he blocked their attacks. Echoes of other bladed weapons clashed, and cries of both anger and defeat rang in his ears, but he had not the luxury of time or rest to warn those on his side of the struggle whom they were meant to fight. He was forced to channel his faith in Raibeart to the soldiers he had trained, hoping they would be able to parry even those who were just as skilled as they were in terms of combat.

The king knew there were other men hoping to take a stab at him and impatiently fighting their opposition in order to race to his side and deliver what could be the decisive blow. Envisioning such a hateful act propelled him onward as his staff shot forward and swept underneath the two soldiers' lances, knocking them upward at an awkward angle. He dropped all his weight into his right foot and then stomped over one set of their feet, only to raise his knee and rush his shin's plate into the gut of the other. In their winded moment, the far end of his staff swung back and knocked his attackers into each other as he shoved them away.

He untangled himself from the fight momentarily, giving himself the time to swat at the lower legs of another soldier who planned to cut him down from behind—the most disgraceful way of delivering an injury.

Rising to his feet, the king aimed the top rim of his staff into the underside of an approaching foe's helmet. The soldier stumbled back a number of steps in the corner of his eye, just as he spun back around to fend off his original pair of opponents returning to confront him. They would attack him together and would attempt to stab him at separate times—they were relentless, and their hatred was on full display with every move they made, all because of his attempt at a worldwide future of peace.

In the instant when he dwelled on their motivations, a single strike narrowly avoided skewering his throat. Blood oozed from the right side of his neck and stung as the sea breeze whipped past his injury. A feral grunt escaped him then in his moment of fury, as he was overtaken by the physical pain coinciding with the insult he felt inside.

"Xerus!" a voice called from above.

He avoided turning his head skyward at first in order to solidify his defense. However, a high-pitched wailing following the cry of his name withdrew not only his focus but also, seemingly, the focus of everyone else involved in the battle aboard the *Nereid*. In unison, every single person lifted his or her head high and was immediately met with a surprising and unintentionally inspiring sight.

Skylar had arrived to come to his aid on the back of a magical boar with an ivory hide.

It was not just any boar, he knew—her steed was Essentia's zenith, Hildesuin, which was rumored to live deep in the Byrinque Thicket. Raibeart was not currently at her side, but it was simple to assume they had been together in the past, given that his signature tartan wrap was visibly fastened around her body. His presence was hardly consequential, as the arrival of the queen of Varon K'aii and a zenith she had befriended was a powerful enough image to quell the clash indeterminately. The exalted swine unleashed a chilling cry as it soared over the reach of the ship's sails and circled the miniscule ferry that barely measured to half of its height. Under the shadow cast by its body, most of the men and women aboard the *Nereid* were either shocked or frightened.

Eyes brimming with awe and pride, Xerus witnessed her leap from the mighty creature's back and descend onto the deck, exuding her natural grace in a manner that was surely comparable to Essentia herself. She stood in the blink of an eye as Hildesuin retreated almost instantly, and neither one acknowledged the other; it appeared Skylar was standing before them as an act of Ordell itself. Even though she had just dismounted the deity of peace's personal zenith, her green eyes had never looked as fierce and provoked as they did in that moment.

As far back as he could recall, Skylar's expressions were always a mere maintained tremor compared to the magnitude of her emotions.

"Soldiers, betrayers, listen well!" shouted the queen, standing tall, her whip still resting in place at her back. "The actions you are committing today are not worthy of the results they will garner. This event will indeed impact the fate of Varon K'aii, but do not assume that striking down the king will guide our land and our people toward any sort of future in which they would all wish to live. To kill one leader and replace him with another will only create a cycle of assassinations; to use aggression instead of words will only revive the struggle and pain felt during the last war, whose scars time has yet to fully heal. To allow your fears to fester and provoke you to betray your king is not what you promised to become when you were given the rank of soldiers in our armies!"

Suddenly, the voices of riled foes cried out to voice the concerns their queen had mentioned.

"We never wanted to join with Viskretta and Hierony!"

"Now you want to waste time with other countries we don't even know!"

"We don't need to unify with anyone! We need to focus on our country first!"

Skylar carried on with the same level of momentum. "I appeared before you on the back of Essentia's personal beast! She is one of our most treasured deities, and she allowed her zenith to bring me here to stop this fight—does that not tell you that your methods won't warrant the peace you desire? We are people, not animals, meaning we have the ability to communicate with words! You are speaking to me now because I interrupted your fight and challenged your ways. Why could none of you challenge yourselves with bravery and visit King Xerus or me to voice these dire concerns of yours? Why must we revert to such animalistic means to convey our feelings?

"We are so much more than just our bodies, our desires. We are Varon K'aiians! We understand how different cities of people can come together and form one country. Isn't that right? We did it once, didn't we?"

Suddenly, one of the two who had deserted Otornot Keep after her arrival to listen to the very concerns that had motivated them that day, cut her off, shouting, "Xerus killed King Tiriaq during our last war! You have no right to lecture us!"

Skylar appeared cross, with the slightest dip of her eyebrows implying her distaste for those words. With her breathing seemingly a tad strained due to her rousing appeal and the remark referring to his past actions, the current king knew it was his responsibility to properly respond to such a remark. Finally feeling free to confront the men himself, Xerus moved to stand next to Skylar, knowing that the two royals paired together would make for a powerful image. The aura he emanated was empowered by her dedication to the peace she had recently set out to achieve, which had brought her all the way out to sea in order to act as the most qualified ambassador for his cause that he had ever seen. "I did indeed kill King Tiriaq. I challenged him in Yukaih Castle and slayed him with my blade. That single decision I made did nothing to end the war with the people and ultimately led to the battle on the Vicis Plain."

The other of the devious duo who stood before him exclaimed, "Don't pretend to regret what you did! You became king because you killed him! You are no better than any of us!"

The snap returned to his tone when he replied directly to that accusation. "I buried my comrades the same way you did and promised to move forward toward a much brighter future than one where the people of the Goodlit Summit were left freezing and starving or where tribes and cities were isolated from one another when they lived within reach. I understand the desire to take hold of your own fate and the desire to achieve what is right; however, the methods with which you choose to achieve these dreams of yours are just as vital as the end result!"

His words were the greatest truth Xerus had learned over the course of thirty or so years of life. As he looked at the spectacle on the *Nereid*'s deck, it was clear to him now—more so than ever before—that his violent ways were just as much responsible for his kingdom as was his vision for the future. The swords he had forsaken had merely been a symbol for the actions that had shamed him on his rise to the throne. A leader of Varon K'aii's future could not act upon his base desires and fight his way toward every goal he wished to accomplish; he could not bully his way into the people's hearts with force.

That sentiment was even truer on the grander scale of his amphitheater's production.

A fire was stoked deep in his belly, and the king felt the weight of his role most prominently since the moment he had captured the title. Indeed, Xerus was so moved that he wished to usher in another exchange of words, but it was naive of him to think that words alone would quell his would-be assassins. The two soldiers who had behaved the most aggressively in attempting to take his life immediately sought to utilize the hefty pause to continue forth in their plan. Lances high, battle cries bursting forth from their armor-covered chests, they charged at the king and his queen while the rest of the ship's passengers remained still. Without looking to the woman at his side, he raised his staff in one fluid motion and held off the strike aimed at his heart.

A whip shot past him in the direction of the other antagonist in the pair as he rotated his lengthened weapon around the hilt of the offensive lance and managed to not only lower its jab but also disengage it from the soldier's hands with an almost parental whack to the bulky metals gloves that encased them. Before he could think to glance over at his wife's handiwork, he called out to anyone capable of further assisting them, "Rope! Someone bring some to me, please!"

"Allow me!"

While frantic men and women of his loyal guard made immediate attempts to locate something useable to bind the traitors with, a foghorn sounded closely from the port side of the ship. All those unfocused by a threat or task looked over in time to witness yet another ship appear on the open waters, with another Goodlit Summit native leading the charge: Captain General Raibeart. The boats had barely aligned, when he wound his arm and tossed something incredibly helpful toward the king and queen; a weighty net shot from his grip like a precisely targeted hit and cast itself sideways over the pair of weaponless soldiers. Many were stunned by the strange sight, as the perpetrator of the impressive throw proudly chuckled while awaiting his chance to board the SR *Nereid.*

A buzz of confusion and conversation hummed along the ship's deck, but it did not register with the king. His steps were heavy as he marched over to the port beam and worked with the slowed sailors in securing the connecting bridge laid across the rails. Xerus huffed as he waited for his captain general to stroll into the awaiting chaos. A small fleet of Summerside's guards followed after him—a gifted reprieve from the mayor, no doubt. The tartanless appearance he donned looked naked on the elder gentleman as he traipsed onto the scene, offering his respects to his superior. "Ah, King Xerus." Raibeart sounded pleased to see his friend. "It seems I arrived at the perfect time. It looks like your trip was just as miserable as mine." Whether belated or not, his revelation of the state of his past travels did nothing for the king in that moment.

"Raibeart." Xerus acknowledged him by name with a heavy tone of displeasure. If not for the concern of managing the remains of the secret rebellion, he might have found the older man's mannerisms amusing.

"I take it you are aware of the current situation we're faced with here," Raibeart said as he frowned at the large crowd of people standing on the deck. Though he would never behave in an undignified fashion, it was clear the captain general found himself frustrated with the tasks to follow this debacle as well. Thankfully, it appeared he had already taken it upon himself to help set up the aftermath of the ceasefire.

"Raibeart, we need to—"

"Mayor Deyvin will be responsible for the rogue soldiers."

"What will happen to them afterward?" Skylar nearly sounded panicked as she suddenly joined their conversation. Given that she had arrived late, she was unaware of the suspected reaction Summerside's elite would take, and her concern was warranted. It was wonderful to note, the king thought in passing, that her journey and its focus on prejudice, such as they had just faced, had not dulled her empathy and sense of duty as a queen.

"She will need to apprehend them since many of these men and women came from Summerside's ranks, but given that we prevented an incident, we hope to argue for their return to our custody once His Highness returns to Varon K'aii. His mission will not be halted by this attack and therefore must be handled by Mayor Deyvin until there is more time to discuss any sort of extradition." Raibeart hoped to calm her and confirm that the belief she had in their righteous intentions was well warranted.

Based on her faint grin, Xerus believed she had been comforted by the answer. Her arrival had been a welcome surprise, and he planned to discuss her adventures up until that moment when he had the time to spare. Under his guidance, the mayor's gifted troop swept the *Nereid* and took with them those who had dared to attack their king. He delegated over the procedure in which to hold them and gave detailed instructions to be imparted to Mayor Deyvin regarding how he preferred to have them dealt with while he was away. Given that his trip could take anywhere from a week to a month's time, potential legal actions would likely occur while he was overseas. Thankfully, he had Raibeart's wise fortitude to rely on in trying times such as these. In his place, his old friend would perform perfectly in his stead.

It was not until the ships had parted ways that Xerus realized his queen was likely assisting the captain general, as she was no longer by his side.

With a crew halved by the incident, it did not take long for him to notice her sly disappearance, nor was the feeling of disappointment and deceit easy to ignore. He felt as though he had looked into the sun itself, witnessed its glorious light, and been forced to look away for fear of losing his vision to its brilliance; her presence had been so fleeting that it would have been questionable if she had even boarded the ship if not for the distinctive memory of Hildesuin's cry and the rallying words she'd spoken ringing in his ears.

"We are people, not animals, meaning we have the ability to communicate with words!" she had said.

How could she have slipped away without his knowledge before giving him the chance to ponder her striking speech? How hypocritical she could be when she failed to give him the chance to prove to her that he was more than just his power as a king—he could find the words he needed to help them bridge the gap between their lives as well. If only she had given him the chance.

It was yet another matter he would need to tend to on his return.

✦ ✦ ✦ ✦ ✦ ✦ ✦

To say he was confused by her oddly timed advance was an understatement; had she attempted to seduce him early that morning, they more than likely would have been late leaving the hot spring resort. However, her sudden display of obvious allurement felt just as desired as perplexing, and the dissociation between the two reactions inside of him helped Xerus to recall the sense of disturbance in his wife the moment he'd laid eyes on her when he awoke from his dream of their honeymoon night.

"Skylar," he said.

"Xerus," Skylar replied, per their ritual, with a type of hooded grin that nearly had the king wishing he could shake this woman for all the turbulence she was causing him.

As quickly as he could manage while remaining unaffected by her externally, Xerus continued on with his original thought. "Why are you doing this now?"

It almost hindered him to see the shock in her eyes; Skylar showed her surprise, but if she was offended by his possible rejection, it did not come through in her emerald gaze. For a moment, the world inside of their carriage stilled, and the existence of time was banned from entering. It was as if it were forbidden to exist as his wife peered into him while attempting to understand his question as well as the motivation behind it. If only their lives could have frozen in their moment of euphoria from the night before instead of this purgatory they had found themselves in.

"Oh." The small sound from Skylar's lips was just as weak as she perhaps felt, but she quickly returned to her previous demeanor of feminine esteem. "I'm surprised you aren't interested in extending our honeymoon by the carriage ride home. It's not as though the driver would know."

"I merely asked you why," he said, but he would not voice the rest of his response. "I never said I was opposed to such a thing." Whether or not he properly answered her original question, whether he was willing to engage in semiexhibitionist behavior, would remain to be seen until he understood her for a moment more than he typically did—and the one time she was honest with him, Xerus wished she hadn't been.

The carriage jumped again just before she spoke, and he did his best to steady her by holding on to her wrists. When it looked as if she might lose her footing, his thighs held her legs in place between them, and one of his hands reached out to wrap around her body. Such a touch never occurred, though, as she finally admitted, "Is it not a wife's duty to service her husband?"

"Pardon?" The word snapped out of his mouth before he knew what to do with it.

Skylar carried on, unaware of his deteriorating sentiment toward her with every word she spoke. "Since you're so busy all of the time, I thought that was why we went to the hot springs; all kings want an heir, don't they? When we return to the Goodlit Summit, we most likely won't see each other until I come to bring you to bed. It's best if we take advantage of the time we have right now."

"No." Again, he fired his single-worded response at her like a weapon.

"No?" Skylar repeated, seemingly unaware of how horrible her explanation had been. After he had organized a trip for the two of them, hoping to rekindle their deep-seated admiration and build upon their bond in the hopes of becoming a proper married couple, she had assumed he brought her to the hot springs merely to procreate? As if he were using her as a breeding stud for the future of his kingdom and only thought of furthering his reign, when in reality, he had been intently focused on the present moment and his time together with her?

The feeling of failure was unfamiliar to Xerus, but he knew all too well just how sickening it felt when his good intentions were ignored. Could she not have had any greater faith in him or believed that he might have hoped to care for her beyond just as a woman he'd married to solidify his line? Her assumptions made him feel as if she had lowered him to the level of some beast she thought she had tamed—some creature that knew nothing beyond her enchantments and mysterious mannerisms—and though he knew he could never be placed on such a low pedestal, it was infuriating that he felt possessed by her misunderstanding.

It plagued him to think that she'd viewed their coupling in the heated waters as something other than the soul-bearing act it had been.

Xerus was a king, and kings were supposed to have unbending composure, so he found himself telling her, "You can return to your seat; we won't be doing that here."

He felt no satisfaction as he witnessed Skylar nearly recoil from the possible damage his denial might have caused her. In the moment, the words he had spoken were a much kinder version of what he wished to say to her—she could handle his blunt answer if it meant avoiding the more honest response the ignoble side of him wished to proclaim. The king felt his queen's wrist slip free from his hold as she fell into her seat once again across from him in the carriage, her expression just as strong as his in terms of concealing the truthfulness it shielded.

CHAPTER 15

As Xerus entered the castle dressed in his image, he felt a singular, familiar sensibility overtake his intuition. It felt reminiscent of the first moment he'd entered the fortress after having claimed it from his most personal enemy, the former King Tiriaq. Copious amounts of wet snow had fallen on that day as well, cloaking the tundra in the mountains with a type of dryness that only harshened under the altitude of the city. Surely his accomplishments during the visit to the amphitheater were equal to, if not greater than, what he'd achieved when he became that united land's king. Yet a rumbling instinct held him captive beneath the strong armor he adorned. A silent siren had the proud ruler of Varon K'aii feeling anxious—misplaced even—within the walls of his own home.

"Good afternoon, King Xerus," said one of his maids as she bowed while scuttling past. His acknowledgment might have been missed as she ran down one of the hallways off to his left, but he paid it little mind as he headed toward another meeting with his fellow leaders of the country, knowing that the group of allotted dignitaries were awaiting him. The wide doorway had not been barricaded properly, and he was able to peer inside from his peculiar stance out in the hall. A huddled group of officials were patiently talking among themselves, but their communal presence was not reason enough to pull him inside. Instead, he turned his attention to the antler chandelier above the star-pointed table in his meeting place and became fixated on the twinkling flames. Their unsteady stances felt reflective of the uneasy sense he could not shake.

Raibeart appeared at his side, escaping the relentless weather and shaking away the slush as he said, "What a peculiar day this is. First, Mayor Deyvin handed over our ex-soldiers to us without any sort of fuss, and then we ran into Miss Shia in Spierté on a field trip with her students, only to find ourselves rained on when we return home, of all things." The heavy doors to the palace slammed shut at the end of the captain general's recollection of their single-day voyage from the Marina Anchorage, as if to say that the unusual and unexpected happenings—though peaceable in their own right—were now exiled to the outdoors, and any cosmic force responsible was forbidden from orchestrating the rest of his day to follow in such a fickle pattern.

"It has certainly been a day of surprises," mused Xerus aloud as he turned to face the man who had been kind enough to join him on his jaunt home once he had returned to his homeland. It was no surprise that his captain general had been the one to oversee every step of his would-be assassins' legal procedures and, as a result, greet him upon his return.

It was, however, somewhat disappointing.

Inhaling with slight distress, the king proclaimed, "There will most likely be tourists and unprepared civilians needing assistance in this weather. Our guests will also most likely need to spend the night. We'll need to—"

"Allow me to handle the people, please," said Raibeart in a tone that bluntly stated his intentions. "You are probably anxious to begin your review of the Luminaries' project that we designed while you were gone, and I'm sure you must require more rest than you're willing to show. I'll wager that the other officials trust me well enough by this point to know that I won't be luring them to their doom if I ask them to allow me to officiate the meeting." The elderly man finished with a pronounced laugh.

If Xerus had been the type to leer at such forms of teasing, he would have.

Seeing he was unconvinced, Raibeart went on. "If the leader of Maxega is also waiting on your correspondence, I would consider that a major priority as well. I can share a review of your trip in the meeting, and I'm sure your fellow leaders will understand."

"This won't become a habit." Xerus thanked him in his blandest tone of voice before taking his leave and unintentionally following after the maid from earlier as he made his way toward his study. He thought of Raibeart's words as he walked and knew he was indeed fretful in naming the peacekeeper who would represent Varon K'aii on an international scale and contemplating the first country to consider his endeavor and their planned negotiations, as they were both tremendous responsibilities. Attaining peace with the first land of many was a great deal different from building his revolutionary army. After all, violence was no longer a viable option to assert one's views, as cooperation, empathy, and a willingness to diversify and understand had become the front runners in favored methods to build a world of multiple nations hoping to function together.

He would need people who were aware of these principles as well as avid practitioners of such values in their daily lives—people who succeeded him in patience as well as ingenuity when it came to handling naysayers. If Skylar's mission had taught him anything, it was that sensitivity was the key to opening the channels between those who were frightened and unsure and those who had already begun to change. Bitterly—in association with her name, most likely—he wondered if it should be the queen's responsibility to construct the mission statement of his project for the Luminaries, given that she would surely protest any claims he had toward empathy or the willingness to understand another.

He surely understood nothing about her, not after her sudden departure from the *Nereid*.

Xerus stood before the door to his study for a moment as he pondered her location with grave concern. She had been unavailable via her totem for the entirety of his mission, and her sudden disappearance after their apprehension of the rebels had been startling and confusing. He had not a clue where his wife was presently, and Raibeart had been unhelpful in answering his concerns. Yet he was expected to continue on with his work as the representative of a country and move forward with his operations toward peace. He wondered if she had returned to the

Nazuré people, but he couldn't determine a motivation that justified her behaving in such a rash way. If she had survived half a year of marriage without his proper companionship, surely she would not abandon him and her queenhood when they had only just begun to understand one another. No, Skylar had a much stronger sense of respectability than what he was giving her credit for.

In tune with his thoughts, the sound of a door opening collected Xerus's attention suddenly, given that he was still staring at the one that led to his study. He turned his head and saw the sister of his late comrade leaving his own bedchamber, Lady Mahina Gaellen of Sailbrooke. She stepped into the hall as if she had every right to be in his private quarters before spinning around and closing the door with the gentlest of touches. After watching it close with a natural grin, she lifted her weary gaze and spied him immediately. "Oh, King Xerus!" she exclaimed before curtsying in his direction.

The king remained still for only a moment, however pronounced it felt in the elongated, empty hallway, and then moved to approach his bedroom door. The young woman remained calm and unaffected by his catching her in such an odd place in his castle, likely due to their history shared, given the allegiance her brother had provided him with. Truly, it was not her location that had him heading in her direction. "How are you, milady?" he asked her genuinely.

"I'm doing very well, thank you. How was your trip overseas?" inquired the regal young lady, clasping her hands behind her back as she awaited his reply.

"It's progressing positively, thank you," he said before cautiously prying. "If I can recall correctly, your two-year anniversary as the duchess of Sailbrooke is coming up shortly. I hope you are finding yourself having an easier time as the years pass." Xerus did his best to speak his words gently, given the reason she'd been forced to take on such a vital role for her city and her people. He stood a few paces back to give her some space after asking her such a thinly veiled question.

Mahina merely blinked at him with slight confusion before regaining her composure as she answered, "Yes, of course. I still don't know if what Jovost saw in me was the truth or something he said to me in order to have someone he trusted take his place, but I like to believe I handle my role to the best of my ability and that my people appreciate my efforts."

Whether it came from a place of emotion or truthfulness in his own right, Xerus addressed her concern at once. "Faith was surely Jovost's most powerful quality. If he believed in the two of us, then we were most definitely worthy of it."

A second passed between them as his assessment of the late warrior brought to the surface memories for them both. Then Mahina graced him with a smile that showed just how much experience she had gained in the years gone by since her brother made her a leader, and Xerus was surprised how the signature Gaellen grin still had the power to impact him so.

With an exaggerated curtsy, the young dignitary took her leave and made her way to the meeting place without expecting him to follow. For a moment, Xerus was so taken aback by her maturity—his recollection of the young girl who'd seemed so unsteady two years ago felt unjustified—that he felt stilled and somewhat proud as he stood there. However, his admiration did not keep him from wondering why she had been in his bedroom. Once Mahina had rounded the corner, he regained control of himself and moved to open the door that led to his most secret den.

Instantly, the room felt warmer than the rest of the castle; with the heat and the scent of earth and laundered towels, Xerus knew exactly why his chambers were as stifling as a sauna. Though he nearly felt deafened by the silence, he sensed her at once. As he approached the door to the adjoining bathroom, he couldn't help but admire the room lit by candlelight against the backdrop of the murky weather outside. Though the tones of red that decorated his home had spilled into their bedroom, that room seemed to hold a warmer, more welcoming and loving tone than the sturdy appearance the rest of Yukaih Castle was dressed in.

He did his best not to sneer as the thought angered him, with flashes of the past few weeks entering his mind the moment he deemed his bedchamber to be loving. He'd considered Skylar missing while he was at the amphitheater, and now he knew she had been there in their home, ignoring any attempt he had made to merely know that she was safe. With little consideration, Xerus opened the bathroom door and walked in on his wife bathing.

Her blonde head of hair was wrapped in her warrior's loop as she rested it against the wall of their pool-like bathtub. The steam immediately battled with his armor, trying to heat his body beneath its metal without consideration. Unlike the bedroom he had just shown a most deplorable expression to, the bath and the room that encased it were tiled in white, as if to emulate a world of nonexistence when one was able to relax in the gentle waters. The lack of windows helped to accomplish this effect, isolating the room's occupants from the rest of the world.

She did exist, though—the boil in his blood told him so.

"Skylar," Xerus said as he took a notable step into the room. He left the door open so as to release some of the steam that could overwhelm his wife, whether she seemed to care about possibly fainting in the bath or not.

At his sudden appearance, he heard the waters lapping at her shoulders as they jolted in shock from the sound of his voice speaking her name. An empty instant passed between them; neither one of them moved, made a sound, or seemed to breathe, until she responded, "Xerus."

In that moment, the king realized he was moving forward without structure, a strategy to guide him on his way, or any semblance of how to handle such furious emotions when directed toward a wrong made against him in such a personal way. The last time someone had truly insulted him had been when his wife accused his romantic gesture of being a means to procreate. Now she sat before him without looking his way, refusing to face him when he had come to speak with her.

He would not stand for this disrespect any longer.

"You have avoided me for long enough—you will face me when I speak to you." His words came out as a command, though he had meant them as a high-handed reminder of proper etiquette. Nevertheless, Xerus found himself in such a state of distress that he dared not waver in rectifying the first string of words that left his mouth. If he could get a rise out of her, even if it was defensive, at least he had engaged her in conversation.

Much to his disappointment, Skylar did not grow angry; almost obediently, she dipped her head backward and stared him dead in the eye. There was not a hint of emotion on her face as she gave him what he wished for, ignoring the depth of meaning and intention that had surely been behind his unceremonious demand. "Yes?" she whispered with a matching voice of vacancy.

The patter of the wet snow against the roof above grew fiercer in the time it took for him to think of a way to respond to her blatant, silent protest to his rudeness. Xerus damned his sense of righteousness with just as much furor; he would not fault her for toying with him after he had initiated their discussion with such an aggressive start. A deep breath filled his lungs and then escaped him as he took a different approach. "You disappeared from the SR *Nereid*."

"Yes."

Unsatisfied, Xerus said, "And did not respond to any contact I made via totem."

Skylar nodded as she craned her neck and positioned herself to sit properly while leaning over the side of the bathtub. Again, she agreed with him. "I didn't."

At that, Xerus felt his authoritative nature demand to overtake him and say whatever he deemed necessary to extradite some semblance of repentance from his infuriating wife. "Why?" he asked, gritting his teeth. Then he was made to wait again.

The candlelight in the bathroom reflected cleanly off the tiles that covered the space from top to bottom, and in its wake was Skylar's expression—contemplative, as if she had been just as unprepared as he was to break through the obvious defensive wall that had been preventing them from having an amicable relationship for many months. Knowing she was just as unnerved as he allowed Xerus to lose some of the edge he felt gnawing at his heels and urging him to charge through the conversation in a belligerent manner that he was unaccustomed to.

She was unaccustomed to him; Skylar made him into someone he hadn't known he could be.

Her mouth opened, but no sound escaped her for quite some time. When she finally did speak, her dazzling green eyes, which he desired to witness burning with as much passion as he himself felt, clashed against his own as she explained, "I felt you wouldn't mind my silence, given that you've had it so many times before."

He appeared just as inquisitive as he was cross. "If I attempt to make contact with you, it means I am trying to—"

"And that you've given me just the same."

If not for the many forms of pauses and hesitations he had endured on both of their parts that day, he might have allowed her words to sink deeper in his mind before propelling himself into formulating a reply. "If you are accusing me of something, it is best to do so outright."

"It is not an accusation." Skylar tried to clarify as she moved her shoulders back and straightened, almost as if she meant to conduct herself cordially until their problems were resolved. "It is an observation at best."

"Of what, pray tell?" Reflexively, the king crossed his arms while entering unstable territory.

The queen appeared unmoving. Her demeanor was neither cold nor welcoming for the moment; something unknown was lurking within the beast master before him, making her cautious while she hunted for something he could not ascertain. "Of our marriage, Xerus."

This conversation had been bound to happen—it should have happened many months ago, yet the time never had been right, or they'd never found the appropriate circumstances. He was a busy king in his own right, and the thought always seemed to occur to him when he was away for work or when he had listened to the problems of some civilians and felt their issues strike a chord close to his own. Neither one of them had been satisfied in their love life since their belated honeymoon, which had deteriorated so quickly the following morning that it was unlikely she considered it to be an enjoyable memory, let alone one in which they had expressed and promised a future of devotion.

If her avoidance of him had anything to do with her pondering such thoughts of severity on her own, Xerus wondered how this spontaneous talk would bode for their future. If he had his way, they would still have a future to look forward to, one that promised more than what he had given thus far, as long as Skylar understood that their partnership required them to adapt to one another.

Considering what she had to say next, the king wasn't sure she understood this about him at all. "Before the conference, I had a mission: to assist Commander Vergil in understanding the men at Otornot Keep who were threatening the peace of mind for our Viskrettan and Hierian citizens, in an attempt to give those opposing peace between the lands a chance to grow. Along the way, I ended up encountering many of your past companions—Cyril, Emery, Dalya. I even came into contact with Shia, who, in speaking to me for the first time, gave me a deeper insight into who you are, Xerus."

Though intent on listening to her speech, Xerus was stunned by the last of the names she mentioned. To his knowledge, Shia and Skylar had never been formally introduced before she had left. He hadn't invited his sister to the castle after the outburst she had had in front of Syvant and the troops he had gathered during one of his visits to the Goodlit Summit. It had never occurred to him that he had not formally introduced them as in laws after the wedding, which helped him to imagine the surprise Skylar must have felt when bumping into her sister through marriage.

In that moment, Skylar reclaimed his attention with a firmer voice. "It was through those encounters that I learned how the world sees you and how your friends see you, and I realized that no matter how wonderful of a man or a king you are, I didn't know you, Xerus."

"You didn't?" He repeated her wording, noting her use of past tense.

"I didn't until I spoke to them, and they each taught me something new about you that I did not learn with you in six months of marriage. Why is that?" Her tone of voice sounded slightly pleading, but he could think of no answer that made sense to him either.

Disappointed in himself, Xerus felt his frown deepen as he tried to assimilate some sort of explanation as to why he had refused to close the irrefutable gap between them when he had brought her into his home, into his kingdom, after taking her from her world in the dunes and marrying her for his own selfish reasons. Some part of him recognized that the young man of twelve who had first witnessed her in all her power and soulful beauty during that night in Spierté had remained alive all these years, influencing him in ways he could never have imagined when he interacted with her the night before their honeymoon and the morning after. He'd taken too great an offense at her actions, regardless of how badly she had smarted him with her assumptions of his ulterior motives regarding his need of her.

Xerus had never needed another human being, and whether or not Skylar was such a person remained to be seen, but the child who had admired her in his memory had felt disillusioned, and the man he had become had allowed himself to carry on in a disrespectful manner.

"If you cared to know me at all, you could have made an effort to speak to me yourself. Whatever you assume of me and our relationship, you cannot speak of one's ability to communicate to the men who tried to take my life and then fail to live up to the words you preach when we are committed to one another. You never once allowed me to show you what I was capable of!" The sharpness of his echo in the confined marble room allowed him to hear just how true his words were, but it also allowed him to hear the rash end to his otherwise substantiated claims. A deep breath filled his lungs before he attempted to carry on.

"That being said, I cannot provide you with a reason that would satisfy you," he said honestly, given how disappointed he felt with justifying it with himself. "All I can say to you now is that if you choose to address these concerns with me, we will begin to better understand each other from this point onward."

"No." The brusque word nearly stole his breath from him, more so than the heat of the bathroom.

The king studied his wife a moment as she stared at the floor with what he assumed to be avid determination, her fingers tense as they held on to the bath's ledge. The drastic change in her expression and her tone alerted him to a wave of emotions about to strike him down, and he welcomed it, though he feared its might. "Skylar?" he said, issuing her a chance to delve deeper.

Delve Skylar did. "Do not treat me like one of your subjects who needs you to save her from some plight. I am supposed to be your wife, Xerus—not a problem you fix with your promises and decrees but a woman you said you wanted to marry and have as your queen." She lifted her gaze to his once again, and the wave he had anticipated seemed to recoil just enough to cause her eyes to gleam. "Do you understand me?"

The woman before him, though riled, truly was a queen. The beast master title she held was reflected in the way she carried herself against what she most likely imagined to be a war waged between them, yet the spirit he saw in her demands of him was just as inspiring as it was aggravating. It was the spirit of the young girl he had met in Spierté— the spirit he had hoped was buried beneath the blonde tresses and royal attire he had had tailored for her. For the first time since they had been named man and wife, it felt as if Skylar had come to life before him.

He believed that being allowed to witness this brightness in her only after all they had been through was a major part of their problems as well.

"I understand," Xerus said, wishing he was certain of their recovery in progression to approach her, "and I did not mean for it to sound as such. I know that I have allowed myself to become distracted more so than my work has deserved, and I now see that it has caused you a great grievance."

Skylar nearly recoiled when he openly acknowledged his treatment of her, and the sight of her slight falter helped him to better understand just how deeply his neglect ran within her. Yes, both he and his queen were immensely powerful and housed unquestionable strength; however, it had never once struck him to ponder what the terms of strength were within them individually. Xerus had assumed too much about the woman before him, and too late had he realized that her unaffected front had indeed been just that—a guise to fool him into believing that the way he had distanced himself from her hadn't affronted her as much as it had.

Fighting the consumption of his regret, the king made his motivations clear. "We have been in this state since our trip to the hot springs, since you told me you assumed I wanted our honeymoon to be a chance to make an heir with you. Given that we weren't as close then as we are now—after speaking through our totem conversations and slowly repairing what was lost—I genuinely wanted to spend time with my wife and get to know the person she had become."

"A king is required to have an heir, just like the chief of a tribe or an alpha male in a pack," Skylar said in a roundabout way of defending her mind-set from months past. "You barely made time for me then."

"Which I was attempting to rectify," Xerus said to silence her less-than-desirable depiction of how he had imagined their first of a hopeful many secret getaways as king and queen.

He watched his wife's eyes flicker under the diminishing candlelight as she took in possibly the simplest response he had ever given. Hearing the words himself, Xerus listened to how simple the entire situation sounded when emotions were removed. If only he had allowed himself the chance to a be a husband, then perhaps they would have been working more as a team rather than behaving like two sides of a raging battle.

As if he knew any other way to live.

A scowl nearly encompassed his face, but the chime of Skylar's voice kept him steady. "You should have told me," she said.

Xerus desperately needed to sigh. "In retrospect, there are many things I should have done then that I cannot go back and change. I—"

"When I completed my mission at Otornot Keep, the first thing I had to do was call you," Skylar said, as if she needed to explain the fact that her first response to accomplishment was to contact her husband, as if a direct apology could not compare to acknowledgment of anything she needed to say to him now.

With bravery riling him in an instant, lighting him like a match against a striking surface before illuminating one of the many candles in the bathroom, Xerus asked her a question she had once asked him: "Why?"

"I had to report to you since you had allowed me leave to take on this mission."

"I did not *allow* you leave." Xerus nearly spat as he took a courageous step forward and then another so as not to appear as though he stomped in defiance. "You are a queen and free to move about Varon K'aii as you so wish."

"Then why am I trapped in Yukaih Castle, always taking lessons on how to *be* a queen? Why have I barely stepped foot into the Goodlit Summit, let alone seen the rest of the world? You showed me Terrinal the day I agreed to marry you, and you showed me the hot springs on our impromptu honeymoon; otherwise, when have I ever left the castle? It's the same reason I did not even know what a totem was until I saw Cyril's."

He had exacted control over too many areas in her life and locked the beast master within her cage.

The unspoken explanation of her stress resonated between them without the need to be said. Xerus had treated his wife like a conquered territory from his early days in his rebellious campaign over the land as the man who intended to unify the world. Without even realizing what he was doing, he had created an agenda for her life and never made the time to learn of her accomplishments, improvements, and needs. Again, his behavior felt reminiscent of his younger self, Van Austiant. He'd desired her much as anything else he ever had in his life, and he'd moved about with the same decorum he showed now as king, only with a greater tenacity that had needed to be jaded in a sense as time passed by.

Growing into a man and a ruler meant forsaking the parts of himself that would become hazardous to him or his people should he behave in an unthinking manner. It was how he devoted himself to the citizens of the world and its betterment—it was not how he wanted to carry on his marriage with his wife. Skylar was much more than a queen on a throne: she was a warrior, a giving and caring soul, and a wise woman who was promising as his equal.

Before the thought of a proper apology could cross his mind, a shiver ran over his wife's bare shoulders. Xerus remembered leaving the door to the bathroom open, which likely had resulted in a significant departure of heat. Still, ever stubborn in her resolve—or perhaps she was undeterred in her desire to finish their conversation—she refused to grab for either of the towels within her reach. He had ruined her attempt at relaxation, and he decided to end her act of decency as he made his way toward the towels himself.

After all, if he recalled, it was she who'd moved on top of him during their night in another set of steamy waters.

Xerus avoided her with his eyes as he reached for the plush cloth and held it up for her, just beyond the step down. "Why else?" he asked as he waited for her to comprehend the gesture and move to accept it with grace.

Skylar sat with confusion on her face for a moment longer than he would have liked before repeating him. "Why else?"

"Why else did you need to call me after you completed your mission?" The king expanded on his question while the queen slowly began to move. Under the glow of candlelight waning in the room, he spied something that nearly struck the proud Xerus down.

Skylar had a heinous wound on her right side.

It appeared as though something large and sharp had dug into her hip and dragged its pointed tip up to the far edge of her waist. Angry looking and likely painful, the injury could not have been old, as he had not seen her skin marred when they had made love that one night many moons ago. The bath must have been a poor attempt at a remedy for any pain she felt. The wound must have been why she'd left the *Nereid* after taking care of the rebels and why she'd been wearing Raibeart's tartan wrap.

In gaining Hildesuin's aid, she must have waged battle with it first.

Xerus's face was blank as he took in her injury, bothered by its plausible torment. Nevertheless, he had asked a question, and Skylar likely had hoped to distract him by answering his curiosity. After placing a hand on his wrist, she climbed out of the bath without so much as a grimace or a groan, as was the Skylar way, and turned as she took the towel from him and wrapped it carefully around her body. While he stood at her back in a state of shock, he heard her gentle voice say, "Because even though I had traveled with many companions and made many friends, I found myself wanting to share that experience with one person specifically."

He felt the way she gasped when he placed a hand on her left shoulder, wordlessly requesting that she face him once again. The patter of the wet snow had not lessened, and it gave the scene a greater sense of isolation for a reason the king could not place. Staring down into her eyes and looking as though there were nothing else he would rather see, Xerus unintentionally lowered his voice as he admitted, "And I cannot convey to you how much those words mean to me."

Skylar, who was just as capable as he of hiding her emotions behind a facade of placidity, suddenly offered her husband the first genuine smile he'd inspired to appear upon her face. The feeling of witnessing it was similar to that of the sun having found its place inside his home, hidden within the heart of his wife. Suddenly, Xerus felt himself breathe such a hefty breath that it was as if he had never truly breathed before. In a desire to make this moment of reconciliation even more believable, he watched as his busy fingers left their perch on her shoulder and gently smoothed her steamed strands of hair off her glorious face.

When she moved her cheek to gently nuzzle his touch, in that moment, he, as her husband, finally believed his wife was indeed his to cherish, as she truly had begun to cherish him. The way in which he gazed at her felt intrusive and intense, but he could not look away from the grin she showed him. Her happiness felt like the first sign that there was hope for mending the injuries they had caused one another, healing together, and moving onward past their discrepancies into a brighter future. Even though they had come together on the day of a messy storm, the elements were not able to take away from them this moment of tranquility in the restive water that had become of their love.

She believed him. Skylar had only ever imagined what it would be like to stand on the same level as her husband—to feel as though their bond were as vital as his conquests and that they were as fortified in their marriage as the keep she had visited in her quest—and she did not know what it felt like just yet. However, the hope of attaining such intimacy no longer felt like a dream to chase or a burden to obtain. Whether or not they managed to thrive as a couple and whether or not they had an heir, all that mattered to them in that moment was the promise that a better tomorrow was something worth having faith in.

After all, she believed they both possessed the capability to work toward it together.

EPILOGUE

H is knock created a hardened sound against the door to their bedroom, booming heavily for a man with a lighthearted intent. The feeling of being on the other side of the familiar scenario—of being the person who was requesting the attention of another rather than being the one sought out—washed over him with a touch of nervousness that was peculiar to him. Xerus was a proud man who possessed a brave heart and logical mind. He could not recall many instances in his life when he'd felt frightened, and those he could remember had indeed been worthy of such a response from his hardened being. However, in the split second of silence he endured while awaiting a reply from his wife, the swift grip of anxiety rose from his belly and squeezed his heart in its grasp, with nails as sharp as his retired swords.

"Come in," answered Skylar with a singsong voice, and at once, his worries dissipated.

Breathing deeply, he quickly yet graciously stepped into the doorway. Xerus's amber eyes found his queen stationed before her wardrobe with a nearly nonexistent smile dressing her face, her muted happiness hidden in the corners of her lips. She stood like a statue meant to denote a sense of culture in their private chambers, adorned familiarly in her regal attire that spoke of her position as the woman who ruled with him side by side. It warmed him to witness her in the specially tailored garb, even though there was a touch of the Nazuré tribe's influence in her chosen designs. After wading through the waters of their mending relationship over the course of the past few weeks, the king had found that one of his most indisputable pleasures was when Skylar looked to be a queen just as much as she genuinely was one. The look suited her beyond his own ability to describe it, even when she appeared to be tense in her stance.

Hands hidden behind her back, her twisted locks tossed over her shoulder, she was picturesque in her attempt to conceal whatever she had been doing before he had arrived, if not for the fact that he had never seen her so still in all his life. "Skylar, good morning." He greeted her normally regardless of her strange behavior.

"Good morning, Xerus." Skylar's grin realigned itself into a more natural state, as she took their words as a gateway to connecting with one another more closely. Approaching him in a matter of steps, she placed herself directly before her mate without any hesitation. "I thought we weren't meant to leave for another hour or so."

"We aren't. I'm not here to retrieve you for our trip," he said. The king understood her assumption that he had appeared suddenly in order to escort her out of the city for their first voyage together to the outer islands. It would surely be a momentous day in terms of experiences and sights for her to behold upon arrival, yet there was something else he wished to show her before they departed and before the citizens of their kingdom bombarded her with knickknacks and blessings the moment they exited Yukaih Castle.

Did she have the same curiosity in her eyes when she left with Cyril all those weeks ago? he wondered. Both king and queen had been so dismayed by their marital woes at the time that she had managed to sneak away from the Goodlit Summit without a farewell, as he recalled. That slight was easily avoidable now that they intended to travel together, something he had promised himself he'd make a greater habit of whenever possible. Her sparkling eyes as she gazed up at him with unbridled wonder were partly a motivator for such a decision.

"Oh? Then what brings you here?"

"Is this not my bedroom too?" he teased. The noises his armor made while he pretended to huff at her question seemed to amuse rather than intimidate.

Skylar huffed back at him in response, saying, "It is. I assume your reason for collecting me isn't something to be found in here, though."

"It is not," Xerus said with a sharp nod.

When he chose to provide no more information than that, his wife's sigh sounded a tad displeased, amusing him. "Well then?" she said. With no torches lit in their bedchamber, the natural sunlight that stayed nestled in the clouds over the city gave a nearly ominous look to Skylar's impatience as she stood with her back to the windows. Even though she appeared to be meekly shadowed, her aura was never to be stifled.

The same could be said about his own energy. "Would you be willing to accompany me, even if I refuse to tell you where I wish to take you or what you are about to see?" His question was a serious one, yet he maintained the gaiety of the scene. The king would require the utmost confidence of his queen before he could disembark with her on his spontaneous excursion, and that was no laughing matter. Should she refuse him, Xerus would simply attempt to garner her favor again at a later date, for she possessed his trust completely.

Thankfully, it appeared as though his wife felt the same. "Yes, of course," she replied. Her interest in the topic was somewhat tempered as she somberly answered him. Expressions were something she occasionally struggled with, but in that moment, her sincerity was genuinely portrayed and received.

"Very well then. Let us move quickly," Xerus said over his shoulder as he swiftly turned on his heel and examined the hallway. He allowed himself to become orderly and analytic in an effort to avoid becoming distracted by the endearment he felt when she put her faith in him. Their time to share in his secret was dwindling, as their departure time would arrive shortly, and he needed to expose his truth to her before their carriage called. Sharing with her something that not even Raibeart knew would be his way of repaying his wife for her immediate response and her genuine devotion, no matter the struggles they had faced while together. He prayed she would understand his impatience and forgive him once she understood why he was seemingly shifting between personas.

"Where are we going?" Skylar said softly, taking it upon herself to behave just as secretively as her mate. Standing directly behind him, she was prepared to follow in his footsteps to his mysterious destination. He took her hand in his and proceeded to direct them away from the main entryway and past his study—away from anyplace she would likely assume to be his intended goal. Guiding them bravely, Xerus's steps corresponded with the beating of his heart while they veered toward one of the exits at the back of the castle. It felt like a grand chase, as if he expected one of the maids or chefs to spy their escape and demand they cease such foolish scampering. He felt young, the king realized. He imagined his secret jaunt as though he were running away with his wife, even if only for a short amount of time.

The frigid gust that greeted them upon their emergence onto the deserted training grounds stole away his oddly childlike delight and reminded the king of his intentions. Squeezing her hand with a tender diligence, the king revealed his courtly side as he helped guide Skylar through the snow, over the many layers that had gathered during the past few days of temperamental storms.

"Where are all of the knights?" asked his partner in crime, her voice slightly louder as she tried to talk over the blistering winds.

"Everyone is on duty today since this is our first voyage after the confrontation at Summerside." Xerus spoke without any reservations or fear in his voice.

"And yet we are heading into the mountains? Away from their protection?" Skylar observed.

The sharp winds struck his cheeks in a blunt way that complemented her inquisitiveness, for she showed no reserve in questioning his peculiarity. He doubted she had ever wandered into the snow-capped mountains that seemed to touch the sky. Staring up at them now, Xerus could not help but feel a great deal of dread at the prospect that had she ever been defiant of the shackles he had once placed her in and wandered through the formidable landscape alone, discovering his secret without him there to provide for her the answers she would need to understand, he could have lost her forever. The thought felt much colder than any of the snow that attempted to slow his venture to right a past wrongdoing.

"We won't need it. I promise you that," replied Xerus with a gentle force in his voice. She said not another word as they slipped away from the castle grounds and made their first few leaps onto one of many snowy ledges; the only indication that she was keeping up with his climb was the second set of footprints he heard pressing forward through the snow. She kept to herself for a great deal of the journey as they traveled from one mountain's base to the next, wandering around through a maze of ridges until they finally found the entrance to a cave. They slipped inside of its coverage from the turbulent weather, and he allowed them both a moment to collect their wits before attempting to observe his wife.

It did not surprise him that her eyes were already on him, the brilliance of emerald taking in the sight of his large body in its entirety after following him blindly on some sort of a miniature adventure. There was a strong note of caution mingling with the eagerness she possessed. Though they had not gone far and had barely broken a sweat during their climb, Skylar had surely begun to run out of patience as to what his mystery would turn out to be, and she had perhaps begun to imagine all sorts of odd conclusions related to the unconventional location he had led her to. Her lips parted as she intended to bother him for an answer to yet another viable query, but he gently placed a finger over them before she could utter a word.

They were caught in a deadlock of silence with eyes staring one another down, postures posed with a great deal of seriousness, and slightly rattled nerves, though they barely cared to show it. The situation, as generous as he knew it to be, was indeed an odd one for her to experience. His behavior in that moment was most unlike him, and it surely would set her off if he were not careful. So the king did the only thing he could think to do: he removed his finger from her lips and used his hand to cup her cheek, stroking her skin with his thumb softly. He could tell in an instant that his lone gesture of affection was enough to steady her against all other concerns she may have had. Skylar nodded, and he saw her response as a commitment that she would continue to follow his lead.

Renewed, Xerus removed his touch and once again turned away from her in order to face the depths of the cave. The quiet of the earthen shelter felt deafening after their escape from the weather outside. It made the thoughts and worries he possessed sound much louder inside of his mind, even while his righteousness willed him onward—not only for himself and for Skylar but also for the secret he kept. It was finally someone else's turn to learn of one of his greatest treasures, and as he thought of his time at war, from which his secret hailed, to this moment, he was astounded to be sharing this experience with someone as close to him as a wife. It was baffling to imagine a world in which he'd never met Skylar and found his motivation to rise above those who opposed him, when the life he now led was surely a state of eternal happiness.

Wasting not another moment, Xerus whistled two swift notes. He did not cease to wander deeper into the cave, nor did he explain to Skylar why he'd made such a sound. Instead, he awaited a much greater response than a mere sound.

With his aurasthesia eyes, the king witnessed the deity Relic's outline appear in a burst of green energy.

A massive man with the features of multiple monsters slowly approached him through the darkness, his caribou-like antlers the most prominent and awe-inspiring feature. Xerus did not need to observe his wife to know she could not see anything through the darkness, for his eyes were a rarity—a specialty that not many people possessed. Skylar's lack of a reaction told him that she only saw the darkness before them, whereas the two men proceeded to partake in a silent conversation of permission and allowance for the queen to share the same privilege as her husband. To his relief, it appeared Relic had no reservations; the governor of prosperity offered a smile and then used his energy to light a fire behind his spiritual body and step aside.

The gasp Skylar released was well warranted, considering her absence of understanding in such a situation. However, what truly deserved her surprise was what lay next to the fire: a small pile of pelts had jumped slightly when the collection of gathered sticks sparked, and in a moment of awe, a small child's head popped out from beneath the layers of fur.

Before them sat a little girl nestled in her makeshift bed, with white hair and eyes like the sun. Her skin denoted her tribal heritage beyond any of her other features, but her smile was her most noteworthy trait, for it reminded Xerus of someone special. Though he did not respond to her with a grin of his own, Xerus gestured to her a silent greeting he had once taught the young babe many months ago. With an uncontrollable fit of laughter, the child raced toward him for a loving embrace. The king's strong hands lifted the giggling child into his arms, but he did not hold her close, for fear of his frozen armor connecting with her bare skin that peeked through the rags that were her clothes. That did not mean he did not wish to hold her, though, for she was indeed precious to him.

"Xerus." After a moment of confusion, Skylar, surely stunned, called to him with nothing but his name. It seemed she was out of questions when she finally had the perfect opportunity to ask him anything.

He turned to face his wife, and before she could decide which emotion would guide her words, he handed her the child. In some foolish way, Xerus genuinely hoped that if she could at least connect with the little girl in her arms, perhaps she would see past his secrecy and focus on his motivations. He hoped she would understand him, the situation he had been put in, and the circumstances that had led to such elaborate and dangerous actions on his part. Surely with the recent reconciliation between them and with her position meaning more to her now than ever before, the queen of Varon K'aii would not return to ostracizing him after his revelation.

She gave no indication of such a response as of yet. Though she held the child in her arms naturally in his eyes, letting them both adjust to one another, Skylar asked, "Whose child is this?"

Without missing a beat, he answered, "She is the last member of the Relic tribe."

"What?" The question flew from her mouth before her thoughts seemed capable of catching up with her. "Is this Léonie's child?"

It was now Xerus's turn to endure surprise. "I was never told of her parentage. Léonie was the one who brought her to me around three years ago, however. She simply asked that I keep her hidden from the world. She said that no matter what happened, this girl needed to survive, even if she was the only Relic to see Varon K'aii be united, as it was the dream of her entire tribe." By the end of his response, his voice had hardened measurably—not due to the remembrance he was forced to endure by bringing Skylar to such a place but, rather, due to the idea that he had not fully achieved his goal yet, not after the attack at Summerside he had endured. It was difficult to know when it would be safe to bring this lonely child into his home, when there was not yet peace among his people. Catching the gaze of the reigning deity as he retreated to his own place in the makeshift den, the king couldn't help but wonder if they were in agreement on the matter.

Then he recalled his wife's presence and realized she had just as much say in the matter as Relic did. While he had been lost in his thoughts, Skylar had put the little girl down, only to endure a giggle fit as the young child ran circles around her with great amusement. He had been concerned about how the child would respond to her; to his surprise and delight, the introduction had begun smoothly. Was it foolish of him to believe that any transition he hoped to create in the future would be just as peaceful? Was it beyond the realm of realism to believe that the child could one day have a normal, blissful life in which she could freely proclaim that she was indeed the last of her once proud tribe? Was it wrong to pray to every deity in existence that Skylar would accept his secrecy and the child together?

"What is her name?" was Skylar's final inquiry.

Xerus explained, "Given that she has not learned to speak and that I never speak of her, she does not have one. Léonie simply referred to her as 'the pup' in order to avoid accidentally revealing her existence."

Skylar digested his answer slowly while looking down at the ground before her. A small silver bob of hair ran past her boots every other second as she contemplated the situation she currently faced. In front of Xerus was a scene that plucked upon the strings that Raibeart had once tuned, the chords in his heart that wanted a family so strongly that he'd gone to the Nazuré people in order to request Skylar's hand in marriage. It bewitched him into stillness, preventing him from having any say in what happened next.

As the young babe ran circles around his wife, Skylar, who had been timing the rhythm of her self-made race, intervened suddenly, shifting their little game into a chase. The little girl squealed and stopped, clapping her hands with a delighted look on her face while receiving such attention. After a moment of pause, Skylar bent down before her, the queen's back to her king, and pointed at the heart of the pup. She slowly said, enunciating each sound, "Rei-mi." The look Skylar received was almost a mimicry of her own expression when she'd first laid eyes on the child—the one she had just named.

The babe's lack of speech made it almost impossible for her to repeat the name she had just received, since most noises she made were merely grunts and whelps. The poor girl, who was unfamiliar with speaking, seemed to be growing a tad overwhelmed at the prospect of being expected to respond using her voice, and Xerus wondered if the calmness of their first meeting had imploded. Just as he was about to intervene, growling emanated from the cave. At first, he believed the sound came from a predatory monster of the mountains, and he prepared to strike it down with his staff, but then Skylar brought a hand to her mouth, seemingly pointing at her face. The little girl smiled in response, her mood easily turned around, and she began to growl with the queen.

"Rrrrr." The noise his wife emitted was a perfect imitation of an animalistic growl similar to those of wild creatures he had faced.

The pup was having a great time playing with both the sound and the woman teaching it to her, giggling as she tried to replicate the noise. "Rrrrr!"

Her enthusiasm ushered in the next set of letters to be taught to her: "Rrrr-ei."

"Rrrrr." The child found her growling to be amusing, and it took a pause in Skylar's noise making to prompt her to complete the repetition if their game was to continue. "Rrrrr-eh!" Her attempt was not perfect, but it was not a failure.

With fascination and adoration, Xerus watched the peculiar moment from his stationary pose behind his wife. Knowing a successful strategy when he saw one, he stayed behind and allowed her to try her hand at such a tall order of a task.

Skylar dropped to her knees on the ground and planted them firmly to give herself balance. This time, as she growled, she patted her thighs along with the rhythm. "Rrrrr-ei!" After finishing the first syllable of the new name, she tossed her hands into the air as though she were attempting to touch the sky or a ray of sunshine.

Even though she remained on her two tiny feet, the young one was thoroughly entertained and drummed an offbeat pattern of claps on the tops of her legs and then threw her hands high and cried, "Rrrrr-ei!"

Again, Skylar tapped on her firm skin, growling all the while, and then shot her hands toward the ceiling. When she intended to lead them both into the last part of the name, she patted her chest with both hands and firmly stated, "Mi!"

"Rrrrr-ei-mi!" cheered the child, pronouncing her new name for the very first time.

Xerus could not believe what he had just seen. He had come by the cave to visit the young girl in Relic's care whenever he had the chance over the last three years, and not once had she shown any interest in speaking. She would try to play games or motion to the deity who watched over her, likely confused by the different states of being her guardian and her king possessed, but never had she pronounced anything close to a word. For a man who had fought in battles that represented peace and unified a land in order to benefit the lives of all its civilians, seeing his wife achieve something he had never had the sense to attempt was inspiring. Even after twenty years, she continued to amaze him in ways no other human being ever had.

Proud of them both beyond comprehension, the king snapped out of his stupor and approached Reimi with his arms open to her. Her pride was brightly illustrated on her face as she dived into his offered embrace, her giggles bounding off his armor and filling the entire cave. Her achievement that day meant so much for her future that he weighed it just as heavily as he did her survival during whatever battle Léonie had rescued her from, because it meant she had a future beyond the cave that had been keeping her safe. Gazing over at his wife's response to such an accomplishment, he whispered words of praise to her with a great deal of heart to them: "Thank you."

As Skylar blessed him with yet another one of her grins, Xerus could feel the presence of Relic as he suddenly began to move about the cave. Slowly but surely, the guarding deity bowed his head in passing while making his way toward the exit. Xerus's amber eyes fixed on the ghostly form; he could feel the weight of responsibility fall upon his shoulders while he witnessed the departure of Reimi's guardian, whose role in her life had come to an end. It was now Xerus and Skylar's role to watch over the pup, he seemed to say—another duty and another trial.

Reimi's care was a new adventure to take on with his wife as his partner, his support, his greatest ally.

Though the storm continued to rampage beyond their safe haven inside the cave, Xerus felt as though the usual storm he endured within himself was lessening slightly as the bright light of Skylar and Reimi reached him amid the once heavy snow.

Appendix

Name: The Goodlit Summit and Yukaih Castle

Description: Yukaih Castle was influenced by adobe houses and has some plank roofs and some tepee-like rooftops, the most distinguished divisions of the structure. The town is mostly decorated with wigwam houses, but the communal areas have longhouses (the only igloos are made by children for play). There is an impression of tradition and olden times in Goodlit Summit, but Yukaih Castle gives the distinct towering awareness of formidability, should anyone think of attacking. No walls cover the city, as Xerus deemed them dissociative and cold as king of the united continent.

History: The Goodlit Summit was established as the revered land for the almighty Relic. Many warriors from Spierté become full of themselves after succeeding in the arena and attempt to challenge the deity, which leads many tribal warriors to go missing and never return. Though generations of the Tiriaq family ruled the city, it wasn't until Xerus's reign that the once scattered land of native homes transformed into the proud city he governs.

Name: Spierté

Description: Spierté is known casually as Spier to some; the name comes from *esprit* (spirit) and *fierté* (fire) in French. The arena is shaped as a circle, and the battleground is surrounded mostly by spectator seats, with the far side open to the mountains; the canopy resting over the seats can be seen from far and wide and is designed to resemble the spear-like digits of the claw of a massive monster escaping through the crust of the earth.

History: Having been designed by a more primitive people—when the tribes were simple-minded and required a designated battleground to wage wars of decisive actions and supremacy—the city stands as a reminder to the once numerous tribes. Only a handful remain on the continent; only the greatest of heroes from the tribes have statues, buildings, pathways, or weapons named in their honor. Given that the city is built on the slope of mountain, the town is in levels and requires transportation to the arena at its peak.

Name: Terrinal

Description: The name Terrinal (Earthen Key) comes from *terra* and *cardinal*. It is an average-looking town divided by a hearty river that leads to a waterfall on its outskirts, as well as a massive area of forestry and a land-contained lake. It connects to the Vicis Plain, but no one dares to step beyond the lake.

History: Once, long ago, a traveling monk appeared and claimed that Terrinal was the Earthen Key because it was the most sacred place on the face of the planet. He gave locals reason to believe—and spread the good word—that Ordell had recognized the city as his most religious territory; as such, it used to be a religious and spiritual spot, but tourism overran the original importance of the city once the continent was united. The massive mind-shaped building is the most well-known landmark; it originally served as both a school and a church but has since transformed into solely the latter with the creation of the Viskretta Center.

Name: Universal Epicenter and Terra Cathedral

Description: Acting as a place to facilitate knowledge about the universe to all who wished to receive it, the Epicenter was revered for its design as well as what was housed within it. Most notable as the largest structure in the city, it was designed to resemble a brain being held by a pair of hands, as if to offer up the minds of its students, teachers, and parishioners to receive divine wisdom from Ordell.

History: It was the original learning center for philosophy, religion, and sciences, but when Viskretta became part of Varon K'aii and the school was founded there, it became solely a church once again. When tourism shifted due to trinkets and the attraction of the lake, the teachers approached King Xerus for a solution, and the building was transformed into a cathedral only, to focus on imparting the legend of Ordell's visits.

Name: Vicis Plain
Origin: Fezebel Marsh
Description: Vicis Plain is a wide-open landscape that is not to be touched; one only travels to the plain if he or she was involved in the war, as all those who died in the war are buried there. Though the area is void of any sign of monsters and plant life other than grass, the grass is lush.
History: N/A

Name: Otornot Keep
Description: Otornot Keep is a formidable fortress that was once captured by a group of rebels during the war. At either end of its passage are guarded gates to remind travelers of the king's guardianship over the keep. It acts as a traveler's rest stop when one is wandering throughout the continent (it has no rooms, but the length of it allows caravans and parties to rest anywhere inside once the sun goes down; they are to leave after the sun rises).
History: The keep originally housed a militia that was not connected to a tribe before it was overrun. When Xerus first approached, he requested to speak with the leader of the rebels and was denied; then he asked to have a group meeting with them but was denied again. Finally, he forced the rebels out by staking claim over the surrounding land and slowly moved in on the defiant group. War was threatened, and the rebels surrendered to him, promising to serve Xerus wholeheartedly after a lengthy set of talks (even though they were too small in number to face the king's army by that point).

Name: Nàmheil

Description: The name comes from *floating* and *peace* in Scottish Gaelic. It is one of the few habitable islands within the large body of water in the middle of the continent. Certain buildings were constructed to stand higher than the trees to guarantee sailors could spot the island as they sailed past. The island houses only a dozen or so people, acting as an oasis on a continent trying to come together. Oddly, the island seems slightly advanced compared to some of the tribal territories, as there are buildings made of brick and cement instead of weaker structures, as well as lampposts (run by a water mill).

History: Legend states that a sole survivor was tossed onto the island after his ship sank in the waters. In need of food, he cried aloud to request something from the heavens, and he found an animal to eat. In need of shelter, he once again proclaimed his need, and a collapsed tree's branches provided necessary shade. Curiously, he asked aloud for a companion to spend his days with, and nothing happened—until a female pirate happened by and rescued him. Once she became pregnant, they returned to the island they'd first met upon, and her crew helped build Nàmheil.

Name: Sailbrooke

Description: The name comes from *willow* in Irish Gaelic and *brooke*. It is a star-shaped fort town covered in cobblestone and excess drapery, as cotton is their major export, making them the most commercial town on the continent. The Gaellen crest is seen nearly everywhere. It was first introduced in order to inspire patriotism and unite under one name many different people meant to live together inside the walls.

History: It was formed as a fort town, with connections to Voulair Port and Otornot Keep, built by the first Gaellen family to protect the town from the tribes and offer refuge to people who escaped the tribes or were cast out. The star shape was chosen to honor Ordell and his confidants; five generations later, Jovost was the first of his name to leave his position of ruler of the city, and Mahina became the first female to stand in for him, believing in her brother's reasons so strongly that she was willing to face those opposed to her rule and ward away suitors.

Name: Tel Adis

Description: The name Tel Adis roughly translates to "Temple on the Hill" in Latin. Inexplicably safe from the unpredictable downpours in the Torrential Ingress, Tel Adis is dry unless the land needs the rain. The citizens feel as though they are guarding a sacred location, but after the unification, they have become open to the possibility of allowing outsiders to visit their quaint town. Huts are their homes. Each houses a star above the doorway that acts as a request for the deities to bless anyone who enters and to watch over any who leave.

History: Until Ordell appeared to the people of Terrinal, Tel Adis was believed to be the only place worthy of its presence, since the other four deities are believed to have their zeniths stationed across the land, ready to appear to those who need them. Even though the Goodlit Summit is the highest point of the continent, it is believed that Varon K'aii was spun from Tel Adis, from which everything originates.

Name: Summerside

Description: Summerside is a port city that serves as the focal point of travel between Varon K'aii and its island territories for anyone brave enough to venture out into the unknown world. The population is large, and citizens are lively and devoted to their country, even though their location is the most diverged from Varon K'aii overall. Most of the territory is covered in shops and indoor activities, with many of the citizens living above their places of work.

History: It is the newest city to be founded since Xerus's rule began. Some of the wealthiest people moved to Summerside when they heard of the project to build it from the ground up and formed their own jurisdiction. Mayor Deyvin was elected via vote, which made Summerside the first territory of the land to use such a modern system of election.

Name: Hierony

Description: An island that is mostly forgotten, Hierony is home to the richest minerals of the entire country. Mining is the most popular profession, but due to the island's isolation, any collapses in the mines or loss of workers heavily hinder the people's ability to flourish. Their other greatest exports are weapons and tools.

History: When Xerus offered to have the island join with Varon K'aii, the people of Hierony were the most cooperative with the merger. They are also the citizens who visit the mainland the most, and they welcome the families of students who are studying on the neighboring Viskretta. They evolved past the hunter-gatherer stage early on in their civilization and have the most knowledge when it comes to the development of construction and transportation.

Name: Viskretta Center

Description: The center is a ten-story building that promises to provide the most elite education to the citizens of Varon K'aii. A typical structural design was chosen in order to highlight the Epicenter in Terrinal, where all religion is exclusively taught.

History: Nicknamed by its students as Credit, the center is new, as it was founded by King Xerus in an attempt to offer proper education to those who wish to learn about the continent. Only those who attend Credit are privy to the knowledge of the amphitheater and the Luminary positions there prior to the international announcement. Given that the rest of the island is relatively unfounded and was in need of support from the continent, the enrollments at the school are helping to support Viskretta overall. Their greatest export is fishing, followed by lumber.

Name: Tundra Walk

History: The Tundra Walk is an ice path that connects the Goodlit Summit and Spierté. Natives who live on either end of the walk check it daily; the blue-to-clear areas are safe ("Thick and blue, tried and true; thin and crispy, way too risky"). It is surrounded by copious piles of snow that thin out near Spierté.

Beasts:

- Owlursus
- Ahklut (a.k.a. alpha aquarius)

- Caribou-like creature (legend)
- Agloolik (zenith of Syvant)

Name: Rivage Docks and Rivage Passage
History: Acting as the main port between the Goodlit Summit and the southern territories, Rivage is home to many different breeds of monsters that thrive off the shifting landscape in a mostly harmonious existence, from a desertlike land to a wetland and a port town.
Beasts:

- Jaculus
- Jackalope
- Hippocampo
- Emela (-ntouka)
- Chimera (zenith of Relic)

Name: Marina Anchorage and Marina Path
History: The Marina Path is a pathway from the sea to the arena of warriors in Spierté. Many rock formations and deformed paths show the influence of impatient challengers making their way toward the tournament; weapons of fallen warriors are left standing in place of their graves—as long as the local monsters leave them be, since two species living in the area hold grudges against one another's kind.
Beasts:

- Werehyena
- Freybug
- Ennedi tiger
- Naga
- Grootslang (zenith of Vaoz)

Name: Byrinque Thicket
History: Most humans avoid this shrouded area. Many monsters have claimed territory within the thicket; most packs live in harmony, given that the thicket is guarded by one of the legendary zeniths.

Beasts:

- Enfield
- Alphyn
- Carcolh
- Gigelorum (rumored)
- Hildesuin (zenith of Essentia)

Reader's Guide

1.) How would you describe Skylar's strength in one word? Would you describe your chosen word as masculine, feminine, or gender neutral?

2.) Out of all the people Skylar met on her journey, who would you say provided her with the biggest opportunity for growth?

3.) If you were a citizen of Varon K'aii, which city would you prefer to live in? Why?

4.) What was your perception of how the author handled the adversaries in the story? What do you think motivated her to write about them the way she did?

5.) In the prologue, readers learn a great deal about Xerus and Skylar's past interactions and what drove him to leave the Austiant tribe in order to pursue greater pastures. Considering Xerus's journey as a character, how would you categorize him in the alignment test? (Search online for more information.)

6.) Considering Skylar's conversation with Shia, in which she learns about some of Xerus's ventures behind the scenes during his takeover, do you think Skylar would have joined him in his quest to claim the Goodlit Summit and unify the tribes with the rest of Varon K'aii during the war? Would she have taken a different path?

7.) Given what you know about Léonie's character, how do you think she would have perceived Skylar as the woman she becomes by the end of the story?

8.) After learning about Ordell and the Four Deities, which deity do you find to be the most compelling? Which one could be the most destructive if left to his or her own devices? Why?

9.) What do you think Reimi's future holds? How do you think she will function in Skylar and Xerus's life after the epilogue?

—

About the Author

J ennifer Anne Gambacorta has dreamed of being a writer since she was twelve, when a teacher handed her back an English assignment with an A grade and she did not believe it could possibly be hers, despite her name being on it. After that, writing became her passion, along with languages, social studies, and traveling. She has a degree in social service work, and her favorite places she has visited are Capri, Athens, Tokyo, and Osaka. She lives in Ontario, Canada, with her family, dog, and cat.

Printed in the United States
By Bookmasters